The episode could not have taken much more than a minute. . . .

The light strengthened. The footsteps stopped. A figure stood in the doorway. If she had been able to think rationally she would have known that the creature could not see her, except as an indistinct shape against the white sheets; but she could have sworn that the glowing eyes inspected her naked body feature by feature, that the dreadful smile broadened, that the hands lifted in an incipient and unspeakable embrace.

Up to that point she had not thought of screaming. Now she did; and that was the worst moment of all. Her hands flew to her throat.

The figure in the doorway recoiled, the face changing from lechery to furious rage. And suddenly the intruder was gone—blown out like a candle flame. . . .

*Also by Elizabeth Peters
published by Tor Books*

ELIZABETH PETERS
DEVIL-MAY-CARE

TOR

A TOM DOHERTY ASSOCIATES BOOK
NEW YORK

DEVIL-MAY-CARE

Copyright © 1977 by Elizabeth Peters

A TOR Book
Published by Tom Doherty Associates, Inc.
49 West 24 Street
New York, NY 10010

Cover art by David Mann

ISBN: 0-812-50789-4   Can. ISBN: 0-812-50790-8

First Tor edition: June 1989

Printed in the United States of America

0 9 8 7 6 5 4 3 2 1

To the Washington Redskins
with thanks
for all the hours
of viewing pleasure
they have given me;
and especially
to the greatest of them all,
Number Nine

CHAPTER ONE

Henry Danvers Willoughby was an extremely fortunate young man. On a marital eligibility scale he ranked slightly below millionaires and well above promising young doctors. He was aware of his status, but was rather inclined to resent people who described him as lucky, for he felt that he owed his success to his own abilities—intelligence, honesty, hard work, and charm. His family connections had nothing to do with it. Undeniably his branch of the family was not overly endowed with money; it had taken every penny his father could save, borrow, or beg to get Henry through Harvard Law. The question of how he got into Harvard Law was one Henry did not discuss. The other branches of the family were happy to use their influence, so long as it didn't cost them any hard cash.

At the age of twenty-seven Henry was a junior partner in one of Washington's dullest and most influential law firms. (It was his uncle's firm, but Henry did not stress that fact.) In twenty years he could expect to be a senior partner and a very wealthy man. He was already comfortably situated financially; he was healthy, reasonably good-looking, and socially popular. His schedule included a daily workout at the gym, for, as he sometimes said to his fiancée, *"Mens sana in corpore sano. . . ."* He had forgotten the rest of the quote, if there was any more, but the point was clear.

Henry looked complacently at the aforementioned fiancée, whom he considered another of his assets. He did not entirely approve of her casually bizarre clothes, but that would change when she became his wife, along with several other defects. They were minor flaws; he had selected Ellie because she met his requirements in all major areas. She was extremely pretty—that went without saying. Blond, of course. Blue eyes, widely spaced; a neat, pointed nose; and a mouth with the full lower lip which, Henry believed, indicated a passionate nature. Henry's smile widened as he contemplated his bride-to-be fondly. Ellie sensed his smile and turned her head to smile back at him. She had excellent teeth—another of Henry's requirements. Good teeth were hereditary and orthodontists were expensive.

"Don't take your eyes off the road, darling," he said.

Ellen returned her gaze to the windshield. Henry had let her drive, although the car was his. Ellie's driving technique was one of the minor flaws he meant to correct before he put her in charge of his car and his handsome, intelligent, white-toothed children. When they had married and had moved to the suburbs, he would buy a station wagon. Ellie would drive the children to their exclusive private schools, wearing slacks and a tailored shirt, her hair tied back in a ponytail.

At the moment her hair was too short for Henry's taste. He was working on that point too, but had grown rather fond of the clustering golden curls.

Yes, he had chosen well. One of his criteria had been Ellie's physical appeal, for he considered sexual attraction important in marriage. Ellie was also intelligent—for a woman—and he certainly didn't mind that; he was careful not to put her down when she tried to talk about intellectual topics. After all, children inherited intelligence from both parents.

And now to discover that, in addition to Ellie's other attractions, she had a rich, childless aunt! It was almost enough to make him believe in luck. Sweet, silly little girl, she had been afraid he would be angry when she told him her Aunt Kate wanted her to spend her two-week vacation house-sitting while Kate went off on some jaunt or other. He had agreed to forgo their planned trip with such magnanimity that Ellie had flung her arms around him and kissed him enthusiastically. They were on their way now to Kate's mansion in Virginia. Henry had offered to come along and on his way back drive Kate to catch her plane at Dulles. As he had explained to Ellie, he wanted to meet the dear old lady. Wasn't he about to become a member of the family?

Henry had no doubt of his ability to charm the dear old lady. Old ladies loved him. They liked his short hair and honest, candid look, and his championing of the good old-fashioned virtues. And yet . . .

The faintest of frowns creased his high, tanned brow (a little too high; Henry would be bald as well as wealthy in twenty years) as he remembered the letter Kate had written her niece. He amended his description: dear old eccentric lady. It had been a rather peculiar letter, and he had taken exception to the postscript when Ellie read it to him.

" 'P.S. Are you sleeping together? I need to know because of the sheets.' "

"What does she mean, 'sheets'?" Henry had demanded.

"Oh, you know. She doesn't want to put clean sheets on two beds unless it's necessary."

"How peculiar."

"I think it's funny," Ellie said defensively.

"Certainly." Henry smiled. "But for a woman of her generation to speak so casually of—"

"It does go on, you know," Ellie said seriously.

"Hmmm," said Henry.

Remembering this letter, Henry's frown deepened. It might behoove him to learn a little more about Aunt Kate. Eccentric old ladies had to be handled with care.

"Darling," he said. "No, don't look at me, sweetheart; how many times have I told you—you must never take your eyes off the road. A simple 'Yes?' will suffice."

"Yes?" said Ellie.

"Your aunt. Is there anything I ought to know about her? Any little foibles or prejudices I should consider? Perhaps we might stop along the way and get some flowers for her."

"She has masses of flowers," Ellie said. "She's an enthusiastic gardener."

"Ah," Henry said. This hobby was quite in keeping with his idea of sweet little old ladies.

"Anyhow," Ellie went on, "I bought her a present. It's from both of us."

"That old book? I don't know, Ellie—"

"She collects old books. Among other things." Ellie was silent, but Henry did not speak, recognizing the silence as one of concentration. Finally Ellie said, "I don't know how to describe her. She's rather—er—"

"Eccentric," Henry suggested.

"Oh, yes, she's damned eccentric! There *are* a few things you might—well, you might avoid. She's somewhat opinionated on certain subjects."

"Politics?" Henry suggested.

"I don't know what her political opinions are. I mean, they change a lot. She voted for Wallace once."

"George?"

"Henry. And she campaigned for Shirley Chisholm."

"Liberal," said Henry. "Women's lib."

"I wish you wouldn't do that," Ellie said.

"Do what?"

"Label people."

"Darling, I'm not. I'm simply trying to sort her out. I shall be careful not to criticize Shirley Chisholm or Gloria Steinem. What else?"

"Well . . . I told you about the cats."

"I can't believe it," Henry said, with genuine feeling. "How many does she have?"

"It varies. Between ten and twenty, most of the time. And the last time I heard from her she had four dogs. Plus the raccoon and the Siamese rabbits and the chickens. The ones that look like Ringo Starr."

"Look like—"

Ellie chuckled. She had a delightful laugh, low and throaty and infectious.

"You know, hair over their eyes and long thin beaks. And she had a lot of hamsters, but I think they got away. And a rat—"

"Never mind," Henry said resignedly. "She's an animal lover. Fine, that gives me considerable insight. What about religion?"

"Oh, Henry, she isn't like that! I mean, religion, politics, and things. . . ."

"I don't understand."

"You don't have to avoid whole categories like religion or politics. She gets excited about specific things. And people. Like Lorenzo the Magnificent."

"Is she for him or against him?" Henry asked wittily.

"For, definitely for. She thinks he's great."

Henry considered asking who Lorenzo the Magnificent was. But that would have been admitting ignorance. It was not really necessary that he know the man's identity—some Italian or other, obviously.

"All right," he said. "No rude remarks about Lorenzo the Magnificent. I doubt that the subject will come up, dearest."

"Aunt Kate brings up subjects like that," Ellie said darkly. "Oh! I almost forgot, and it's very important. Don't say anything rude about Sonny Jurgensen."

"Who?" Henry stared.

Ellen stared back. This necessitated her removing her gaze from the road again, to the imminent peril of a pickup truck and two bicyclists. Henry pointed out the peril, somewhat acrimoniously, and Ellen swerved the car back into her own lane.

"I'm sure that was the name," she said, frowning. "He's a football player. I thought you knew all about football."

"I do," Henry said, without false modesty. "Naturally I know who Jurgensen is—was, insofar as the active sport is concerned. Before he retired he was the Washington Redskins' quarterback. My exclamation of surprise was prompted by the question as to why your Aunt Kate should care what I say about him. Are they related?"

"No, no, nothing like that. Aunt Kate is a rabid football fan. Most football fans are excitable and when Aunt Kate gets excited, she . . . oh, I can't explain it. All I know is, I never saw her so mad as she was the last time she visited me and one of my friends made a critical remark about Mr. Jurgensen. The next day poor Tony came down with a terrible case of shingles. He had to go to the hospital."

Henry thought seriously for a moment. Then he said,

"I fail to understand the connection between the argument and the shingles."

"I think," Ellie said thoughtfully, "it was what he said about Mr. Jurgensen's age. Kate seemed to be very sensitive about his age."

"That's the craziest thing I ever heard," Henry said sincerely. "You mean she's sensitive about *her* age. How old is she?"

"I'm not sure. But I don't think she's sensitive about it. She got mad when Tony said—"

"Wait a minute," Henry interrupted. "I have told you before, Ellie, that you must learn to concentrate on the thread of a discussion and not wander off into side issues. Let us return to my initial question. Granted that your aunt was annoyed. What is the connection between that fact and the fact that the unfortunate gentleman came down with shingles?"

"She gave them to him," said Ellie. "I forgot to tell you that. She's a witch."

"My dear girl!"

"A white witch, of course," Ellie said quickly. She frowned. "The shingles were—was?—an exception. She doesn't do that sort of thing very often, only when she loses her temper, and she's always very sorry afterwards."

"You're joshing me," Henry said. "I wish you wouldn't, darling, not when we're having a serious discussion. It is very important to me to understand your aunt. I wouldn't offend the dear old lady for the world. How marvelous that she is interested in football! I can help her understand the complexities of the sport. I presume she is a Redskin fan?"

"I suppose so," Ellie muttered.

Henry regarded her with affectionate amusement. She looked cute when she was sulking, like an irritated kitten or baby chick. (Henry's figures of speech were not very original.) She would soon learn to accept his gentle corrections gratefully; in the meantime he simply ignored her ill humor until it went away. That was the way to train people, show them that temper tantrums and pouting didn't have the least effect.

"That gives me a good conversational lead," he said cheerfully. "I shall praise the Redskins."

"Why don't you make a note of it?" Ellie inquired.

"I think I can remember it," Henry said, chuckling to show that sarcasm did not affect him either. "Is there anyone I can safely criticize? There must be someone she dislikes. I always say nothing makes people friends more quickly than a shared enemy."

"Oh," Ellie said, "well, yes. She does dislike quite a few people."

"For example?"

Ellie took a deep breath.

"Joe Namath and Dr. Joyce Brothers and Roger McGrath—he's the head of the local schoolboard and he has been trying to censor the high-school library—and *All in the Family* and TV commercials about deodorants—she adores the cat-food commercials, of course—and Howard Cosell, but I guess that isn't unusual . . ."

"No."

". . . and Norman Mailer and Plato—she says he's a fascist—and Tricia Nixon and Gore Vidal—"

"I'll go along with that," Henry said approvingly.

"But probably not for the same reasons," Ellie said, with a swift sidelong look. "She's mad at him because she says he is almost a great writer, and he won't take the trouble to be a great writer because he despises people so much."

"I see. Who else?"

"Poor Henry," Ellie said, laughing. "Don't sound so depressed. I can't think of anything else at the moment, but I'll mention subjects as they occur to me. Oh, and, Henry, if you start to say something wrong, I'll raise my eyebrows, the way Meg did in *Little Women*. You just watch me."

"All right," Henry said morosely. "Damn it, Ellie, this is ridiculous. Are you sure you aren't joshing me?"

"I wouldn't josh you, darling," Ellie said. Her voice had a peculiar note. Henry had heard that tone rather often in the last few months. It did not occur to him to wonder about it, which was perhaps unfortunate for him. On the other hand, things often turn out for the best—another of Henry's favorite quotations.

"Then *she's* joshing *you*. How serious is she about these things?"

"I'm not sure," Ellie said. "Sometimes she jokes about things she takes quite seriously; and sometimes she keeps a straight face when she's joking. It's hard to tell, with Kate."

"I wonder that people bother trying," Henry grumbled.

"People love her," Ellie said. "I'm afraid I've given you the wrong impression of her. She is a little odd, but she is the kindest, most tenderhearted person alive. She is hard on people she considers pompous or snobbish. . . ."

Her voice trailed away and she stared fixedly at the road. Henry was glad to see that she was concentrating on her driving, but he was feeling abused.

"She sounds most peculiar," he said. "Not at all like your mother. Now there is a splendid woman! Down to earth, competent—"

"No," Ellie said. "She's quite different from Mother. . . . Kate said something to me once. She said she spent the first forty years of her life worrying about what other people thought. She figured half a lifetime was long enough. She is utterly honest in her peculiar way, Henry; no pretense, no living up to the Joneses. Oh, yes, I almost forgot; she's very critical of Freud just now, so don't tell her about your shrink. And don't say anything nice about monotheism."

There was a short silence.

"What?" said Henry.

"Monotheism," Ellie said patiently. "Last year she decided that monotheism has caused more trouble than it is worth, what with all the pogroms and persecution and religious wars, and things, so she—"

Henry shook his head.

"Darling, she *is* joshing you."

From Ellie's general direction came a soft grating sound. Henry peered under the dashboard.

"I must have the car checked. Something is grinding."

"It's not the car," Ellie said.

II

Ellie's description of his future aunt-by-marriage disconcerted Henry, but he consoled himself by enumerating her positive qualities: the estate in the Virginia horse country, the antique-jewelry collection, the stock portfolio. However, his rising spirits were dashed when Ellie turned off the highway onto an unpaved side road that deteriorated rapidly into a rutted, boggy trail lined with brambles and poison ivy. His head hit the roof of the car. He complained.

"Aunt Kate likes privacy," Ellen replied, slowing down a little.

Henry was plunged into gloom. Privacy, for the wealthy, was attained, in his experience, by walls, guards, dogs, and heavy gates. Neglected driveways meant poverty. This driveway went on for over a mile, and by the time they reached the end of it he was prepared for the worst—a tumbledown sharecropper's shack inhabited by a crazy old crone without teeth or shoes. They came out of the woods and Henry's eyes literally bulged.

A wide green lawn, smooth as clipped velvet, three or four acres in extent, was dotted with handsome old trees, including two giant, symmetrical magnolias flanking the entrance gates. Henry caught a glimpse of a formal continental garden, with clipped boxwood hedges, behind the house, before Ellie swung the car around the graveled circle and stopped.

The house was originally eighteenth century, but its red brick central core had spread out into innumerable wings. Half a million dollars, Henry thought, taking in the magnificently manicured lawns and the limitless expanse of slate roofs, chimney-crowned. Six hundred and fifty thousand. . . .

A broad, roofed veranda enclosed part of the west wing. It looked like a comfortable place to sit on a warm afternoon, with its wrought-iron furniture,

softened by bright cushions; but at the moment it
was not as impeccably neat as the other parts of the
house and grounds. The furniture had been shoved
into a huddle at one end. Henry revised his opinion
of his hostess to fit the total image he had received
thus far: old and a bit doddering, perhaps, but a delightful old lady. . . . By this time he would have considered Kate delightful if she had had tentacles and
practiced cannibalism.

A door led onto the veranda from the house. It was
closed; but as Ellie got out of the car and started
toward the steps it burst open and a figure emerged,
waving its arms and moving its feet with insane agil-
ity. Its movement was so rapid that Henry could not
see it clearly, but it seemed to be a child; the dimin-
utive stature, the blowing locks of silver-gold, and
the costume—jeans and flapping shirt—suggested
late adolescence.

The creature was dancing. A blast of sound issuing
from the open door assured Henry of the correct-
ness of this deduction. As he watched, openmouthed,
the dancer's steps took her away from the door,
along the length of the veranda; and then a second
figure appeared, also dancing. This was presumably
a male person, although it wore a short pleated skirt
that barely reached its knees, and a sport shirt of
violent purple. Silvery hair, lifted by the vigor of his
movements, formed a halo around his flushed face.

The music ended, with a blare like the moan of a
dying cow. The male figure collapsed onto one of the
porch chairs and sat panting, its neatly shod feet extended. The female figure turned and descended the
steps.

It was not a child. The hair was more silver than
gold, the narrow pointed face was not free of wrinkles—or of freckles. The features were undistin-
guished, except for a pair of remarkable eyes,
somewhat shadowed and sunken, but of a shade of
azure so deep as to be almost cobalt—the true, rare

sapphire-blue. Glowing like gems, they matched the woman's sapphire earrings, stones the size of lima beans, framed in small diamonds. The earrings did not match the rest of the costume—jeans, dirty white sneakers, and a man's blue work shirt.

This, no doubt about it, was Aunt Kate.

Henry got out of the car, mashing his knee on the door handle in his haste. Without breaking stride Kate advanced upon him, her eyes fixed unwinkingly on his face. Henry was suddenly reminded—although there was no physical resemblance—of a schoolteacher he had once had, an outspoken old termagant who had terrified him.

"Henry?" Kate said, extending a small ugly hand—calloused, square-fingered, covered with a network of half-healed scratches. The questioning tone in her voice implied that she was hoping against hope the answer would be No.

"And you're Aunt Kate," Henry said heartily. "I hope you don't mind my calling you that; after all, I'm almost one of the family. And I feel I know you, Ellie has spoken so often about you—"

"Lies," Kate said. "All lies."

She turned to Ellie. They did not embrace; instead they stood grinning foolishly at one another. For a moment the resemblance was uncanny, and all to Kate's advantage. Her blue eyes danced and her face looked softer and younger.

"It's been a long time," she said, and smiled even more broadly, as if the triteness of the phrase pleased her.

"You're pretty good," Ellie said. "Since when have you taken up Scottish dancing?"

"Last month. The reels are not coming too well. Ted is in rotten shape and he won't exercise." Kate cast a critical glance at the man in the skirt. Henry still had not accustomed himself to her voice, which was too low and too deep and far too emphatic for her small frame. She couldn't be five feet tall. . . .

"Leave the luggage for now," she ordered—most of her remarks sounded like orders, whether they were meant that way or not. "You can unpack later. I need a drink. Ted wears me out; he's so inept."

"Delightful suggestion," Henry said heartily. "You and I are going to be pals, Aunt Kate."

Kate turned and gave him a long, thoughtful look.

Ted struggled to his feet as they approached, and Kate, without stopping, threw a casual introduction over her shoulder.

"Willoughby, Fraser. You remember Ellie, Ted."

"Indeed I do," said Ted. He might have traded voices with Kate, to the benefit of both. His was high-pitched and drawling, with an affected stress on the vowels. He was a tall man, a little flabby around the middle, but otherwise in excellent condition for his apparent age. On closer inspection the garment that covered his lower torso seemed to be a kilt rather than a skirt, but Henry had no doubt as to Ted's nature. The way he stood, with one hand on his hip. . . . He nodded coolly to Ted, who nodded back at him without enthusiasm, and followed his hostess into the house.

There he found himself confronting a suit of armor that appeared to be about to topple off its pedestal on top of him. Henry stepped back and stared. The rest of the decor went with the armor. The hall was determinedly medieval, from the flagstone floor to the oak-beamed ceiling. The furniture was scanty, but one piece caught Henry's calculating eye—a long, low chest, intricately carved. Sixteenth century, at the latest, he thought. It could not be a reproduction. The blackened, satiny surface was the product of centuries of use. It must be worth at least . . . And the tapestry over the chest looked like one he had seen in a museum somewhere, with unicorns and ladies in pointed hats enveloped in a misty green twilight.

As he followed Kate through room after room, he

had the feeling that he had stumbled into a museum. The drawing room was a pleasant relief to the eyes after the gloomy bareness of the hall; long windows let in a flood of sunlight that warmed the Aubusson carpet, the rosewood piano, and the eighteenth-century furniture.

The next room was a library. The decor here was Gothic. A massive stone fireplace occupied one entire end of the room. The other three sides were filled with books. A gallery, with more bookshelves, ran around the upper portion of the room, reached by a curving wrought-iron staircase. The high ceiling was beamed, gilded, carved, and painted to a dizzying degree.

Finally Kate opened a door at the end of a long corridor.

"My workroom."

The room was enormous—thirty by fifty feet at the least. There was another fireplace, with a white carved mantel, and a wide bay window filled with plants. Some of them were withered. The outstanding quality of the chamber was the incredible litter that filled it. The furniture consisted mainly of chairs and tables; the flat surfaces of both types were covered with objects, many of them cats.

Henry had never seen so many cats. Fat cats and lean cats. Short-haired cats and cats that looked like animated mops. Blue cats. White cats, tabby cats, gray cats. Siamese cats, Persian cats, and cats of indeterminate species. Kittens. Cats with long tails, cats with no tails at all.

Kate had left the room, presumably in search of refreshments, so Henry was able to stare unobserved, which he did. The cats weren't the only kind of clutter. A long table in the center of the room was heaped with miscellaneous objects, ranging from fabric and tangles of bright-colored wool to tools such as pliers and hammers; scraps of wood, papers (newspapers, carbon paper, sketching paper), pencils, scissors, an orange rind, and four coffee cups, all of them dirty. The chairs and the floor contributed musical instruments (guitar, zither, lute, and a set of trap drums), sporting equipment (a tennis racket, a baseball bat, and a jump rope), several pieces of unfinished embroidery, a quilting frame, with a quilt on it, and two plastic do-it-yourself models of monsters (Dracula and the Wolf Man). The parts of the floor that showed between cats were tiled in a creamy marble pattern. The walls were pale green, but very little of their surface was visible; pictures and posters covered them, as in an overcrowded and bizarre art gallery. The only painting that rated a clear space, above the mantel, was a Japanese water color of cherry trees in bloom. Henry's superficially educated eye recognized its quality, which made some of the other pictures even more appalling. Many framed photographs depicted cats and kittens, sickeningly maudlin in style. There were several photographs of statue heads, one of a man in a femininely draped hat, and another of a personage with a weird crown on his head and features so exaggeratedly ugly that they verged on caricature.

The posters included a map of Middle Earth, an profanely belligerent piece of propaganda for women's liberation, and, occupying the center of the longest wall, a near life-sized representation of a large gentleman in the act of throwing a football. The face guard of his helmet obscured his features, but Henry did not need the number 9 stamped across the ample front of his jersey to identify him.

Henry sighed involuntarily and turned to meet the unexpectedly sympathetic eye of the kilted person named Ted.

"It is a bit overpowering," said Ted, with an engaging smile.

Shaken out of his usual composure, Henry spoke without affectation.

"Is she for real?" he asked.

"That's very perceptive of you," said Ted. "How much of Kate is for real? God knows. There's a germ of truth behind all her peculiarities, but . . . I've often wondered myself."

"A germ of truth," Henry repeated. "Including her claim to be a witch?"

"Ah," said Ted. "Now that is the most interesting question of all."

Before Henry could decide whether or not he wanted to pursue this subject, the door opened. Kate and Ellie entered, carrying trays. Henry leaped to take Kate's from her; but as he reached out for it he was paralyzed by an outburst of sound from far down the corridor. It sounded like a pack of wolves approaching.

"Damn it," Kate said. "I forgot the dogs. Ted, get the door, quick—"

Ted was too slow again. Before he could reach the door, a furry avalanche was upon them.

The intensity of the sound was diabolical; the shouted orders of Ted and Kate mingled with the howls of angry cats and the baying of the dogs. Furry bodies flew in all directions. Henry stood frozen as an animated, fragmentary rug swirled around his feet and battered his ankles. When a huge, liver-colored mastiff launched itself at his throat he closed his eyes, but stood firm.

The crash of his fall stunned him. He could feel the dog's weight on top of him; the hot, slobbering breath was only an inch from his face. Henry opened his eyes on a vista of white fangs and drooling red tongue. He closed his eyes again. The dog moistened his entire face in one long loving swipe from chin to hairline.

Kate's voice snapped out a command. The dog slid off Henry and crouched, cowering. Henry didn't blame it for cowering. The next command was directed at him; it brought him staggering to his feet, although for several reasons he would have preferred to remain prostrate.

Kate looked him over.

"Are you all right?" she asked; and answered her own question. "More surprised than hurt. Here, have a drink."

Henry took the glass Ted handed him. It was excellent Scotch.

"What an affectionate dog," he said, glancing at the mastiff. Its teeth were bared in what might or might not have been a canine grin, but when Kate turned cold blue eyes in its direction it sobered immediately and lowered a pensive muzzle onto its paws.

"She is completely undiscriminating in her affection," Kate said. "And completely fickle. Any new face . . ."

The rest of the afternoon passed like a horrible dream. Ted took his departure, and although Henry did not care for his type, he was sorry to see him go because Kate was then free to turn her entire attention to him. It began to rain. One of the dogs—a Saint Bernard—was afraid of rain. It wanted to sit on Henry's lap. Kate finally removed it, but not until it had deposited considerable hair on Henry's beautifully tailored knees.

Eventually Kate led her guests upstairs and showed them their rooms. She had some regard for the proprieties after all, Henry decided; not only did he and Ellie have separate rooms, but they were separated by the full length of the house. Ellie went off with her aunt to help prepare supper and Henry collapsed onto the bed, where he remained for some time.

He was aware that he had not made a smashing impression, but an interval of peace and quiet restored his natural egotism and he decided he would win the old lady over during the evening. In the handsomely appointed private bathroom he made a finicky toilette and assumed his second-best suit.

Then he set out to find his hostess. It was not an easy job. The house was big and rambling. Henry didn't mind; it gave him an opportunity to inspect the premises. As he wandered from room to room, counting antiques, he was more and more inclined to overlook Kate's eccentricities. Even the dogs.

Finally he located the two women in a small cozy parlor in the east wing. The theme here was American primitive. The furniture was eighteenth century and the walls were covered with antique samplers and paintings of puffy-faced children. The cats were modern.

There were three of them—an ageless Siamese, an enormous orange beast with a tail like Cyrano's plume, and a smaller, long-haired silver tabby with malevolent yellow eyes. Henry leaned over to stroke the Siamese. "Nice kitty," he said. The Siamese gave him a long, thoughtful look, very much like the look Kate had given him earlier. Then it rose to its feet, stretched, and walked away. Even Henry, who was not sensitive, got the point.

However, he was sensitive enough to realize that he had interrupted a heated discussion between Ellie and her aunt. Ellie was flushed and suspiciously moist around the eyes. Kate looked pensive, and, for her, almost subdued. She greeted Henry and removed a cat from a chair so that he could sit down.

She was wearing a long skirt embroidered in silks of varying shades of blue, a pale-blue silk blouse, and enough jewelry to stock a store. Diamonds blazed and sapphires glowed in the soft light of sunset. There were opals on her small ugly hands.

Ellie's only ornaments were her engagement ring and a copper-colored pendant that resembled a petrified fried egg. Her long skirt was of faded blue denim, with a ragged fringe around the bottom instead of a hem; her sleeveless T-shirt had a print of an Hawaiian sunset, with palms. She looked absurdly pretty in this ridiculous outfit; Henry made a mental note to help her select more suitable evening attire when they got back to Washington.

"Have a drink, Henry," Kate said sweetly. "My dear boy, don't be so abstemious, a big man like you *needs* a stiffer drink than a woman does. Here, let me. . . . There you are. Now sit down and tell me all about yourself."

Henry was still describing his high-school career when the dinner guests arrived. One was Ted, wearing a faultlessly tailored tuxedo and a ruffled shirt. The other guests were a couple named Grant. Mrs. Grant was a slim pseudo-blonde whose type Henry recognized; her daytime attire would consist of slacks and a tailored shirt, and her hair would be tied back with a scarf when she drove the station wagon, taking the children to their private schools. Her evening wear was just as conventional—a long skirt and silk blouse. Henry hardly noticed; he was more interested in greeting her husband, a craggy-faced, broad-shouldered man with streaks of gray in his dark hair.

"Senator," he exclaimed, extending his hand. "It's a pleasure to meet you."

"Just call me Al," Grant said with a practiced smile. "I mustn't get too accustomed to that title; who knows, I may lose it in November."

"I admire modesty, Al," Henry said sincerely. "But everyone is predicting a landslide victory for you."

"There's one vote I won't get," Alan Grant said, turning to his hostess with the same bland smile. "Unless Kate changes her mind about my platform and qualifications."

Kate returned the smile. Hers was distinctly feline; you could almost see the whiskers vibrating.

"I wouldn't vote for you for dog catcher," she purred.

The comment, and the haste with which Grant

changed the subject, confirmed Henry's earlier hunch—politics was not going to be a safe topic. Grant's platform was conservative, to say the least, so it was not difficult to imagine where Kate's political sympathies lay. Henry had suspected from the first that she was a left-winger. He was tempted to start a discussion so that he could impress Grant with his knowledgeability. Grant was definitely a comer. Still in his early forties, he would be a national figure by the time he passed the half-century mark. But if he pleased Grant he would alienate Kate, and he didn't want to do that. Better leave politics alone. He would find an opportunity to make use of the introduction to Grant some other time.

Apparently Grant and Kate were old acquaintances, if not friends, and Grant knew how to get his revenge.

"Have you been meddling with the electricity again?" he demanded, glancing at a coil of wire and pair of pliers that had been shoved not quite out of sight under a chair. "Kate, why the hell don't you call an electrician?"

"And pay him twenty dollars to rewire a little old plug?" Kate demanded indignantly. "I can manage a simple thing like—"

"The last time you tried it you blew every fuse in the house," Grant said.

"She fixed that table lamp for me," Anne Grant said.

Her voice was placid and there was a pleasant smile on her exquisitely made-up face. But Kate glanced sharply at her and then exchanged a quick look with Ted.

"Thanks, Anne," she said. "Testimonials and recommendations appreciated. I always say—"

"Alan can't plug in a lamp without blowing a fuse," Anne said. She was still smiling.

"I'm afraid Alan has a point when he criticizes me, though," Kate admitted. "I am, of course, an expert in practically everything; but even Leonardo da Vinci had a few failings; and electrical work still baffles me at times. But I've got a book, Alan—*The Practical Home Electrician*. I'll lick it yet."

Henry wondered whether he should say something complimentary about Leonardo da Vinci. "What a painter!" or something like that. . . . No, wait a minute; that wasn't the name Ellie had mentioned as being a favorite of Kate's. Lorenzo. Not Leonardo, Lorenzo. Another Italian.

The conversation had become light and casual, following Kate's lead. Grant kidded her, not without malice, about her enthusiasm for new hobbies and her frequent failures. Kate defended herself vigorously and Ellie and Ted took one side or the other as the spirit moved them. Only Anne Grant sat silent, smiling—a Mona Lisa smile, Henry thought. He knew what Anne's problem was. Quietly and inconspicuously she had already put away three stiff drinks. She was able to get away with it because they were serving themselves—except when Kate pressed a refill on one guest or another. She had not pressed any on Anne. (Henry was unaware of the fact that he had been favored by Kate more frequently than anyone else, but he undoubtedly would have misinterpreted her attentions even if he had noticed them.) He had already been struck by the absence of servants. Odd, but then everything about Kate was odd. Except for her Scotch. She served excellent Scotch, and she wasn't stingy about it, either. Henry felt fine. He was having a wonderful time with a lot of swell people. Sweet pretty Ellie, sweet, rich Kate—good old Al—poor Anne, the lush—Ted . . . Oh, hell, Henry thought tolerantly; it takes all kinds to make a world.

The next time Anne reached for the decanter Kate rose smoothly to her feet without interrupting her speech:

". . . and I also have a new cookbook. *Recipes from*

the Yurts of Turkey. My abgushti will be completely ruined if we don't eat it now."

"If abgushti is what it sounds like, I don't imagine time will make it any worse," Grant said.

"You're mistaken." Ted had also risen. Smiling, he offered Anne his arm. "Abgushti needs all the help it can get."

Henry, who enjoyed his food and had a delicate stomach, was relieved to learn that the Turkish cookbook was another of Kate's little jokes. The main course was an excellent pot-au-feu, accompanied by salad and rolls. They served themselves and then took their plates to the long dining table with its magnificent lace cloth. The wine was magnificent too. After taking one sip Grant lifted his eyebrows; the smile he turned on Kate had more genuine warmth than it had held all evening.

"Good Lord, Kate, where did you get this?"

"My little old wine merchant," said Kate. "Is it any good?"

Henry decided it was time for him to shine. He had not spoken much up to this time; the social chit-chat the others engaged in was too frivolous for him.

"Superb," he exclaimed, before Grant could answer. "Wonderful bouquet—authority—mellow—uh . . ."

Kate's smile became seraphic.

"How lucky that I should have selected it. I didn't realize you were such a connoisseur, Henry. Have another glass."

"Thank you. It reminds me," Henry said, "of a Château Margaux I had once in a tiny restaurant in Paris—not mentioned in Michelin, the best places never are, you know. . . ."

"Is that right?" Ted asked.

"Oh, yes. Don't want the hoi polloi finding out about-'em. Know lots of places like that. This wine—"

Henry went on at some length. He really did know

quite a lot about wines; he had spent hours reading up on them. After a while he noticed that Ellie, across the table from him, was making the most extraordinary grimaces. He stopped in the middle of a sentence.

"Is something wrong, darling?" he asked.

"Uh—no. No. What makes you think something is wrong?"

"You were making such funny faces," Henry said simply. "What was I talking about?"

"Wine. But," Ellie said, "I think you've covered that subject very thoroughly, darling. Let's talk about something else."

"Pick a subject," Henry said cheerfully. "Any subject."

Ted leaned forward.

"Are you a football fan, by any chance, Henry?"

"Am I a football fan!" Henry eyed the older man's smiling face owlishly. He winked. "Hey. What about those stories I been hearing? You know what I mean, ol' boy—you know any of those guys? You know who I mean. Can't say anything more; ladies present. But you know—"

"Oh, yes," Ted said. "I know what you mean."

Henry was feeling no pain, but he was dimly aware of an aura of disapproval emanating strongly from certain quarters. He was relieved when Grant said pleasantly,

"I suppose you're a Redskin fan, Henry? Season-ticket holder?"

Now it must be explained that season tickets to Washington football games are a prestige symbol. They are jealously guarded, and it is almost necessary to inherit them from a friend. Henry hesitated, but not for long.

"Not that enthusiastic anymore," he said nonchalantly. "Oh, I enjoy a good game now and then; go with friends when I'm in the mood. Team's gone downhill lately."

"How true," Grant said. "Actually, I'm a Baltimore fan myself. They're a young team, with a great young quarterback. I think he'll be as great as Tarkenton one of these days."

"No." Henry shook his head. Once he had started shaking it he couldn't seem to stop. "Tarkenton's the greatest. Of all time. Broke all the records."

"Not quite all," Kate said.

She was sitting with her elbows on the table—uncouth, Henry thought dimly—and her chin propped on her hands. Her eyes were enormous; her hypnotic blue gaze held Henry, so that he was able to stop shaking his head. The eyes seemed to be getting bigger and bigger, and he had the strangest feeling that he was going to be drawn into the blue depths and drowned.

"All the records," he said firmly. "Used to be Unitas. The greatest. Now it's Tarkenton. The greatest."

"Do you really think so?" Kate said flatly.

Grant chuckled.

"No fair, Kate. Poor Henry doesn't realize he's treading on sacred ground. You see, Henry, Kate has a favorite—"

"Oh," Henry said. Now he knew why Ellie was making faces at him again. He had forgotten their conversation in the car. Ellie should have reminded him. But it wasn't too late. He could still retrieve his near error. He smiled widely at Kate.

"Not quite, not quite. Thought you'd catch me, didn't you? Oh, no. Not me. Greatest of 'em all. Greatest quarterback the Redskins ever had; any team ever had . . . uh . . . Billy Kilmer!"

CHAPTER
TWO

It was necessary to leave early the next morning, since Kate's flight from Dulles departed at ten. Henry's alarm woke him at six. In the first moments he couldn't tell whether the pounding noise came from rain on the roof or the interior of his skull. He had not been aware of drinking that much, but his physical symptoms and the haziness of his memory indicated that he had.

Maybe haziness wasn't the right word. He couldn't remember a damned thing that had happened after dinner, and his memories of the period before that were somewhat chaotic. They had talked about wine, he remembered that much; and then about football. . . . Kate had tried to trick him—or maybe it was one of her jokes—she had a peculiar sense of humor, that woman. But he hadn't fallen for the trick.

Thinking was a strain. It was too much for his poor head. Groaning, he dragged himself out of bed and got dressed. As he shaved he remembered the rutted road leading from the estate to the highway and groaned again. His car would be absolutely filthy.

In this he was correct, but he had no time to brood about it beforehand. Kate was affable enough—suspiciously so, if Henry had been in any condition to notice—but she kept him busy with chores and rushed him out of the house as soon as he had forced down some breakfast. She was wearing slacks and a trench coat buckled tightly around her impossibly small waist; before they went out the door she added a hat to this costume. It was a sou'wester, of a particularly virulent crimson.

Ellie hadn't dressed. She was wearing a soft, flowing robe; her curls were tumbled and her eyes were heavy. She embraced her aunt and mumbled, "Have a marvelous time, darling, and don't worry about a thing."

"I'm not worried," Kate said, frowning distractedly. "Did I tell you one of the neighbor boys is coming to look after the lawn? Oh, I did. Don't forget to keep an eye on Sapphira's gingivitis and that funny place on Duke's back. The vet knows all about it. You will count them all at night, and make sure everybody is in? Albert chases cars—"

"I know all about the animals," Ellie said. "You've told me a dozen times. Just take care of yourself. . . . Henry, what's the matter?"

Henry, who had been absentmindedly scratching his midsection, flushed irritably. Ellie should know better than to draw attention to such a crude gesture.

"Nothing," he said repressively. "Good-bye, Ellie, I'll call you as often as I can. Do take care to lock the house up at night, you are careless about such things. I'm not sure I like your being here alone, in such an isolated place—"

Ellie was looking at her aunt, who avoided her eyes. Staring at the beamed ceiling, Kate was whistling under her breath. She interrupted Henry, whose tone was decidedly petulant, with a brisk "Nonsense, she's perfectly safe here. You aren't worried, are you, darling?" Ellie opened her mouth to answer, but before she could speak, Kate went on, "Because there's nothing to worry about. The dogs are all the protection she needs, they are all trained watchdogs, and brave as lions. And the ghosts are no trouble, they are very quiet types. No chains, or banging around in the night, or anything like that. Good-bye, Ellie, enjoy yourself."

And out she went, before Ellie could say more. Henry gave her a rather formal kiss and followed. Ellie noticed that he was scratching his stomach again.

She stood at the open door watching as Henry drove away. There was a flash of crimson as Kate pressed her face and her hat against the car window. Ellie waved. Then the car disappeared into the trees. The rain made a soft beating sound on the saturated ground.

It was a warm, sticky morning. Ellie stared blankly out at the rain. She didn't know whether to laugh, or swear, or cry. Laughter won, and she stood giggling feebly for some time. The expression on Henry's face when Kate told her not to worry about the ghosts. . . . In all fairness to Henry, she had to admit that she herself wasn't always sure when Kate was joking—what was that awful word Henry used? "Joshing." Good God.

Deep down in the hidden recesses of emotion, she had come to a decision about Henry; but, like many drastic decisions, it did not surface for some time. She knew only that instead of missing Henry, instead of anticipating lonely hours, she felt only an overwhelming sense of relief. The old house radiated welcome and comfort; she could almost feel it, like warm hands bracing her. Ghosts, indeed! Kate was really a little obvious at times. And yet Henry had definitely been scratching. He never scratched. Scratching was lower class. Was it possible that Kate . . .

The soft silkiness of fur brushed her bare ankles, and she looked down to find herself calf-deep in cats. The dogs had their own house, an elaborate heated kennel that resembled a Walt Disney castle—one of Kate's more revolting architectural conceptions. They spent part of their time there and part of it in the house, to which they were admitted, on rainy days, via a system of mud rooms, drying rooms, and the like, as complex as the air locks on a space vehicle.

But the cats had not gone out and they were not about to do so. When Ellie opened the screen door the assorted eyes, green and gold and baby blue, contemplated the rain, and then turned to Ellie with critical contempt. It was obvious what they were thinking and it put Ellie on the defensive, as it was meant to do.

"I can't help it if it's raining," she said loudly. "It isn't my fault."

Nobody in the crowd believed a word of it. Under their contemptuous regard Ellie began to doubt it herself.

She fled from the cats into the kitchen, where she found Marian Beaseley clearing away the breakfast dishes. Kate's arrangements about domestic help were as peculiar as her other habits. She didn't like live-in servants; in fact, the whole master-servant relationship irritated her considerably. Yet it was impossible to run the big house single-handed. Kate had solved this dilemma in a characteristic manner and with the uncanny luck that usually accompanied her most eccentric ideas. Who else but Kate could have discovered a family that felt just as she did about privacy, and who were willing to work only for someone who ignored their presence as thoroughly as they ignored hers?

The Beaseleys, husband and wife and assorted children, did most of the work in and around the house, with the assistance of a commercial cleaning team that came several times a year, but it was rarely that one actually saw a Beaseley in action. They functioned like the little elves that helped the kindly shoemaker, although their big-boned, harsh-featured faces were not at all elfin—sliding smoothly out of a room as one entered it, and vanishing without comment when the work was done. They didn't need to be told what to do, they simply did it. The Beaseleys refused to work for anyone else. This was understood by the other families in the neighborhood after an unfortunate encounter between Marian Beaseley and an innocent new resident, who had visited the Beaseley house in the hope of hiring a "daily."

Kate's peculiar reputation in the neighborhood hadn't been helped by this relationship. Although there had been Beaseleys in the area for two hundred years, people had a tendency to regard them as Kate's familiars, or as victims of a form of occult blackmail. Some of the more superstitious residents really did think Kate was a witch. Oddly enough, this idea increased the respect in which she was held; people were afraid of her, but they thought of her as basically benevolent—if she was not provoked. Indeed, Ellie thought, Kate's reputation was probably as much protection as the dogs.

The Beaseleys had one defect as servants—they never waited on anyone. Indeed, the idea of Marian Beaseley, hawk-nosed and leather-skinned, bending servilely over a tray of canapés was enough to boggle even Ellie's excellent imagination. If one had the inclination, it would be interesting to trace the conglomerate ethnic groups that had contributed to the Beaseley heritage. There was Indian blood there, surely; some black genes, some Scotch-Irish—heaven knew what else. They were inbred to a shocking degree, but the results were surprisingly efficient. And perhaps no one but Kate, who had her own form of pride, could have understood the fierce independence and pride that moved the Beaseleys.

Ellie had a lot of respect for it; she nodded to Marian, who replied with a grunt—a surprisingly affable response—poured herself a cup of coffee, and left the kitchen.

She headed for Kate's workroom—the one room in the house the Beaseleys never touched. It was a wonderfully comfortable room. Odd, that the word "comfort" should come to mind so often about a house as grandiose and bizarre as Kate's home; but for all its pretentiousness and elegance the house had nothing in it that had been selected for the purpose of impressing anyone. Every object was something Kate liked for its own sake.

Ellie was one of the few people who knew where the money for all this had come from, one of the few who knew of Kate's brief, unhappy marriage. She had inherited a modest fortune from her husband, but it was she who had built it into a large fortune through judicious and inspired investments. That was Kate's undeniable talent, a talent so great as to verge on genius, and the one thing that bored her to the point of nausea. As soon as she had made the money she needed, she had dropped out of the market and proceeded to spend the income doing the things she loved—and doing most of them rather badly.

Ellie grinned as she looked at the piece of embroidery on the top of the pile. Kate still hadn't really mastered the satin stitch—that deceptively simple and most difficult of all embroidery stitches. She was still trying, though. The overall effect wasn't bad. Kate could do most things competently; it was probably because she tried to do so much that she had occasional, and often spectacular, failures. Grant had been fairly kind about Kate's failure with electrical work. She had been accused of blacking out the entire town on one occasion, although she strenuously denied this, pointing out, with some justice, that even if she had tried to she could not have produced such massive effects. And there had been a storm that night. . . . Old Man Fletcher, the chief proponent of the witchcraft theory, insisted that Kate had called up the storm to get back at him for hunting on her property. Lightning had struck his still and reduced it to a rubble of fused copper coils.

The day passed with exquisite slowness. Ellie embroidered, played the guitar, got herself some lunch, demudded four dogs, fed twelve cats, and again denied responsibility for the rain. The cats reacted variously; some kindly overlooked her inadequacy and wanted to sit on her lap, some sat and sulked ostentatiously at her, some left for parts unknown. Ellie did a crossword puzzle and practiced throwing darts, and read, and played the piano. She got herself some supper, demudded six dogs, and counted cats—and repeated, rather shrilly, that she could not make it stop raining.

The phone had rung several times; enjoying her solitude, she had not answered it. Kate had a recording device attached to the phone, although she usually wiped the messages without listening to them. After supper Ellie watched television for a while, finished the crossword puzzle, and then decided to go to bed. The sound of the rain made her sleepy.

She checked the doors downstairs before she went up, although she was not at all nervous. The dogs *were* a security factor, though not in the way Kate claimed; they were all idiotically friendly, and most of them were arrant cowards. Ellie assumed that they would make enough noise welcoming a burglar to awaken her, and that if she were in any danger of sleeping through the welcome, she would certainly wake up when William, the Saint Bernard, tried to climb into bed with her. The last time she had visited Kate, William had encountered a large clicking beetle in the hall, and had fled to Ellie's bed, trembling with terror.

Normally the dogs didn't sleep upstairs, so Ellie was accompanied by only half a dozen cats when she started up. She was accustomed to weaving around them, even when they suddenly lay down on the step under her poised foot, but the climb did require a little concentration; she was gazing at the floor and thinking of nothing in particular except falling—certainly not of Kate's final words—when a slight change in the light above made her look up.

She was almost at the top of the stairs. To left and right the long upper hall of the west wing stretched out. She had a clear unobstructed view of a considerable section of bare wall. Only it wasn't bare. Not exactly.

The man was young, and not really handsome; but he was a pleasant-looking person, with an attractive smile. His hair fell in long, wavy locks to his shoulders. He wore a brown coat with lace at his throat, knee breeches, and white stockings; and, at knee level, a low table with a vase of flowers on it. The table was the one that normally stood in that part of the hall. The man was, in a word, transparent.

As Ellie stood transfixed he went out—disappeared, vanished—like a light when a lamp is switched off.

CHAPTER THREE

Ellie was aroused from her stupor by a feline wail. She was standing on someone's tail. She lifted her foot, but remained where she was, uncertain whether to retreat or make a dash for the presumed safety of her bedroom. In order to reach that shelter she would have to pass the spot where the man had . . . "stood" hardly seemed an appropriate word.

Strangely enough, her uncertainty was not tempered by fear. A certain degree of disquiet was present; the occurrence had been unequivocally abnormal. But the apparition had brought with it none of the customary characteristics of visitors from Beyond the Grave—no blast of icy air, no sensation of indescribable terror. He had seemed a rather pleasant ghost. Had he smiled at her, just before he vanished? Ellie wasn't sure. She rather thought he had.

She went on up the stairs. Stopping by the table, she extended a tentative hand and touched the wall above it. It was a smooth, flat wall, painted pale blue. It felt cool and slightly damp.

Ellie walked along the hall to her room. It was the one she always used when she visited Kate, and it was still furnished in the style she had selected when she was twelve. Early French boudoir, Kate called it. Ruffled skirts on the dressing table, gilt cupids holding up trails of muslin that framed the mirror; a ruffled canopy over the four-poster bed, a ruffled skirt on the overstuffed chair. . . . There were rose-buds all over everything. Kate had "done" the room, as she did everything, with a thoroughness that bordered on excess, but tonight Ellie found its overwhelming cuteness comforting, a reminder of childhood and the welcome this house and its owner had always extended to her. The fire in the fireplace—a sign of the presence of one Beaseley or another, earlier in the evening—was flickering low; it added the final touch of cozy security to the walled-in brightness of the room.

In the white-painted bookcases on either side of the fireplace Kate kept a selection of childhood classics. After she had undressed, Ellie selected *Anne of Green Gables* and climbed into bed. But she did not turn at once to the bucolic innocence of that vanished world; instead she sat propped up against her frilled pillows and stared at the opposite wall.

Four of the cats and one of the dogs had decided to sleep with her. The cats occupied the entire lower half of the bed; Ellie had to sit with her knees pulled up. The dog was Kate's Pekingese, Franklin; although he was the smallest of all the canines, he was probably more capable of repelling burglars than were the larger dogs. Kate insisted that Franklin was always sorry after he bit someone, but he had a quick temper and was getting too old to learn new habits. As Ellie looked at him where he lay, on the old sea chest at the foot of the bed, he raised his head and gave her an affectionate curl of the lip. Ellie glanced from his silky russet shape to the furred piles of sleeping cats—silver tabby, blotched calico, tawny Abyssinian, orange Maine coon—and thought about the ghost.

None of the animals had seemed to notice the apparition. That fact didn't fit the mythology of the su-

pernatural. Animals were supposed to be sensitive
to such things; in all the ghost stories she had read
they snarled, or fled, or bristled—or something. . . .
The only reaction she had observed was a yowl when
she trod on someone's tail.

Ellie glanced involuntarily at the open doorway.
She had to leave the door open, since the animals
insisted on going and coming during the night. Like
most old houses, this one was never silent. The tim-
bers moaned and whispered with changes in weather
and humidity, and some members of Kate's zoologi-
cal collection were nocturnal creatures. Ellie was
accustomed to these sounds, including the heavy,
plodding footsteps of Ambrose, the thirty-pound
Maine coon cat, which sounded exactly like the tread
of a large man.

A rustling, scrabbling sound might have been unnerving if Ellie hadn't known what it was; she continued to watch the open doorway, and when the
shining white shape appeared, she greeted it famil-
iarly.

"Hello, Roger. I haven't seen you all day."

The rat squeaked at her, and two of the cats stirred
uneasily. They were terrified of Roger. They had been
taught that he was sacrosanct, but Roger didn't feel
the same way about them and they knew that he was
capable of royal displeasure if they got in his way.
Roger the rat was the undisputed head of the house-
hold pecking order; his progress through the house
resembled that of an emperor, as all creatures fell
back before him.

After a moment Roger left; he obviously had other
plans in mind, and had only stopped by to pay his
respects. Kate had kept him away from Henry—
whether for Henry's sake, or Roger's, Ellie had no
way of knowing. Her face twisted in a grimace that
Henry would have described as "cute." She wasn't
feeling cute. Kate really was a demon. She had taken
an instant dislike to Henry, and her behavior. . . .

Ellie had spoken to her about it, just before dinner; and Kate, appearing contrite, had promised to behave herself. She had then proceeded to encourage Henry to drink too much.

In all fairness Ellie had to admit that Henry probably would have made a mess of things even if he had been completely sober. He was not sensitive to atmosphere, or to other people's feelings. Though how anyone, drunk or sober, could have been unaware of Kate's outrage. . . .

Some form of mental telepathy must have been in operation, for at that precise moment the telephone by the bed rang. It was Henry.

He had called, he explained, to see how she was getting along. Ellie started to say that she was getting along fine, except for the rain. . . . She had no time to say more, since Henry was more concerned with telling her how *he* was.

He was not well. The drive back to Washington had been frightful; the weather had been terrible, and Kate had hardly spoken, even in response to his repeated thanks and his praise of her lovely house. It was a fairly normal series of petty complaints, to which Ellie had become accustomed, but tonight she found them unusually irritating. And there was something else. . . .

"You sound funny," she said suddenly, interrupting a description of the imbeciles who had been driving the other cars along Route 40 that morning. "Are you sick? Have you caught a cold?"

"No."

"Then what's the matter?"

"Nothing."

This was so unlike Henry, who usually gave her detailed descriptions of each sneeze from a head cold, that Ellie began to get a horrible suspicion.

"Henry, something is wrong. What is it?"

"I have a sort of a—you might call it—well—"

"A rash?"

"Well, yes. But don't get any crazy ideas, Ellie. I'm very sensitive to certain foods, you know. Maybe the strawberries in the dessert . . ."

"Damn it! Henry, I warned you, you know I did. What did you say? I knew there was something the matter, I've seen that look on Kate's face before, but I didn't understand any of that nonsense about football. You must have said something. . . ."

"I don't remember what I said," Henry muttered.

"You don't?"

"I mean, I wasn't paying that much attention. It was such a puerile conversation, and I was exhausted from driving and from those repulsive dogs jumping all over me—"

His voice was rising; it always did when he got panicky or offended.

"You drank too much," Ellie said coldly. "Alan Grant didn't help; he was trying to heckle Kate, he always does, and he didn't mind using you to annoy her. All that stuff about Tarkington and United—"

"Tarkenton and Unitas," Henry said. His voice was quite shrill. "Oh, God, yes; we did talk about quarterbacks. But I remembered what you said. I saw the trap; I did not claim that Francis Tarkenton was the greatest quarterback of all time. I remembered what you said about Sonny—"

"But that wasn't the name," Ellie interrupted. "That wasn't what you said. It was some other name. Billy something."

There was a long pause. She could hear Henry breathing heavily.

"Not Billy Kilmer?" he said after a while. "I didn't. Don't tell me I said Billy Kilmer."

"I think that was it. Why is that so terrible?"

"Oh, damn," Henry whispered. "It's all your fault, Ellie. Why didn't you stop me?"

"But what difference does it make?" Ellie asked gently. "You don't believe in Kate's black magic, do you? Even if she was mad she couldn't do anything to you."

"Naturally I don't believe in such nonsense. I wouldn't even have mentioned my illness—that sort of self-pity is totally alien to my personality—but you insisted—"

"You'd better go see a doctor tomorrow," Ellie said resignedly. "I believe it takes several weeks to get over it."

"I'm quite sure it will be gone by tomorrow. I used the ointment your aunt gave me, and—"

"Henry, you didn't!"

It was inevitable that they should have a fight then, a good old-fashioned shouting match that ended with Ellie's hanging up on her fiancé. It was the first time they had ever had that kind of argument. Ordinarily Henry didn't yell back; on this occasion Ellie was able to gauge the degree of his discomfort by the failure of his self-control. Shingles was, she had heard, very painful. Not that she really believed Kate could inflict disease on people by ill-wishing. But if Henry had had some kind of psychosomatic itch (it had not been wise of her to mention that other case of shingles) and if he had mentioned it to Kate (which was typical of him, he adored complaining) and if she had produced some peculiar medication from the bulging handbag she always carried . . . Ellie remembered that at one time her aunt had gone in for homeopathic medicine, growing her own herbs. . . .

She groaned aloud, but it must be admitted that the groan turned into a laugh. It was not until she had turned out the light and was half asleep, lulled by the soft breathing of the cats and their warmth on her feet, that she realized she had not told Henry about the ghost.

And that, even if she had not been distracted by their argument, she had never had any intention of doing so. The last thing she saw in her mind was the smiling young face of the boy in his old-fashioned costume. He had had a small, sickle-shaped scar on his chin, it looked almost like a deep dimple.

II

The rain continued all next day. The phone didn't ring. Ellie knew Henry wouldn't call, he never took the first step toward a reconciliation. She was alone in the house, except for the animals and the scarcely felt presence of various Beaseleys. She had no difficulty amusing herself with Kate's variety of hobby materials, but she was rather pleased when, late in the afternoon, the doorbell rang.

It was impossible for her to go to the door, not only because she was some distance from it, in Kate's workroom, but because William, the Saint Bernard, had her pinned in her chair. She had, with some difficulty, prevented him from trying to climb into her lap, but his heavy head, laid across her knees, weighed her down like a sandbag. But Kate had provided for such an eventuality by having the house wired with an intercom system that usually worked, except when she had been tinkering with it. So Ellie shouted, inquiring the identity of the caller; when the familiar voice answered, she invited him in, knowing he had his own key.

When Ted reached her, he was carrying a tray with glasses, bottles, and ice.

"The sun is definitely over the yardarm," he announced cheerfully. "I won't stay long, if you are enjoying your solitude, but I hate drinking alone."

"I'm delighted to have some company," Ellie said. "You're a darling to come out on a day like this, Ted. And don't kid me; you came over to see how I was getting along."

"Never. It was pure selfishness. I feel the same way

William does about rain. If I weren't so inhibited I'd howl and try to put my head on your lap the way he does."

"Feel free," Ellie said, smiling.

Ted gave the dog a disparaging look. It rolled its eyes at him and did not move.

"I'd have to wrestle William. And I'd lose. How are things going? Everything okay, or has Kate bollixed up the plumbing or the wiring?"

"Everything in the plumbing line is fine." Ellie hesitated, but not for long; she had known Ted since childhood, and he had always been the most admirable of adopted uncles, with an intuitive understanding of a child's illogical fears. "Ted, I did have a funny experience last night."

She told him about the "ghost." Ted listened, as he always did, with complete attention. His ruffled silvery hair, slightly damp with rain, made him look like one of the meeker saints.

"Very curious," he said, when she had finished. "Very curious indeed. You say the animals sensed nothing?"

"Not a quiver. Ted, has anything like this ever happened before?"

She had wondered, as she first spoke, if there had been some slight trace of reserve in Ted's manner, but his answer to this question was prompt and sincere.

"Never. You know how Kate likes to joke about her ghosts, Ellie. Actually she's been furiously disappointed at the absence of any such manifestations. When she furnished that ghastly Gothic library she was hoping for a spook or two to go with the decor."

"Then why—"

"There are several possibilities," Ted said calmly. "Perhaps your presence is the catalyst. Oh, I know, you've visited before and never brought any apparitions with you; maybe you have changed in some fashion as to produce a latent—well, what does one call it?—an image, perhaps, of someone who once lived in the house. It's old enough, at least the central portion is, to have harbored a gentleman in ruffles and knee breeches."

"That's silly."

"Of course, the most obvious hypothesis—the one an investigator would check first—is that there is a purely material cause. Did you look for wires?"

"You mean the image was a projection of a picture or slide? No, I didn't look. I never thought of such a thing."

"Let's look now, then," Ted said.

They looked, William having been persuaded to remove his head. He followed Ellie, snuffling pathetically, and got in everyone's way by trying to sit on some part of her whenever she stopped moving; but it did not take long to verify the fact that there were no visible wires on the stairs on in the upper hall. They went back to the workroom, escorted by William, and Ted freshened their drinks.

"Let's chalk it up to hallucination and forget about it," he said comfortably. "These things happen more often than people realize. It doesn't worry you, does it?"

"No. He was a very pleasant-looking ghost." Ellie smiled. "I don't mind if he wants to hang around."

"If you'd feel more comfortable, I could move in for a few days, or nights—"

"That's not necessary. Honest, Ted, I'm not at all afraid."

"Okay." Ted looked relieved. Ellie knew how much he enjoyed the comforts of his own charming little house. He had a fetish about privacy, just as Kate did; that was one of the reasons why they got along so well.

"I enjoyed meeting your fiancé," he said.

"You did not."

"Oh, yes I did." Ted grinned; there was no other word for the expression, it was too broad to be called a smile, and it transformed his face, from the faintly aesthetic to the gently malicious. "You ought to be ashamed, Ellie; subjecting that boy to Kate was like tossing a kitten into a tiger's lair."

"Ted . . . I'm sorry he was so rude to you. He was drunk, or he wouldn't have . . ."

It was a subject they never discussed, not because either of them was particularly embarrassed by it, but because there had never been any reason to mention it. Ted looked slightly embarrassed now, but Ellie knew he was only concerned about her feelings.

"I've been subjected to worse," he said dryly. "And from people who were sober. Your young man has all the usual hang-ups, Ellie, but his manners aren't all that bad. . . . Er—have you spoken to him since he left? I hope he didn't take cold or anything?"

His eyes were bright with malice. After a moment of stunned surprise Ellie began to laugh.

"Ted, you devil. How did you know? Henry is itching."

"Ah," said Ted.

"But you know she can't do that," Ellie argued. "You know that, Ted. It's impossible."

" 'There are more things in heaven and earth . . .' " Ted said dreamily.

"Anyway, what was so terrible about what he said? I asked him, but he just kept muttering 'Damn.' "

"About Kilmer?" Ted began to laugh. "Oh, God, that was funny. I knew Kate was trying to loosen his lip by plying him with drink, but I never hoped for anything that rich. Don't you remember seeing those bumper stickers all over the Washington area a few years back—the ones that said 'I like Billy' and 'I like Sonny'? The two were competing for the quarterback spot and the Washington fans thought it was a more important issue than Vietnam. People used to have fistfights in bars about who ought to be Number One. You couldn't support one without despising the other, and Sonny's fans were—and are—more fanatical than most."

"Oh," Ellie said. "Henry always did get names mixed up. He couldn't have said anything worse, could he?"

"Oh, yes," Ted said, still choking with amusement. "He could have said a kind word about George Allen. Kate never forgave Allen for firing Jurgensen. If Henry had praised Allen he'd probably have leprosy today instead of shingles."

"I never heard of anything so silly," Ellie exclaimed.

"Kate is pretty silly," Ted said. "That's why I love her. Now your Henry is silly in an entirely different way. He is not at all lovable."

"Are you suggesting I shouldn't marry him?"

"I never make such suggestions. Giving other people advice is one of the most irritating and useless activities known to man."

They sat in silence for a while, since Ellie could think of nothing to say in answer to that indisputable statement. It was a comfortable silence; the rain pattered softly against the windows, and growing dusk made the room a bright oasis of warmth and comfort against the dark. Finally Ted, whose eyes had been wandering around the room, reached out a hand and picked up an object from the littered table.

"What's this? Something new?"

"I don't know how you can tell, there's so much stuff in this room. That's a present I brought Kate. In all the furor yesterday I completely forgot to give it to her. I found it this morning when I finished unpacking."

Ted turned the slim volume over in his delicate long-fingered hands. It was bound in limp leather, which had become speckled with spots of mildew and damp. The rubbed gilt lettering had faded, but was still readable.

"*Vanished Grace: legends of Burton, Virginia, the Homes of Gentlefolk who are no more,*" he read aloud. "Where did you find this, Ellie? It's quite a rare book."

"Is it? I hate to tell you how little I paid for it. I found it in a secondhand bookstore in Georgetown, and thought Kate might get a kick out of it."

Ted opened the book and began turning the pages.

"Have you read any of it, Ellie?"

"I glanced at it, but it looked pretty dull. I did recognize a couple of the names."

"Oh, yes, some of the old gentlefolk are still in residence. . . ." Ted continued to turn pages. His thin, sensitive lips twisted. "And they are just as pompous and hypocritical as their ancestors were. You were right about the book being dull, Ellie. The usual collection of sanctimonious lies. If the truth about these so-called ladies and gentlemen were ever printed, it would make *Peyton Place* read like Elsie Dinsmore."

"That's probably true about most towns. I thought you were one of the gentry yourself, Ted. You don't mean to say your ancestors were among the pompous hypocrites?"

"The worst of the lot, my dear. It's just as well the line is dying out—as it will with me. The last degenerate descendant of a decadent breed . . ."

Ellie shifted uncomfortably. Ted glanced at her; his smile broadened and his face lost its bitterness.

"I do adore alliteration," he said. "And self-pity. Excuse me, Ellie."

"Rain is depressing," Ellie said. "But you usually aren't. . . . Then you think I should just forget about my ghost?"

"I'd be tempted to encourage his visits." Ted sat in silence for a few moments, his long fingers drumming lightly on the cover of the book. "I wonder . . ."

He didn't finish the sentence, but Ellie was sure she could follow his train of thought.

"Oh, no, you don't. No séances, Ted. I don't mind my young man, but I don't intend to encourage him."

"If you say so."

"No, I mean it," Ellie insisted. "I know that look, Ted. No tricks."

"Now, sweetheart, would I play tricks on you?" Ted stood up. "Don't move, I'll let myself out. You have a phone right by your bed. Call if anything bothers you."

"Nothing will."

Yet after he had left, Ellie was aware of a faint uneasiness. Not that she was afraid, nothing like that. She was just not looking forward to going upstairs.

She put it off longer than she might otherwise have done, sitting up to watch an old Humphrey Bogart movie. The rain stopped during the evening; when she looked out the parlor windows, the sky was bright with stars. It was almost two thirty before she started up the stairs, accompanied by the usual procession of animals. In spite of her resolve, her steps slowed as she neared the top, and her heart was beating faster than usual.

Nothing happened. Not a sound, not a flicker of movement. Ellie stood on the landing, looking up and down the dimly lighted corridor, and wondering whether the empty sensation she felt was one of relief or disappointment.

She had scarcely slid down into the bed, wriggling her body between cats, when she heard the sound.

She knew the normal sounds of the house—if Roger's rustling could be called normal. This sound came from outside. She had opened the windows, to enjoy the sweet, rain-washed air, so she heard it distinctly. It was a soft, calling sound, like a human voice raised in wordless song. As Ellie lay staring open-eyed into the darkness, it gradually grew louder—or came nearer.

She got out of bed, in a sudden abrupt movement,

because she knew if she didn't move immediately she would simply pull the sheet up over her head and lie there shivering. Her plunging feet dislodged Jenny, the Siamese, who swore at her in a raucous voice. Ellie ignored the complaint. She went straight to the window.

The ruffled muslin curtains were swaying gently in the breeze. It was a beautiful night. The sound still rose and fell, an inexplicable music.

Ellie unhooked the screen and leaned out as far as she could. In so doing she extended the area of her vision; from her second-floor room she could see across the entire western lawn. At first there was nothing visible that should not have been there—the twin magnolias, the shapes of shrubbery and flower beds, the sweep of the graveled drive. Could it possibly be a night bird that was emitting that strange, beautiful song? None of the native Virginia birds made such noises. She thought of nightingales, which she had never heard, and wondered whether some imported rarity could have escaped its owner, to serenade the night. . . .

Then she saw it—or rather, she saw *them*. There were two figures, indistinct in the starlight, but unquestionably dual. They came out of the trees beyond the lawn, moving quickly, but with uncanny smoothness, as if they were sliding or skating instead of walking.

One of them was a woman. Colors were bleached by night, shapes were uncertain, but the long, full skirts were unmistakable. They belled out, at the waist, as if they were supported by hoops or panniers. The upper part of the body was muffled in a shawllike garment, and the hair caught the starlight with a faint, fair gleam. It might have been silver, or golden blond, or powdered white.

With the woman was another . . . person. The billowing skirts concealed much of his body, but Ellie had a fleeting impression of shoulder-length hair, a dark coat, a flash of white at the throat, before the two skimming, graceful figures were swallowed up by the trees again.

The sound had stopped too. Ellie wasn't sure precisely when it had stopped; she had been so startled by the vision that her ears had stopped functioning for a second or two.

They were functioning now. She heard herself gulp, felt the painful weight in her throat as she swallowed. The sound of her own heartbeat drowned out the gentle drip of water from the eaves.

For some time she stayed where she was, searching the darkness with eyes that began to ache with strain. Finally she drew back, and refastened the screen. Her first, instinctive need was for light. She found the switch and stood blinking in the flare of brilliance. When her eyes had adjusted she stared bewildered at the animals.

They were all awake. Two of the cats had already curled themselves up, preparatory to sleeping again; only slitted eyes betrayed their curiosity about her unorthodox behavior, and their annoyance at being disturbed. Franklin was sitting up, his long silky fur puddling around his haunches, his melting dark eyes fixed on her. He too was curious, but not alarmed. The concentrated regard of all the eyes made Ellie feel self-conscious, like a child who has committed some gaucherie in front of grown-ups.

"A lot of help you are," Ellie said, addressing the group in general.

Franklin yawned. He lay down.

Ellie got into bed. Her feet were cold, although the night was not. She thrust them down into the warm areas produced by huddled cats, and looked at the telephone.

It was a terrible hour to call anyone. But Ted had said . . . Ellie reached for the phone.

It took him some time to answer, and when he did

his voice was fuzzy with sleep, but he brushed Ellie's incoherent apologies aside.

"I know you wouldn't call unless you had a good reason. What happened? Your handsome ghost again?"

"No," Ellie said, and then, surprised: "Maybe. He might have been the second figure; it was the same general shape. . . ."

She found it surprisingly difficult to produce any specific detail in her description, except for the shape of the woman's skirts.

"It was pretty dark," Ted said. He sounded thoroughly wide awake now. "I don't suppose you could make out details. I'm afraid I can't hand you a neat rationalized explanation, Ellie. There were no costume parties in the area tonight. I'd know about them even if I weren't invited—"

Ellie's nerves were keyed up; she found herself unreasonably annoyed at this touch of self-pity.

"That's beside the point," she said sharply. "This place is off the beaten track; no one would take a shortcut through Kate's shrubbery. Whoever it was came here deliberately. And what about the music, Ted?"

"That's unaccountable," Ted admitted. "Unless it was a bird—"

Ellie's snort of disgust made him drop this feeble suggestion.

"I'll get dressed and come over," Ted said.

"No, that's not necessary. I'm sorry I disturbed you, Ted. I—wait a minute."

"What's wrong now?"

"Wait a minute," Ellie repeated. She put the telephone down very gently; her eyes were fixed on Franklin, who had suddenly risen to his feet. His upper lip was drawn back. He was growling faintly, and his head had turned toward the open window.

Ellie ran across the room. This time she did not unhook the screen. She didn't have to. The figure stood out with a queer distinctiveness against the dark background of trees. It was the figure of a tall man wearing a black suit of peculiar cut. The trousers were unusually narrow, and the coat was so tight that he resembled a stick figure. As Ellie stared she heard Franklin's growl rise to a queer keening note. Then the figure raised one black-clad arm in a gesture of menace. For a second Ellie fancied that she saw its face—a narrow, fanatical face with knife-narrow lips framed by a black beard. The eyes blazed under heavy brows.

She ran to the telephone. Ted didn't let her say more than a few words.

"I'll be right over," he said, and hung up.

Ellie sat on the edge of the bed holding the telephone. The echoing silence at her ear made her feel absurdly alone, as if Ted's voice had been a lifeline from which she was now cut off. Then the dial tone began. With a shiver she hung up the telephone and forced herself to stand.

Franklin had stopped growling, but he was still looking at the window. As Ellie passed the dog she put one hand on his soft head and felt him start, in a disconcertingly human fashion. She sidled up to the window.

The starlit lawn was deserted.

How long she stood there she did not know, but it could only have been a few minutes before Ted appeared. His house was only a quarter of a mile away by the wood path he and Kate habitually used. She jumped nervously when he appeared from among the trees, but there was no mistaking Ted, even in the faint light. His eyes went at once to her window.

"Ellie?"

"I'm here. He's gone. . . ."

"So I see." Ted switched on the flashlight he was carrying. "I had hoped to catch your intruder by surprise, but there's no point in stumbling around in the dark any longer. I'll have a look around and then come in. Stay where you are."

"I will," Ellie said.

She watched the light until it vanished around the corner of the house. A few minutes later she heard Ted's voice from the hall.

"It's me."

"I'm coming down," she called, and did so.

Franklin and two of the cats went with her; the dog seemed completely relaxed now, and delighted at this activity at an hour that was usually pretty dull. He flung himself on Ted, yapping shrilly.

Ted was dressed casually but impeccably, as usual, from his Givenchy sport shirt to his Gucci loafers. The latter were muddy and leaf-stained. Standing by the open front door, Ted stepped out of his shoes and grinned cheerfully at Ellie.

"How about a cup of coffee?"

"Ted, you're a hero," Ellie said. "You can have coffee or anything else your little heart desires. Bless you for coming."

"Nothing heroic about it." Ted followed her toward the kitchen, pushing cats out of his way with the ease of long practice. The animals, especially the nocturnal varieties, were assembling from all parts of the house. "Either you were having another hallucination, in which case there was no danger to me—or else your visitors were supernatural, in which case my curiosity is strong enough to override my naturally timid disposition. Good Lord, girl, I'd walk miles to see a genuine, honest-to-God ghost. I'm only disappointed that I didn't."

"You and Kate are disgusting," Ellie said sternly. " 'Curious' isn't the word for you; you're plain nosy. Even about the hereafter!"

"At my age, curiosity concerning that particular region takes on a poignantly personal edge," Ted said. He settled himself at the table.

"I don't believe in ghosts," Ellie said.

"Why didn't the dogs bark?" Ted asked.

"Maybe they did and I didn't hear them."

"Possible, but unlikely. They do bark at intruders, you know; they aren't the useless, spoiled hulks they appear."

"They're supposed to bark at ghosts as well as burglars," Ellie said stubbornly.

"Not bark. They cower, whining abjectly." Ted was smiling. But Ellie felt a shiver go through her, as she remembered the Peke's soft, disturbed whine.

"This is a silly discussion," she said. "What should I do, Ted?"

"You could call the police. Or Kate. I doubt that you'll get much sense out of either. Or you can just sit tight, see what happens next."

"I hope nothing happens next," Ellie muttered.

"If you'd like me to move in temporarily—"

"No. What good would that do? No insult intended, Ted."

"I know," Ted said soothingly. "I've always wondered, myself, why the presence of a single man in the house is supposed to deter malefactors. Or why wives in cartoons are always waking up their paunchy, flabby, middle-aged husbands and sending them downstairs to confront burglars who are presumably desperate, possibly armed, and probably high on something or other."

Ellie brought the coffee to the table and sat down. They drank in silence for a time, both thinking their own thoughts.

"You do think it was supernatural, don't you?" Ellie asked, at last.

"It makes such a lovely story," Ted said dreamily. "First the couple—man and woman—gliding across the lawn, obviously in haste. Then the man in pursuit—dark, menacing—the outraged husband? A hundred years ago there was a road to the West. A carriage might wait there, for someone who wanted to make a getaway from one of these houses, through the woods. . . ."

Ellie put her cup down with a clatter.

"There's a story," she exclaimed. "Out with it, Ted."

"It's more than a story, it's fact. One of those escapades I mentioned last evening, when we were talking about the hypocritical residents of the county. He—the young man—was the brother of one of my ancestors. The woman was the wife of his neighbor, Jeremiah McGrath—one of those self-righteous, prim-lipped, Bible-reading town dignitaries, a sanctimonious swine any woman—or man—would want to escape from. He had three wives after her; killed all three of them with over-breeding and mental torture."

"Good Lord," Ellie said, genuinely shocked. "But how could he marry again if she—"

"Oh, she never made it," Ted said gently. "She and her lover were found the following spring—what was left of them. Only bones, and enough fragments of clothing to identify them. The conclusion was that they had been set on by animals—wolves, bears—in the woods."

"There weren't any bears in this part of the country a hundred years ago," Ellie said.

"Very true." Ted sipped his coffee. "But there were juries open to bribery."

"Are you implying that her husband—"

"He claimed he didn't realize she had left him until he discovered her note the following day," Ted said. "But suppose he found out earlier—in time to pursue them? What you saw tonight suggests—"

"Ted, stop it!"

"I'm not trying to frighten you," Ted said. "Don't you see, Ellie, if this is true, you simply saw a replay of an event that happened a century ago—shadow figures, as unaware of you as they were conscious of their own paradoxical survival. Nothing threatening about that, is there?"

"Oh, I don't know," Ellie said wearily. "I'm too tired to think. You must be exhausted, Ted. Go home to bed—unless you want to sleep here for the rest of the night. Don't do it on my account, though. It's near dawn, and I'm not at all nervous."

"Okay. Don't hesitate to call. I'm absolutely fascinated, Ellie—or I would be if you weren't worried about it."

"That's what is so funny," Ellie said. "I'm not. And I wonder if I shouldn't be."

III

Tired as she was, the sun awakened her next day before noon. The air coming in through the open window was balmily warm. When she sat up Ellie was confronted with a row of expectant, waiting forms. The cats looked like a row of schoolchildren, trained to await the ringing of a certain bell. Blue eyes, green eyes, and eyes of all shades of yellow, from amber to citrine, were fixed unwinkingly on her face. Ellie laughed and swung her legs out of bed, and the cats broke formation, bouncing ahead of her down the stairs and bunching up near the door. The sun had returned, and they were anxious to greet it.

Ellie let them out and then went to the kitchen. Last night's coffee cups still stood on the table. Apparently the Beaseleys were not due until later. They might not come at all that day; their schedule was one that even Kate had never tried to figure out.

As Ellie stood waiting for the water to boil she considered the Beaseleys as suspects. In spite of Ted's theories she was determined to regard what she had seen as a trick, designed and carried out by human agents. Were the Beaseleys capable of such a trick, intellectually and emotionally?

The tricks had been engineered with some degree of cleverness, especially the first one. She had to concede that, since she had no idea how it had been done. That sounded conceited—and it was conceited. All the same, she was unwilling to admit that the Beaseleys, singly or en masse, were that much smarter than she was.

The Beaseleys seemed equally improbable suspects on the grounds of motive. They had no reason to want to frighten her; and indeed, if the aim of the trickster was to scare her, he was not being very thorough about it. The apparitions had not been particularly terrifying.

After she had washed the dishes she went upstairs to get dressed. She could sympathize with the cats. The sun was calling her too, and she lost no time in getting outside.

She released the dogs, bracing herself to withstand their tumultuous greetings, and then filled their water dishes. It took a good half hour to feed the various fauna Kate had accumulated, including the wild birds and the squirrels. Kate had the most obscenely fat squirrels in the county.

When her chores were finished she dragged a deck chair out onto the flagstoned patio and stretched out. The sun felt divine. Her own favorite among the dogs, Toby the bloodhound, had stretched out beside her, his long, mournful muzzle resting on his front paws, and the beautiful thoughtful eyes that are characteristic of the breed fixed on Ellie's face. His name, derived from that of the fabulous mongrel in "The Sign of the Four," who had so often assisted Sherlock Holmes in his cases, was another example of wishful thinking on Kate's part. Toby had something wrong with his sense of smell; he didn't even recognize his friends by nose, but barked at them until they were close enough to be identified. He had an angelic personality, however, and his very appearance was imposing enough to scare off strangers.

Ellie put her hand on the dog's head, and felt him respond with a wriggle of pleasure. Once again she wondered about the strange behavior of the dogs in the night. What was it Dr. Watson had said? " 'The dog did nothing in the night-time.' 'That was the curious incident,' remarked Sherlock Holmes."

Franklin had not barked at the first pair of "ghosts." Did that suggest that they were people he knew? Or that the old folk superstition, that animals were aware of the presence of the supernatural, was false? Maybe dogs didn't bark at ghosts. Maybe they only barked at unfamiliar ghosts. Kate's dogs might be as wildly unpredictable as their mistress. . . . Before her thoughts could wander farther away from sense, Ellie fell asleep.

She awoke with a start, having dreamed that someone was standing over her, to find that it was not a dream. The first thing she saw was an earth-stained trowel, held in a tanned brown hand, and two jean-clad knees, stained with stripes of green and brown. Her eyes traveled up the man's body— flat stomach and narrow hips, a bared torso in tanned Indian-brown, where the ribs stood out with unhealthy distinctness—till they reached the face. Ellie gasped; and the dog, whose head had been quiescent under her trailing fingers, stiffened alertly as her shock communicated itself. The costume was not the same, but the face was the face of the young man who had smiled at her from the upper hall. Feature by feature identically the same, even to the small sickle-shaped scar on the chin.

CHAPTER
FOUR

Slowly and ponderously the bloodhound got to its feet. Ellie was unable to remove her fascinated stare from the face she knew so well, but out of the corner of her eye she saw that Toby was not registering hostility. His tail was moving from side to side and his big brown eyes were bewildered as he looked from her to the newcomer, whom he obviously knew and trusted.

"Who are you?" Ellie inquired.

"Donald Gold. I'm your yardman. Or do you prefer yardboy?"

He grinned broadly at her. The transformation resulting from a simple smile was amazing; Ellie thought of leprechauns, the Cheshire Cat, and a very young boy cousin whose cherubic face looked particularly innocent just before he reached the punch line of a dirty joke. The newcomer had one of those faces that are pure India rubber, capable of unlimited mimicry. The sort of face that is a tremendous asset to an actor, or a spy.

However, it was also unmistakably the face of her first ghost. There were some differences. This man was darker-skinned—which might have been simply a matter of suntan—and thinner. His cheekbones stood out too sharply, like his ribs. His eyes were hazel flecked with brown; green in some lights, dark in others.

As Ellie continued to study him, her fixed stare began to bother the newcomer. His smile faded, and he shifted uneasily from one sneakered foot to the other.

"You must have seen uglier people," he said. "Or has my nose turned bright green or something?"

Ellie was groggy from heat and sleep, or she probably would not have spoken so unguardedly.

"You look just like my ghost," she said.

Donald sat down, in one smooth movement, his legs crossed and his feet tucked in.

"You're the first person I've ever met who had a personal ghost. Since you're a relative of Kate's, I'm not surprised. But I am interested. Tell me more."

Ellie sat up, pushing the damp hair back from her face. She was wearing shorts and a skimpy T-shirt, and Donald's eyes followed her movements with candid appreciation.

"No, you tell me more," she said firmly. "Who you are, for instance, and why you were hovering over me like Count Dracula."

Donald's upper lip lifted when she mentioned the classic vampire; she could have sworn, for a moment, that his canine teeth elongated. Then his face relaxed.

"I was admiring your figure," he explained.

"You must be the neighbor Kate told me about," Ellie said. "She said you'd be coming to mow the lawn, but I didn't visualize—"

"You thought of a Beaseley," Donald interrupted. Ellie could not have explained how he did it, but his face was suddenly pure Beaseley—long jaw, jutting nose. . . .

"No such luck," Donald went on, letting his features slip back into their normal shape. "My dad is the local doctor. We live over there." He waved vaguely at the row of spruces that loomed up beyond the herb garden.

"Oh," Ellie said grudgingly. "I guess I have heard of you. Why didn't I ever meet you?"

"I guess you were never here when I was home from boarding school and college. I know about you, though. Kate brags about you a lot."

"And what are you doing now—besides cutting lawns?"

"Nothing." Donald smiled. "Absolutely nothing."

"Oh, really. How old are you?"

"None of your business."

"Twenty-six?" Ellie guessed. "You mean you haven't got a permanent job?"

"Listen, taking care of Kate's grounds is a full-time job for four men," Donald said indignantly. "I work like a dog. Not like one of Kate's dogs," he added, with a disparaging glance at Toby, who had fallen asleep and was snoring lustily.

Ellie refused to be distracted.

"Cutting grass is a ridiculous way for a man like you to earn a living. You let your father put you through college so you could cut grass? You ought to be ashamed of yourself."

"You're cute when you get mad," Donald said. He added, "I suppose that's why you've developed such filthy rude manners. Blondes always think they can get away with things that would earn anybody else a punch in the nose. Now why don't you get down off your soapbox and tell me about your ghost?"

If it had not been so warm and pleasant in the sun, if Donald's smile had not been so ingratiating, and if Ellie had been a little less worried, she might have sent him about his business. But she did not analyze these motives until much later. She simply talked.

Donald was fascinated. A flicker of emotion that might have been embarrassment crossed his face when Ellie mentioned his startling resemblance to the first apparition, but as she went on he forgot his self-consciousness and listened raptly. Cats came and went, Toby awoke and wandered off, and a goat began eating the roses that lined the patio.

Donald shied a pebble at the goat, which looked outraged but moved away, and Ellie went on with her story. When she had finished, Donald's first comment told her a great deal about the way his mind worked.

"So the night specter couldn't have been Ted."

"No way. Anyhow, you don't think Ted would—"

"I no longer make didactic pronouncements about what people will or will not do. Given sufficient provocation, the mildest of men and women—"

"Soapbox yourself," Ellie said.

"No, no; I'm stating an essential truth. Motive is the last thing you look for in detective work. Means and opportunity—"

"But this isn't a detective story. It's a—"

"Gothic novel," said Donald. His eyebrows went up, and his face became a caricature of enthusiastic surprise. "By God, that's just what it is. A beautiful young heroine in a strange old mansion, beleaguered by—"

"What do you know about Gothic novels? They're women's—"

"I spent six weeks in a place where there was nothing to do but read and very little choice of reading materials," said Donald. His face momentarily lost all traces of amusement. "What I am trying to say—"

"What do you mean, trying? You're the one who keeps interrupting me, and if . . . ."

Her voice trailed off into silence. Donald sat looking at her with an expression of polite patience, and after a moment she began to laugh.

"All right. No more interruptions on either side. What I meant to say, before we wandered off into a morass of non sequiturs, was that you seem to assume that my experiences were deliberately produced by a material agency."

"I don't believe in ghosts," said Donald.

"I don't either."

"Then what do you propose as a working hypothesis?"

"I haven't got a hypothesis, working or unemployed. Not enough data."

"You have the rudiments of a logical mind," Donald said approvingly. "Tell you what; come to supper tonight and tell my dad your wild tale. He does have a logical mind. Maybe he can suggest something."

"I don't know . . ."

"That's why I came, actually. To invite you."

"I thought you came to mow the lawn," Ellie said pointedly.

"I can't mow today. The grass is too wet."

"Then shouldn't you be digging or something?"

"Is that a subtle hint?"

"Not subtle."

"True." Donald stood up, in a single economical movement. His bones and muscles stood out too sharply, but they seemed to be in excellent working order. "All right, I'll go dig. We'll expect you about six. Turn left when you get to the highway. . . ."

Ellie let him finish the directions, which were not complex; the house was only two miles away by road. Then she said, "Are you sure your mother is expecting me? I mean, you didn't just cook this invitation up on the spur of the moment, did you?"

"My mother is dead," said Donald. "My father is expecting you."

He turned on his heel and walked away.

II

When Ellie left the house early that evening, the shadows of the trees and shrubs were elongated shapes of darkness across the sunlit lawn. It had been a golden afternoon, surprisingly cool for that time of year. The grounds had never looked lovelier. The grass was a little long, but everything else was in perfect condition. Ellie had to admit that Donald seemed to be doing a good job. But it was a stupid way for a man of his age and background to spend his time.

The Golds' home was another eighteenth-century charmer, its red brick Georgian facade mellowed by centuries, its fine old lawns and trees golden green in the late-afternoon sunlight. But the house and grounds were not so well tended as Kate's; like the cobbler's shoeless children, the grass indicated that Donald exercised his gardening talents elsewhere. The house appealed to Ellie at once. A little shabby, a little neglected, it suggested an elderly aristocrat who has allowed himself to spread out and slump comfortably.

There was another car parked in the drive when Ellie pulled up. It might have belonged to Donald or his father, but the long, sleek lines and prestigious emblem didn't go with the house, and Ellie was not surprised to learn that it belonged to a visitor. Donald, meeting her at the front door, had time for a hastily whispered warning before he led her into the parlor.

"Sorry, we've got company—we'll get rid of him as soon as we can. An old enemy of Kate's, maybe she told you. . . ." And then they were in the parlor; smoothly Donald raised his voice and went on, "Ellie, I don't know whether you've met Mr. McGrath, the head of the local schoolboard. And this is my father."

Ellie liked the note of pride in his voice, especially

since the man who had risen to greet her was not an imposing figure. Like the house, he had let himself spread out. He was as tall as his son, but his stomach hung comfortably over his belt and his shock of iron-gray hair needed trimming. Keen dark eyes inspected her with friendly approval and a big, warm hand closed firmly over hers.

"Now I remember you," Ellie said, returning his smile. "The year I got measles. I was ten."

"It would be trite but true to say you've changed considerably," the doctor said. "And for the better."

It was trite, but it didn't sound trite, not in his deep, sincere voice. He didn't give her time to reply; still holding her hand he turned her toward the stranger.

"Mr. McGrath dropped in to discuss some of the issues we'll be voting on in November."

McGrath was dressed with a fussy neatness that contrasted with the rumpled clothes of the Golds; but then, Ellie thought involuntarily, his face needed all the help it could get. His hair was snow white and so was the moustache that bristled out on either side of his long, pointed nose. His chin had no chance at all against the nose. His eyes were a pale, washed-out blue. And when he smiled, Ellie conjectured that his parents had not patronized orthodontists.

Reluctantly Ellie surrendered her hand into McGrath's; it was pinkly clean and a little damp.

"Goodness, yes, you have indeed changed," he exclaimed, squeezing her fingers. "I remember you as a little pigtailed charmer. But I daren't hope that you remember me. We met only briefly."

"You look very familiar," Ellie said truthfully. She did not mention that she had never in her life worn her hair in pigtails. "Are you running for reelection this fall, Mr. McGrath?"

"Let's not talk about politics," Donald said. "It's so dull. What'll you have, Ellie? Martini, gin and tonic, Scotch, sherry?"

Mr. McGrath gave her barely time to express her preference before he burst out.

"If I didn't know you were joking, Donald, I would scold you severely. What would we do without politics? Why, they are the basis of our democratic system! I am indeed running for reelection, dear child, and I hope I may count on your support."

Ellie saw the Golds, father and son, exchange glances of amused despair.

"But I'm not a resident," she protested. "I couldn't vote for you if I wanted to, Mr. McGrath."

"You wouldn't want to," said Donald, not quite *sotto voce*.

McGrath gave Donald a spiteful glance, but pretended not to hear.

"No, of course not, my dear; but you could influence your aunt's vote."

Ellie laughed. "I don't think anyone can influence my aunt, Mr. McGrath. Anyway, what does one vote matter?"

McGrath's eyes narrowed. Again Ellie was conscious of a sense of familiarity. Where had she seen that face before?

"For some unaccountable reason your aunt carries considerable weight in this county, Ellie. She is not even a member of one of the old families, and yet—"

"Oh, come, Roger," the doctor protested. "This isn't the eighteenth century; old families don't mean a curse these days, and I for one am glad of it."

"There were only six of them to begin with," Donald said, before McGrath could reply. He handed Ellie a tall glass, frosted with cold, as he continued smoothly, "Six Cavaliers, fleeing Cromwell—or was it Cumberland the Butcher?—who settled in this peaceful valley. I'm going to write a book about it someday. One of those decadent Southern novels that are all the rage. You know, miscegenation and incest and rape and other popular subjects."

The doctor's smiling glance at Ellie was casual, but for some queer reason she already felt as if she could read his mind. He and Donald were trying to keep McGrath off the subject of politics; now it was her turn to contribute a distraction. Valiantly she plunged in.

"How interesting! You know, I found a book about the county in a secondhand bookstore. I brought it for Kate as a housegift."

"What book is that?" McGrath asked sharply.

Ellie told him.

"Oh, yes," McGrath said. "The local library has a copy. I believe it is quite a rare book."

"That's what Ted said." Ellie added, smiling, "He also said it was a pack of lies."

A spark of anger flared in McGrath's pale eyes; for an instant they looked red instead of blue, and once again Ellie was struck by that jab of familiarity. Once again she failed to pin it down.

"Ted!" McGrath snorted. "He ought to know about lies. Perverted, sick, disgusting—"

"That's enough, Roger," the doctor said. His voice was quiet, but it held a note that stopped McGrath's tirade.

The man was quivering with genuine indignation. Ellie could understand why he and Kate didn't get along. Kate could never resist the temptation to jab pins in pompous, inflated egos. Yes, Ellie thought, as she studied McGrath's twitching moustache—the temptation *is* almost irresistible.

"Ted told me one strange story," she said innocently. "You mean that was a lie? About his ancestor who ran off with the wife of some local dignitary, and they found the bodies the following spring?"

Donald gurgled into his glass and tried, unsuccessfully, to turn the sound into a cough. McGrath turned crimson.

"Is he spreading that outrageous story again? I

told you, Doctor, he is out to destroy me. Such incredible malice—"

"Now how could that story harm you?" the doctor broke in. "True or not, it happened a century ago. Really, Roger, nobody cares any longer."

"Of course they care!" McGrath's voice rose a full octave. "I tell you, Doctor, I shall sue if Ted continues this sort of thing. I won't have my family traduced, insulted—"

Donald rose to his feet with a cry of alarm. Even McGrath was silenced, and all eyes turned toward Donald.

"My casserole," Donald exclaimed, in a dreadfully accurate imitation of McGrath's squeak. "It will be ruined. I do hate to end this fascinating conversation, but I cannot see my beautiful casserole overdone—burned, perhaps! Roger, you will excuse us?"

Not even McGrath could ignore the directness of the hint. He rose to his feet; with a visible effort, he summoned up his most engaging smile and turned it on Ellie.

"My dear wife's dinner will be ready, too. I must go. We'll talk again, my dear. I am sure you don't share the calloused indifference of the younger generation toward the vital issues that concern this nation. The old-fashioned virtues that are, alas, dying amid a morass of apathy, sex, drugs, violence. But they are not yet moribund—no! I have dedicated myself to the task of reviving them—"

"You'll have to meet my fiancé," Ellie said, without thinking. Then she added quickly, "No, Mr. McGrath, sorry; he doesn't live here either, he's a lawyer in Washington."

"My casserole," groaned Donald. His father took McGrath by the arm and led him out, still talking.

Donald dropped into a chair.

"That was a mistake," he said. "No, don't get up, love; we have plenty of time for another drink, uncontaminated by the taste of McGrath. I had to think of something to get him out of here."

"What was a mistake?" Ellie demanded.

"Mentioning that you have a fiancé who is a Washington big shot. Oh, I know you didn't say that, but that's how McGrath will interpret it. How did you happen to get engaged to a pompous windbag?"

"How did you—I mean, what makes you think he's a pompous windbag?" Ellie demanded indignantly. She had to raise her voice for the latter part of the sentence to be heard over Donald's laughter.

"Gave yourself away there, didn't you?" he said, between chuckles.

"I know Kate didn't like him, but she had no right to discuss him with you."

"Now, be reasonable. When did Kate have time to discuss him with me?"

Ellie was silenced. She really couldn't visualize Kate calling Donald in the middle of the night to gossip about Henry. Donald went on, "So Kate didn't like him. That's interesting."

"Why?" Ellie demanded suspiciously.

Before Donald could answer, his father came back. He was mopping his forehead.

"Hot out there," he explained ingenuously. Then, as he saw Ellie's flushed face, he demanded, "Another argument? Donald, how many times have I told you—"

"I don't know why everybody always assumes it's my fault," Donald complained. "Sit down and relax, Dad. You're too good-natured. You should tell that creepy character you've no intention of voting for him, then he'd stop coming."

"He wouldn't believe me." The doctor sat down, stretching out his long legs with an air of pleased relief. "The best way to stop his coming is to tell him he's convinced me. I can't quite bring myself to do it."

"What are his policies?" Ellie asked.

"Can't you guess?"

"Stricter discipline? Back to the basics, no frills, the three R's?"

"The trouble is, it sounds so reasonable," the doctor said mildly. "We're all in favor of discipline, and there is certainly some justification for the complaint that the children aren't being taught basic skills adequately. But McGrath and his crowd are primarily interested in cutting expenses and, consequently, taxes. They want to cancel all the extracurricular programs—music, art, driver training—"

"And censor the library," Donald said. "That's where he and Kate came to blows, Ellie. Last year the schoolboard insisted that *The Lottery* be removed from the English curriculum. McGrath said they didn't want the children to read a book that showed kids stoning their mothers to death."

"The story by Shirley Jackson? But it's a modern classic. The whole point of the story was that people shouldn't stone other people to death. Any people, for any reason."

"You can't expect Roger to understand subtleties," the doctor said, his eyes twinkling. "He lost the fight. As he said, Kate can muster a lot of support when she tries. In the process she said a number of—er—critical things about Roger—"

"I can imagine," Ellie murmured.

"Now Kate's friends have nominated a new slate of candidates," the doctor went on. "They stand a good chance of getting in this fall, and if they do, good-bye to Roger's platform. He's getting worried, poor devil."

"Yes, isn't it fun to hear his voice get shriller and shriller," Donald said happily. "But you underestimate his influence, Dad. The old families still do carry weight in this backward part of the world. More's the pity. I except myself, of course. . . ."

"You're one of the six?" Ellie asked, glancing at the doctor. "I mean, are you descended from—"

"I know what you mean. Donald doesn't get his blue blood from me. My wife was a Morrison. We moved here after her father died and she inherited the house."

The way his voice changed as he spoke of his wife reminded Ellie of Donald's reaction to her mention of his mother. It must have been instinct—or that strange rapport she had already felt—that told her not to shy away from the subject.

"I don't remember Mrs. Gold," she said.

"She died last year," the doctor said. "Cancer."

"I'm so sorry."

"Thank you." The doctor smiled at her. "Did anyone ever tell you you have a lovely voice, Ellie? I think it's because it reflects your feeling so accurately. We were a very close family, you see. I'm afraid I can't talk about her, even yet, without sounding . . . sentimental."

"No," Ellie said quickly. "It's so nice to find families that really like each other. Rare, these days. If you don't mind—"

"Talking about her? No, it's a pleasure to me."

"I hate to drag in my casserole again," Donald said. "But this time—"

He was at his most flippant during the simple meal, bragging outrageously about his cooking but finally admitting, under pressure, that he could make only three dishes—spaghetti, beef stroganoff, and a chicken-and-rice casserole. The casserole was excellent. Ellie said so. However, she agreed with the doctor that Donald's repertoire should be broadened, and she offered cooking lessons.

While she carried on her share of the lighthearted banter Ellie studied both Golds with increasing interest. The doctor was a darling. He had come to terms with the loss of his wife, although it still hurt. Donald had not become reconciled, and that was unusual in Ellie's world. It was not in style to love one's mother. In fact, some people would consider it downright peculiar. Of course Henry loved his mother. At least he said he did. . . . How long had it been since he had gone to visit her, in Minneapolis, or asked her to visit him? Five years, if she remembered correctly. Henry always regretted being so busy he couldn't visit his mother. . . .

Ellie wrenched her thoughts away from that new and disconcerting idea. Donald was talking about the Great Six, as he called them.

"You're forgetting the Beaseleys," his father said. "Old Josh Beaseley was one of the earliest settlers."

"But he wasn't gentry," Donald said solemnly. "We don't count peasants, Dad. Besides, the Beaseleys didn't emigrate; they've always been here, like the rocks and the moon shining down on the mountains. . . . They're weird people, you know that? Really weird."

"The genetic heritage is fascinating," his father agreed. "They are hopelessly inbred, of course; and the good Lord alone knows what the original stock may have been."

"Martian," Donald suggested. "One of the Ten Lost Tribes of Israel? A refugee family from sunken Atlantis, passing on the cryptic learning of that eon-old civilization . . ."

"Cut it out," Ellie exclaimed. "You know the Beaseleys are in and out of the house at all hours; are you trying to scare me?"

"Pay no attention to Donald," his father said, glancing at his wayward offspring critically. "The Beaseleys are . . . Do you know, Ellie, now that I stop to think about it, not a single member of the family has ever been involved in an act of violence. Rather remarkable."

"And more than can be said of any of the first families," Donald said.

"Any family has its share of black sheep," the doctor said. "Even your mother's, Donald."

"At least none of my ancestors was mixed up with John Wilkes Booth."

"What?" Ellie exclaimed, startled. "You mean the man who assassinated Lincoln?"

"Ted didn't tell you?" Donald grinned. "It's one of our juicier local legends. Quite unsubstantiated; just a rumor that one of the local gentry was involved in the plot. Booth wasn't the only conspirator, you know. They hanged several people, after Booth was killed."

"Including that unfortunate woman," the doctor said soberly. "Who may or may not have been guilty ... Donald, you're in a grisly mood tonight; change the subject."

"Not quite yet." Donald looked meaningfully at Ellie. "Now's the time, girl. Tell Dad about what happened last night."

When Donald first suggested that she talk to his father Ellie had not been receptive to the idea. Now she did not hesitate.

He listened as she had somehow known he would, gravely, with growing concern, and no trace of skepticism or amusement. When she had finished, he said,

"Come and stay with us, tonight. Donald will drive you home to pick up your things."

Ellie was a little taken aback. She had expected sympathy, but not such alarm.

"But, sir, I'm not afraid. Do you really think—"

Her tongue faltered on the question, but the doctor understood.

"No, no, I most certainly don't believe your apparitions are supernatural. That is precisely why I am alarmed."

"But why would anyone want to frighten me?"

"I don't know. If I did, I wouldn't worry so much."

"Now, Dad," Donald said easily, "you're getting too uptight. Nobody can get in the house, not with all Kate's dogs around. Anybody who tried to break in would be in serious danger of tripping over some animal or other and breaking his neck. Anyway, aren't you being a little dogmatic? You were the one who used to quote Horatio at me."

They had reached the after-dinner-coffee stage and were sitting at ease, elbows on the table. The doctor ran agitated fingers through his gray hair so that it stood up like a mop.

"Stop playing devil's advocate with me, you ungrateful child. I never said—"

"That's 'thankless child,'" Donald interrupted. His hazel eyes looked almost green. "Get your quotes right, Dad. Just for the sake of argument, suppose it is supernatural?"

"Of all the idiotic—"

"No, but just suppose it is. There wouldn't be any danger to Ellie; none of our local ghosts have any reason to threaten her. She has no family connections in this part of the world. So if the ghosts are ghosts, Ellie is in no danger; if the ghosts are fakes, she's still in no danger, because the house is secure."

"Wait a minute," Ellie said, as the doctor shook his head. "I agree with your conclusions, Donald, but you're getting off the subject. I'm not afraid, but I am curious. I want to know what's behind this. The first—er—ghost. The one that looked like you, Donald—"

She stopped, unable to complete the sentence, which was beginning to sound like an accusation, although she had not intended it that way. From the first moment she saw Donald she had realized that he was the most conspicuous candidate for the role of practical joker; but she didn't want to accuse him in front of his father.

The doctor got the idea, though. He jerked upright in his chair, his eyes widening.

"Donald! You wouldn't—"

"No, Dad." Donald met his father's eyes squarely.

"I'm sorry." The older man relaxed. "I believe you."

"I didn't mean that," Ellie said. "I just meant, does Donald have an ancestor who looks like him? Because the resemblance was really amazing. Even the scar on his chin."

"It's not a scar, it's a birthmark," his father muttered. "We never had anything done about it, since it is not disfiguring; but I suppose . . ."

"No family portraits?" Ellie persisted. "No young Squire Morrison, who just happens to be the identical twin of his descendant?"

"Those things do happen," Donald said seriously. "The birthmark is a family trait. Dad, you remember Great-uncle Rudolph—"

"There are few family portraits," the doctor said. "The Morrisons were strict Calvinists; they didn't approve of vanity, or of graven images. But there is one portrait head that I'd like you to see, Ellie."

Donald made a quick movement, as if of protest; but when his father looked at him, he nodded, smiling.

"Sure, go ahead. We'll have brandy in the parlor."

It was a reasonable excuse for not accompanying them, but it gave Ellie a clue as to the identity of the portrait. She was not surprised when the doctor led her into a pleasant sitting room across the hall from the more formal parlor. Set on a pedestal and framed by a simple arrangement of russet draperies, the sculptured head was done in a medium Ellie didn't recognize. Softer than bronze, the pale-gold surface gave the smiling woman's face tenderness and warmth and captured the true color of the hair that was knotted casually on the nape of the long, slender neck. It was not a beautiful face, but the sculptor had caught a quality of eagerness and candor, a trusting joy that enabled Ellie to say sincerely,

"She was lovely. Really lovely."

"Ted did it for me," the doctor said. "Six months ago. I came in one evening and found it here—just as you see it. He had worked from memory and a few old snapshots, and experimented with various media before he found the right one. Bronze was too hard, he said, and marble too cold, for her . . . Ted *is* irritating, I know, but I won't hear a word against him." His voice became brisker, more matter-of-fact. "As you see, Donald takes after his mother's family. Not that I'm admitting that his nonsensical theory makes any sense, mind—"

"Neither am I. But, honestly, I don't think there's anything to worry about. I'm more intrigued than anything."

When they returned to the parlor, Donald had brandy glasses set out. Ellie refused a liqueur but accepted more coffee, and they talked idly for another hour. In spite of her brave talk Ellie was reluctant to leave, but the doctor's unsuccessfully repressed yawn reminded her of what a busy medical man's schedule must be like, and she finally rose.

"Are you sure?" the doctor began, looking at her anxiously.

"Absolutely. I have a telephone, you know; I'll call if I'm the least bit worried."

"Please do. Donald will see you home—no," he cut off her protest. "I insist on it. And you must let him go through the house. Good heavens, child, that's the least we can do."

The night air was warmly clammy; the summer stars were dimmed by heat haze as they drove back. Slumped down in the seat, Donald seemed to be half asleep. He didn't speak until Ellie pulled up in front of the house.

"Every light in the place on," he said, jeering. "And you said you weren't nervous!"

"I'll tell your father you aren't taking my danger seriously," Ellie remarked; and Donald cowered, clasping his hands.

"Ah, no, ma'am, ye wouldn't be so cruel! Ye couldn't betray me to the old gentleman, not the sweet, bonny lass that ye look—"

"What a ham you are."

"Star of the South Burton Amateur Dramatic Society," Donald said.

"How are you going to get home after you get through playing hero here?"

"Villains were my specialty," Donald said. "I admit it took me a while to convince them that I could play Richard the Third; I'm too handsome, that's my trouble. . . . How do I plan to get home? Through the woods, of course; it's only half a mile."

"Rather you than me," Ellie said maliciously.

She would never have admitted it, but without Donald she would have had a hard time summoning up the courage to enter the house. Not that it was empty, or silent; as soon as the door opened, a mob of furry forms swept down on them, barking, mewing, and generally complaining. With a deftness that suggested long practice, Donald stretched out a long leg and hooked his foot around Ambrose, the orange Maine Coon, just in time to keep him from bolting out the door.

"Can't you get it through your thick skull that you can't do it anymore?" he demanded of Ambrose. The cat glowered at him and then deliberately sat down with his back turned; he looked like an improbably colored fur muff from behind.

The mob trailed along as they started their tour of inspection, but one by one they dropped out of the procession as it became apparent that nothing interesting was going to happen. Most of them stayed in the kitchen, squatting suggestively in front of the refrigerator; but William, the Saint Bernard, stuck to their heels. He didn't appear to be worried.

"Clear and sunny tomorrow," Donald remarked, glancing at the dog. "He's as good as a barometer."

William drooled delightedly onto his shoes as he stopped to check the dining-room window.

When they started upstairs, William left them; Ellie glanced over her shoulder at the big furry bulk, which was scuttling along at a pace quite inappropriate for a dog of William's size, and trying, unsuccessfully, to appear inconspicuous.

"It's all right, William," she called. "You don't have to hide, I'm not going to throw you out."

"A big help he would be," Donald said. "Unless he took a fancy to the burglar and sat on him."

It was with some trepidation that Ellie showed Donald into her room, but beyond a caustic "What were you reading that year—Elsie Dinsmore?" he made no comment, and looked under the bed with a completely sober countenance. On their way downstairs Donald paused to examine the stairs.

"Ted thought of that already," Ellie said, watching him prod the stair carpeting. "No wires, no nothing."

"So I see." Donald straightened. "Just a thought."

He refused her offer of refreshment, saying that he had to get up at dawn to prepare his father's breakfast.

"Otherwise he goes till noon on one cup of coffee. Lock the front door, Ellie; I'll wait outside till I hear the bolts and bars bang into their sockets."

"Thanks, Donald. Good night."

Ellie offered her hand.

Donald contemplated it soberly for a few seconds, cocking his head on one side. Then he took her by the shoulders and kissed her.

Never in her life, not even at the unsophisticated age of twelve, had Ellie wanted to slap a boy for kissing her. She had no idea why she did it this time. Even more surprising was the fact that Donald didn't duck. They stood staring at one another stupidly for a moment, while the echoes of the slap died, ghostily, in the high-beamed ceiling. Saint Thomas, the black-and-white Manx, bit Donald on the ankle. He jumped and swore and—it must be admitted—kicked. Saint Thomas, who was not a stupid cat, had already departed. Donald grinned.

"There you go. All sorts of brave defenders on hand. See you tomorrow."

Gallantly he closed the door for her, while Ellie still stared. She had rarely felt such a fool. Then she heard Donald's voice, through the door:

"Lock it, stupid."

Ellie obeyed, and then fled upstairs. She reached the window of her room in time to see Donald's tall figure moving quickly across the lawn. At the edge of the woods he turned; although Ellie knew he could not possibly see her, he raised one arm in a jaunty salute. He had known she would watch for him. . . .

"I hope," she said aloud, "that something with long sharp teeth drops down out of a tree and sucks your blood."

But of course nothing did. There was not even a ghastly, wavering scream after he vanished into the woods.

Ellie got into bed and started *Anne of Green Gables.* She was well into the second chapter when she heard the familiar scraping scuttle in the hall. The bed was thick with cats, as usual, and Franklin was sound asleep in his usual place on the chest. Ellie looked up from her book.

"Hello, Roger," she said—and then gasped, in mingled surprise and delight as the rat squeaked affably at her, its white whiskers twitching. Now she knew whom Roger McGrath had reminded her of. Kate must have named the rat after him.

CHAPTER FIVE

Ellie sat up with a start. The bed was cat-free, but Roger the rat was standing on the chest at the foot of the bed. Since the top of the chest was about six inches below the surface of the mattress, Ellie could see only Roger's long, pointed nose resting on the coverlet between his neat white paws. He looked like one of the weird little drawings of Kilroy that were popular during the Second World War.

Ellie was accustomed to the migrations of the animal population; she had not been awakened by Roger's arrival or the cats' departure. For a moment she blinked sleepily, trying to think what *had* wakened her. Then she remembered. She had been worried about the Beaseleys. Presumably they had keys to the house (and that was not entirely a comfortable thought), but she had bolted and barred and chained every door the night before. The Beaseleys wouldn't be able to get in, and their touchy pride might interpret the barricading of the house as a personal insult.

Ellie tore downstairs, without waiting to put on a robe or slippers. She was too late. Marian Beaseley was already in the kitchen.

She glanced up from scouring the sink as Ellie came to a rocking stop.

"I made coffee," she said.

"I need it." Ellie went to fetch a cup. She was still too dazed to be tactful. "How did you get in?" she blurted. "I was hoping I could get down here before you arrived, but . . ."

Any other woman would have asked a leading question. Marian didn't even look at Ellie; she had turned back to the sink, which she was scrubbing to a state of whiteness that dazzled the eye. Ellie knew there was no choice. She had to tell Marian the truth. The Beaseleys might walk out if they thought the house was haunted, but that was preferable to having them quit because they felt they had been insulted. There was no danger of them spreading the story around town. They kept to themselves.

"Something funny has been going on," Ellie said, filling her cup and sitting down at the table. "That's why I locked the door last night, Marian. Night before last I saw three . . . people outside on the lawn. And the day Kate left there was—I thought there was a man here in the house."

"Who?"

"It couldn't have been Donald," Ellie said, half to herself. "I must have been hallucinating. It's the only explanation. Sometime, somewhere, I must have seen a picture of him. . . ."

"Hmph," said Marian, her back still turned.

"It must have been imagination, Marian. The man was—uh—I could see through him. He sort of faded away. . . ."

"Francis Morrison. Young Donald's the spitting image of him."

"Who was Francis Morrison?"

"Killed at Saratoga," Marian said briefly. "Second son. Nice young fella."

There were several things Ellie might have said. She did not say any of them. As she sat staring at Marian's uncompromising back, straight as an arrow in its faded print dress, a shiver ran through her. The Battle of Saratoga . . . She didn't remember the precise date, but it had been during the Revolutionary War. Two hundred years ago . . . yet something in Marian's voice implied that she had known the said Francis personally. It wasn't *what* Marian said, it was the *way* she said it. . . . Of course she might have seen a picture. . . . Or she might be inventing the resemblance between Donald and his remote ancestor. There was no sense in questioning Marian. She hardly ever answered questions.

She had not answered the question as to how she had entered the house, through chained and bolted doors.

"The people outside," Ellie began.

"Must of been Mrs. McGrath and that young man of hers. And the old squire, after 'em. The bodies was buried in Kate's woods."

Again Ellie gaped, speechless. Marian filled a pail with water and began mopping the floor. As the mop came closer and closer to Ellie's feet she took the hint.

Once she was out of Marian's presence she was tempted to go back and ask the obvious questions. But she knew it would be useless. Marian's flat, expressionless black eyes were as effective as those of a rattlesnake in paralyzing its victim. You couldn't really call an exchange with Marian conversation. Her comments were as unanswerable as stones dropped into a well.

Anyway, Ellie thought, Marian didn't seem to be perturbed by the idea of ghosts. Why should she, when she spoke of them as old acquaintances?

Ellie lingered in her room, reading *Anne of Green Gables*, until she thought she had given Marian time to finish her work. When she went downstairs, taking the book with her, the kitchen was shining and deserted. Ellie got her breakfast and sat down. She continued to sit, drinking coffee, until she had fin-

ished the book. After all, what else did she have to
do? This was supposed to be a vacation. The house
was unusually quiet, the animals having been fed and
let out by one Beaseley or another. Ellie didn't need
to look at the glaring sunlight to know it was hot
outside. July in Virginia was always hot.

She was a fast reader and she had risen early; it
was only a little after ten by the time she closed the
book and stretched luxuriously. Anne's adventures
were very soothing. What an innocent world it had
been, that remote Canadian province in the last years
of the nineteenth century. A cynic might claim that
such innocence existed only in fiction; that the real
world had had just as much misery, poverty, and sin
as this present decade. Fictitious or not, it was a
nice world to escape into from time to time.

A sharp snapping sound announced the appearance of a pair of cats through the swinging panel
Kate had had cut into the outer kitchen door. One of
them was Abu Simbel, the Abyssinian, a handsome,
ruddy aristocrat; the other was his inseparable com-
panion, George. George was a scrubby white mongrel with one black spot under his nose, like a
Hitlerian moustache. No amount of grooming or
cream-rich diet could make George look anything but
lower class; but he had been Simbel's protegé ever
since the night Simbel had carried him in by the
scruff of the neck, a skinny, half-drowned kitten.
Kate never turned anything away from her door, animal or human, two-legged or four-legged, feathered
or furred or bare, but George's adoption had been
foreordained. He was several pounds heavier than
Simbel now, but the Abyssinian still treated him like
a spoiled baby, washing him several times a day and
standing back from the food until George had finished.

The two of them sat down on very solid bottoms
by the empty food dishes and stared compellingly at
Ellie.

"You already ate," she told them. "You're both too fat anyway. You can't have any more until . . ."

She filled the food dishes with dry food. Then she picked up the piece of paper that had drifted to the floor on the current of air from the animals' passage into the kitchen. Marian had left a shopping list. Bleach, paper towels, cat food, dog food, goat food, birdseed . . . Ellie winced as she thought what Kate's monthly bills for animal food must come to. A number of people had challenged Kate on that subject— once; they never challenged Kate more than once. "How can you spend so much on animals when there are babies starving to death in India?" was one objection; the other end of the ethical spectrum was represented by comments along the line of "Dumb critters oughta feed themselves, they don't need all that fancy food." Kate's reply usually expressed her preference for animals over people; animals, she said, might occasionally bite the hand that fed them, but they never stabbed it in the back. Kate never worried about mixed metaphors so long as she got the point across.

George slobbered noisily over his food. Ellie left him to it. She got her purse and went out the front door.

Ow. It *was* hot.

Ellie opened all the car windows and then went back into the shade to let it cool off. As she stood there, fanning herself ineffectually with the shopping list, her ears were assailed by a mounting roar. A bright-red rider mower came ponderously into view around the corner of the house; it looked and sounded like a mythical monster. Donald was driving it.

As soon as he caught sight of her he began veering in eccentric circles and swaths, cutting insane patterns across the lawn. Ellie glowered at him. Donald steered the mower up to the porch steps and shut it off. Silence, exquisite and calm, descended.

"Hi," Donald said.

"Hi."

"Where are you off to?"

"Town. Shopping."

"You've been talking to Marian," Donald said. "I recognize her rhetorical style. Or are you still mad at me?"

"Why on earth should I be mad at you?" Ellie inquired loftily. She got into the car. The steering wheel was still so hot she could hardly bear to touch it.

"Mind if I come along?" Without waiting for an answer, Donald got off the mower and into the car. He instantly got up again. He was wearing shorts.

The agonized expression on his face broke down Ellie's reserve. She whooped with laughter.

"Oh, cruel," said Donald, his posterior two inches off the seat. "I may be permanently maimed. Get moving, will you? And turn on the air conditioning!"

Ellie did as he suggested, not because of his discomfort, but because of her own. As the car rolled smoothly down the driveway she inquired, "What do you want to go to town for?"

"You don't talk right," Donald said, sitting gingerly on the seat. "You should say, 'Why do you—'"

"What do you want to go to town—"

"Just to keep you company." Donald beamed at her. "I'll finish the lawn later."

"What about the animals? Should we leave them alone?"

"There are assorted Beaseleys all over the place. Anyhow, animals are a lot more competent than people."

Ellie steered deliberately for the first pothole she saw and observed, with pleasure, that Donald's head contacted the roof of the car quite smartly.

"No disturbances last night?" he asked, rubbing his head ostentatiously.

"I said I'd call if anything happened."

"I don't believe you. You might be more inclined to call Ted."

"I'm sorry I called him in the first place," Ellie admitted. "I adore him, but he is an awful gossip. I don't want that story spread all over town."

"He's probably spread it already."

"He didn't talk to the Beaseleys."

"Nobody talks to the Beaseleys. Hey—you mean the exquisite Marian communicated with you? How did you ascertain that she was unaware without giving the show away?"

"I didn't." Donald looked at her in surprise, and Ellie added defensively, "I had to tell her something. I didn't want her to think I was locking the place up because I didn't trust her."

"I forgot about the Beaseleys when we locked up," Donald admitted. "You must have had to get up at dawn to let her in. No wonder you look so hollow-eyed and sickly."

Ellie ignored this gratuitous insult. Donald's comment reminded her only too clearly of the unanswered question.

"I didn't get up at dawn. But she was already inside."

"What? How?"

"She didn't say. You know how she is, I couldn't . . . We must have forgotten to bolt one of the doors or windows."

Donald shook his head.

"No chance."

"Then how—"

"Either she is a witch, which wouldn't surprise me. Or there is some way of getting into the house we don't know about."

"I don't know which idea is worse."

"Forget about the Beaseleys. You don't really believe they're responsible for your ghosts, do you?"

"No."

"Neither do I. What's bugging you? Something Marian said?"

His insight verged on mind reading. Ellie had never thought of herself as having one of those candid, transparent faces that revealed every passing thought. Certainly Henry had never been able to tell what she was thinking. Which was just as well, for Henry . . .

"Maybe Marian is a witch," she said, morosely. "When I described what I had seen, she identified the people. 'Old squire McGrath and his wife and her lover.' She said the bodies were found in Kate's woods."

"Go on," Donald said, after a moment. "That's not all."

"The man in the hall. She said he must be young Francis Morrison. You're the spitting image of young Francis, in case you didn't know. How Marian knows I can't imagine; according to her, Francis was killed at Saratoga."

Donald said nothing. The big car was cool now; he had settled comfortably onto the seat and was staring out the windshield, as if there were nothing on his mind beyond the passing scenery.

"Well?" Ellie demanded.

"What is this, a court of inquiry? I have never heard that I had an ancestor who was my twin, if that's what you want me to say. The name is vaguely familiar, but . . ."

"Then how would Marian know?"

"Maybe she just made it up. I don't know why I should feel so guilty," Donald said irritably. "If one of my ancestors should take a notion to haunt you, it's not my fault. Furthermore, I don't believe a word of it."

Ellie was silent. Donald wriggled uncomfortably, as if the seat had become hot again.

"Oh, all right," he said, as if in answer to a comment Ellie had never made. "We'll look him up. The town library has a good collection of local stuff."

"What about the McGraths?"

"We don't need to look them up. Everybody knows the story. It's true, the bodies were found in the woods not far from the house. The country was a lot wilder in those days."

Ellie slowed the car to a discreet thirty. They had entered the outskirts of Millbury.

The town had been the county seat ever since there had been a county. Never large in population, it had passed through the usual pattern of growth and decay until, in the late nineteen sixties, the craze for antiques and handicrafts and quaint old towns hit Millbury as it had hit so many other communities. The old tavern, the Silver Fox, was still the center of town; its sprawling roofs and gables covered a full city block. The owners had added bathrooms and a new dining room, but the old bedrooms with their fireplaces and sloping floors looked as they had looked in 1753 when the inn was opened. One row of old houses had been converted into smart shops and boutiques, and many others had signs that said "Antiques" or "Katie's Krafts," or something of the sort. The town was on the Washington-Baltimore-Richmond weekend circuit, and was popular with townies exhausted by paperwork, who wanted to get away from it all. But beneath the superficial veneer of new chic Millbury had not changed greatly; the old inhabitants still went to Joe's market instead of to the new A & P outside town. Joe charged and Joe delivered, and Joe still carried the diverse products he had carried for fifty years—caviar for the aristocracy, feed and sheep dip for the farmers.

Ellie had always loved Joe's—the worn bare boards of the floor, the poorly lighted corners, the seemingly disorganized piles of merchandise. Joe knew where everything was, but no one else did; you could lift up a pair of overalls and find a fifty-dollar tin of pâté de foie gras underneath.

She hadn't seen Joe for several years, but he recognized her immediately. His casual nod made her feel as if she were still wearing her hair in ponytails (not pigtails). He had not changed at all. Perhaps there were only six strands of iron-gray hair laid carefully across his bald head, instead of ten; surely a few more wrinkles had been added to the weathered map of his long, dour face, but in all essentials he was the same.

Ellie was so delighted by the store and everything in it that it took her a while to realize that the atmosphere was peculiarly strained. She didn't recognize any of the other shoppers, so there was no reason why they should have spoken to her, and Joe had never been one for light chitchat. He started collecting cat food even before she handed him Marian's list. Donald, alert and unusually silent, had taken one of the worn kitchen chairs that stood in a circle around the potbellied stove—an item that indicated that Joe was not entirely immune to the curse of quaintness, for he had installed an adequate heating-and-cooling system years before. Ellie rummaged, finding unexpected treasures.

A jangle of bells announced the arrival of a new customer. Hearing the tapping of heels on the wooden floor, Ellie glanced up from the pile of old comic books she was investigating and saw Anne Grant bearing down on her.

"I saw Kate's car, so I figured you'd be here," the other woman greeted her. "How are you feeling?"

"Fine," Ellie said, bewildered.

Evidently Anne had not yet reached the Bloody-Mary-for-breakfast stage of alcoholism; her eyes were tired and a little bloodshot, but she was entirely sober and was dressed with the expensive casualness of her social class. The shining blond hair was tied back with a printed black-and-fuchsia scarf that matched her sleeveless, low-necked T-shirt and black pants. A leather bag was slung over her arm. From it she extracted a list, which she tossed at Joe, who took it without comment; but Ellie noticed that he gave her a sharp look before he turned back to his shelves.

"Sit down," Anne said, gesturing at the chairs.

"I haven't time, really."

"It'll take Joe forever to get your stuff together." The other woman took her arm; the clasp of her long, thin fingers was uncomfortably tight. Her eyes sparkled. "Come on, sit down and have a Coke or something; you must tell me all about it, I'm agog with curiosity."

Ellie was conscious of a sinking feeling in the pit of her stomach. It had nothing to do with the fact that the older woman's slim elegance made her feel like a grubby infant in her faded shorts and shirt, or that Donald was eyeing Anne's figure with cool approval.

"Tell you about what?" She allowed herself to be deposited on a chair. Anne took another and pulled it up so close that Ellie felt trapped between Anne's knees and the stove.

Lighting a cigarette, Anne made a wide gesture as she tossed the match away.

"Don't be coy, darling, the whole town knows about your ghosts. What are you up to?" And, as Ellie's expression changed, she added cheerfully, "Not that I blame you, sweet. In fact, I'm with you every step of the way. This town needs shaking up."

"What makes the town so sure Ellie is making up these stories?" Donald asked, since Ellie was too furious to speak. Anne glanced carelessly at him.

"Well, it did occur to me that Ted might be the one who's making them up; but it would be stupid of him, wouldn't it, when Ellie could simply deny them? Ted does have a tendency to exaggerate, bless his little heart, but he isn't an out-and-out liar. And even allowing for exaggeration . . ."

Her wide blue eyes were fixed expectantly on Ellie; and although she was still angry, Ellie felt an unexpected uprise of pity. None of Anne's malice was directed against her; it was the town she hated, the town and . . .

"Does Mr. Grant think I'm inventing stories to stir people up?" she asked bluntly.

"Oh, Alan . . . He's reserving judgment. Very ostentatiously." The woman's lips twisted unpleasantly. "What did you see, now, really?"

Ellie had never been very good at telling people to mind their own business. In this case she realized that Ted's version of the story might be worse than the truth and that this was a chance to correct it. So—although Donald's vigorous headshake warned her not to do so—she told her story, again. She was getting very tired of it, but apparently it lost nothing in the telling. Anne's eyes opened even wider.

"How divine," she said, with a long breath. "Absolutely super. I wish I'd thought of it. Listen, honey, I could tell you a few stories you could use—"

"Now wait a minute," Ellie interrupted. "I didn't invent any of this, Anne. I really saw those people. You and the rest of the town are so quick to judge; hasn't it occurred to you that someone might be playing a trick on *me?* And I don't like it, not one bit."

"But, darling," Anne said. "Did anyone else see your spooks?"

Ellie felt as if she had gotten a hard jab in the diaphragm. She looked at Donald; he was contemplating a row of plaid shirts that hung over the notions counter. It was true. She had no witnesses. Did Donald's father think she was a liar, too—or, worse, sick in the head? Was that why he had suggested that she stay with them, to protect her from her own fantasies? The idea that the doctor might doubt her hurt worse than anything Anne had said.

Ellie stood up. Her legs felt as if they had gone to sleep. Joe had already started carrying boxes and bags out to the car. Probably he was as anxious to get rid of her as she was anxious to leave.

"Good-bye, Anne," she said.

"Be sure to let me know if anything else happens." Anne grinned. She had gotten what she wanted, and she was not much interested in other people's feelings.

The car had been standing in the shade; it was not as hot as it had been earlier that morning. Ellie let herself slump forward over the steering wheel. Donald, sliding in beside her, gave her a critical look.

"Sit tall," he advised, in a passable Western drawl. "Sit tall, li'l gal, and tell all them sidewinders to go to hell."

"You're one of those sidewinders yourself," Ellie said.

"Oddly enough, I am not."

"You mean you believe me?"

"Why, li'l gal, from the moment I saw your purty face I knew—"

"Cut it out or I'll slug you. This is no time to be funny."

"On the contrary," Donald said, with unexpected sobriety. "The time to be funny is when things get nasty. I guess I should have warned you. But I thought you would realize that Anne's interpretation is the one that comes first to mind—to someone who doesn't know you. Now don't get mushy," he added hastily, as she turned toward him, her face alight. "It isn't your purty face that convinced me, it's your air of innocent stupidity. You have no rational motive for inventing wild stories, and you aren't the type to do it for fun."

"Thanks—I think." Obscurely cheered, Ellie started the car. If Donald felt that way, then his father must agree with him. "Where to now?" she asked.

"The library. If you still want to check this thing out."

"More than ever."

"Atta girl, *Excelsior. Illegitimae non . . .*"

It was amazing, how many mottoes and phrases there were encouraging the faint of heart. Donald knew them all. He didn't stop quoting till they had stopped in front of the library.

"I remember this place," Ellie said, looking admiringly at the handsome old house, with its white pillars and wrought-iron fence surrounding a neatly clipped lawn. "Kate brought me here once."

"Then you remember Miss Mary."

"Kate once introduced me to the librarian. Somebody tall and fierce and old—at least that's how she impressed me when I was about ten."

Donald opened the gate for her and they started up the walk.

"She's sill fierce and old. This was her home—the Lockwood house. When Miss Mary's daddy died, bankrupt, the town bought it and turned it into a library. She's got a little apartment on the top floor. It was a nice gesture; she had no money and nowhere to go, and they made it possible for her to stay on. They aren't such bad people."

"Who said they were?"

"Anne Grant."

"It isn't the people she hates, it's the whole way of life," Ellie said soberly. "Because it's her husband's milieu?"

"They say she was a singer in New York—not too successful—when Alan married her and brought her here," Donald said.

"And having presumably fallen in love with her, he promptly tried to turn her into something different. Typical male."

"Don't be such an FCP," Donald said. "There are

as many revolting women in the world as there are men."

"Sometimes I doubt that."

"Wait till you see Miss Mary."

Remembering that the librarian had been gray-haired and wrinkled when she last saw her, Ellie expected to find a withered, fragile old woman. But the intervening years had not left any visible signs of decay on the woman who sat behind the desk as a ruler might occupy a throne. A commanding figure, whose white hair was set precisely in the marcelled waves of an earlier period, she had a nose like George Washington's and piercing gray eyes. The eyes passed over Donald and settled on Ellie with intense interest.

"Ah. Kate's niece. I have been hearing some extraordinary stories about you."

"I suppose you think I invented them, too," Ellie said. She was to learn—indeed, she had already learned—that Miss Mary never wasted time on social amenities.

"I have not yet reached a decision. My mind is open to any reasonable hypothesis."

"She means she believes in ghosts," Donald said brightly.

"You're a fool, young man." Miss Mary looked at him with unconcealed contempt. "Your mother's family had its share of fools. . . . I don't believe in what you ignorantly call 'ghosts.' I do believe in the existence of evil."

There was no doubt that she did. The word, in her deep, almost masculine voice, had a heavy significance that made Ellie shiver.

"You know Donald's family?" she asked.

"I know everything about the six families," said Miss Mary.

Turning, she indicated a portrait that hung over the mantel, in the place of honor. The room had once been the drawing room of the house. It was lined with bookshelves now, but the space in front of the handsome Adam fireplace had been kept clear except for a few easy chairs and low tables, arranged in a casual grouping.

It was a full-length portrait. Ellie had not noticed it before; at the first sight she clapped her hand over her mouth to repress a gasp. The tight, dark suit was the same style as the one that had been worn by the apparition that had shaken a fist at her bedroom window. A second look told her that there was no other similarity. She had not seen the man's face clearly, but she had received an impression of dark hair and beard, and an aura of malignancy. This face was almost saintly. Ellie was reminded of Robert E. Lee, who had had the same gentle expression, the same white hair and short beard.

"My grandfather," said Miss Mary. "Albert J. Lockwood the Fourth. There are no such men nowadays."

"Is that why you remained a spinster, Miss Mary?" Donald asked guilelessly.

This seemed to Ellie to be going too far, even for Donald. She scowled at him; but Miss Mary did not seem to be annoyed by the question.

"Precisely," she said crisply. "He was a scholar and a saint, the kindest, most benevolent man this town has ever seen. He made a great fortune, after the family had lost everything in the war; and he gave it all to charity. He founded the orphan asylum, the humane society for our little four-footed brothers and sisters—built the new church—"

"And tore down the old one, which had stood since 1750," Donald put in. "An architectural gem, that one was. How did he make his money, Miss Mary? Those were the good old days, no labor unions, no child-labor laws. . . ."

Miss Mary ignored this feeble malice with the lofty contempt it deserved.

"I presume you came here for some purpose," she

said, addressing Ellie. "Your generation does not visit libraries for pleasure."

"I just finished *Anne of Green Gables* this morning," Ellie said indignantly.

"Good God," Donald said. Miss Mary's harsh visage softened slightly.

"I'm happy to hear it. It is a very wholesome book, not like the trash that is published nowadays. What can I do for you?"

"We want to look up one of my ancestors," Donald said. "His name was Francis Morrison."

"Which Francis? The one who was born in 1805 or the first Francis, who was killed at Saratoga?"

"Oh," Ellie said damply. "Oh. You mean—there was one who was killed at Saratoga?"

"Yes. You may check my statement in the family genealogy, if you like, but I assure you I am never mistaken about these matters. What do you want to know about him?"

"What he looked like," Ellie said.

"There is no portrait in existence."

Donald leaned across the desk.

"No description? No reference to his merry hazel eyes or—or a birthmark—?"

Miss Mary did not answer immediately. In a leisurely fashion she inspected Donald's face from forehead to chin.

"Ah," she said softly. "Then it is true that the first visitant strongly resembled this young man?"

"Yes," Ellie admitted reluctantly.

"But why should you suppose that it was Francis? You may be sure I am correct when I say that there is no way of knowing what he looked like."

"It was Marian Beaseley who suggested him," Ellie said, even more reluctantly. "And don't ask me how she knew, Miss Mary. She said—"

And then she stopped speaking, alarmed by the change in Miss Mary's face. It had darkened to crimson with anger or some other strong emotion; the eyes flashed like sword points.

"Marian Beaseley! What does she know? The woman and all her filthy tribe are a disgrace to the town. We should have driven them out years ago. Don't talk to me about Marian Beaseley."

"They seem perfectly harmless to me," Ellie said.

"Harmless!" The crimson faded from Miss Mary's face. She snorted. "You don't know anything about spiritual evil; you are only a child. Come here, I want to show you something."

When she stood up Ellie was surprised to see how short she was. Her massive torso and commanding personality suggested a taller woman. She walked with a tread that shook the flooring.

Ellie followed her to one of the bookshelves. Donald's expressive face indicated that he knew what was about to happen and intended to have no part in it. He dropped into one of the armchairs and picked up a copy of *American Heritage* from the table.

Miss Mary's long, knobby finger ran rapidly along the books until she found the one she wanted. She pulled it out before Ellie could see the title, and opened it.

"Here," she said, jabbing the page with her finger.

The paragraph read:

"The pernicious work of Satan goes on; truly is it said, 'He walks the world seeking to do mischief.' Only last year, in the county courthouse of—— a trial for witchcraft was held, with the woman M—— B—— being brought under the complaint of her neighbors that she had done them hurt, drying their cows and afflicting their swine with sickness. One woman, Goodie Curtis, swore that the said M—— B—— did ride her about the country through all of one night, so that she was in the morning much afflicted with soreness in all her limbs and scratched by brambles and suffering from ague because of the wetness of the streams through which the said M—— B—— had ridden her . . ."

"This is ridiculous," Ellie said, turning back to the title page. "Are you trying to tell me that M.B. was an earlier Marian Beaseley? This book was published in 1790."

"The trial was held in 1788," Miss Mary said. "It is on record. Unfortunately, the miserable woman was acquitted."

Her voice held sincere regret. Ellie stared at her.

"I didn't know they still believed in witchcraft then."

"There are several cases on record during that period," Donald said, looking up from his magazine. "But by the end of the eighteenth century only ignorant farmers still believed in it. The justices were more sophisticated, thank God."

"Amen," Ellie said.

Miss Mary looked pityingly at her. "You'll find out," she said, taking the book from Ellie. "I only hope the lesson won't be too painful. You have been chosen, and you must learn."

She restored the book to its place. Next to it was one Ellie recognized.

"Oh, there's the county history I bought for Kate," she exclaimed, reaching for it.

Miss Mary's hand closed over hers. It was a strong, hard hand, in spite of the arthritis that had twisted the joints so badly that it looked deformed.

"You have a copy of that book?"

"Yes, I found it in a secondhand bookstore," Ellie said.

"It is very rare. I thought I had the only copy. Would you consider selling it?"

"Kate hasn't even seen it yet," Ellie said. "I bought it as a present, but forgot to give it to her. It's her book; you'd have to ask her. Why do you want another copy?"

"Sheer acquisitiveness," Donald said before Miss Mary could answer.

"I think we'd better go," Ellie said quickly.

Miss Mary made no attempt to detain them. Once again Ellie saw that queer flash of pity in the woman's face before she turned back to her work.

After the cool of the house the air outside felt like a Turkish bath.

"I'll treat you to lunch at the Silver Fox," Donald said. "I need a drink."

"You act as if you already had a drink, or three. Why were you so rude?"

"I can't stand that old hag," Donald said. "She terrified me when I was a kid."

"That's no excuse for being rude to her now. Maybe I ought to get these groceries home."

"Looks like all you've got is canned stuff and cleaning materials. It'll keep. Come on, the Silver Fox is a showplace. People come from miles around to have lunch there."

The tavern's dining room was crowded, but they didn't have to wait for a table. Ellie wondered whether Donald had insisted on coming here in order to prove to her that he had some prestige, and some friends, in town, even if Miss Mary didn't approve of him. The hostess was a good-looking girl, about Donald's age. . . .

They ordered drinks and inspected the menu, which was printed in type so desperately old-fashioned that it was very difficult to read. At leisure, then, to look over the charming decor of the low-ceilinged room, with its fireplace and leaded windows, Ellie realized that Donald might have had another motive for bringing her to the Silver Fox.

Many of the customers were tourists, but a good half of them were local people; and most of that group were looking at her—some openly, some making a pretense of not looking, which was almost more conspicuous. Donald waved cheerfully at several tables. Then, half rising, he gestured hospitably to a man who had just come in the door.

"Did you know Ted would be here?" Ellie demanded, as Ted started toward them.

"He often is. Why, do you have any objection to talking to him?"

"No," Ellie said grimly. "There are a few things I want to say to him."

They had a table for four—a flagrant example of favoritism on the part of the hostess—and Ted took one of the vacant chairs. He was wearing a brightly vulgar Hawaiian sport shirt and his silver hair, curling with damp, framed his tanned face. He smiled at Ellie.

"Hello, love. Heard anything from—anybody?"

"Why the sudden discretion?" Ellie asked sarcastically. "Ted, I could kill you. You didn't have to spread my adventures all over town."

"You know how untrustworthy I am," Ted said. "Besides, I don't remember you asking me to keep it quiet."

He looked chagrined. His big dark eyes reminded Ellie of William's.

"Oh, well," she said, softened. "I didn't realize what a furor it would cause. Haven't these people anything better to talk about?"

"No, not really," Ted answered. He glanced around the room with an expression of disdain; meeting his eyes, several of the watchers found matters to interest them elsewhere. "They are very dull people, my love. This is a small town, in every sense of the word. And, of course, many of them make their living from the tourist-antique trade—including our gracious host here. They aren't quite sure whether the ghost element will increase business or discourage it."

"There's no question about that. People love ghost stories." Donald looked alarmed. "For God's sake, Ted, cool it; Ellie doesn't want reporters beating at

the door. And if Kate hears about it she'll hex you
with something particularly nasty."

Ted's mouth curled down like that of an unhappy
baby.

"Honest to God, Don, the thing's gotten out of
hand. I didn't talk to that many people. I don't know
how it spread so fast. Maybe you should deny the
whole thing, Ellie. I don't mind. Everybody thinks
I'm a liar anyway."

"It's too late for that," Donald said. "Ellie has already spilled the beans to Anne Grant and Miss
Mary."

"Oh?" Ted's bright eyes darted, birdlike, from one
face to the other. "So you've been to the library.
What did Miss Mary have to say?"

"The usual lecture about her revered grandfather," Donald said. "She's a sucker for the supernatural; belongs to some weird society or other, doesn't
she? She wouldn't think it was so fascinating if
Grandpa turned up in the shrubbery some night."

"How true," Ted murmured. His lips curved in a
smile.

"She also showed me a paragraph from some disgusting old book, about a case of witchcraft," Ellie
said, and Ted nodded to indicate that he knew the
case she was referring to. "Why is she so down on
the Beaseleys?"

"She tried to play lady bountiful with our Marian
one time when she was young," Ted said, with a gig-
gle. "What a confrontation that must have been!
Anyhow, she is a hidebound old Puritan; that type
instinctively dislikes anyone who lives outside the
conventional boundaries of society."

While they ate, Ellie told Ted what Marian Beaseley had said that morning. Ted was delighted.

"God, she's a marvel, isn't she? What about it,
Don? I remember reading about your gallant ancestor, but I didn't know he was your double."

"Neither did I. What's more, I don't know it now.

Marian likes to play witch; it amuses her. She doesn't know any more about my ancestors than anyone else does."

"Everybody seems to know too much about everybody else's ancestors," Ellie said. "Such snobbery. Who are the six families you keep talking about? I know Donald's family, and yours, Ted—"

"The Morrisons and the Frasers," Ted said. "You also know McGrath; that line is still—shall we say flourishing? No, let's not. Miss Mary is the last of the Lockwoods—thank God. That makes four, right? Well, there's our Senator, Alan Grant. . . ."

"And the sixth?"

"If you read the *Post* or the *Star Dispatch* or any of a hundred newspapers, you must know the sixth," Ted said. "Her maiden name was Selkirk; she married a man named Stewart; but neither was euphonious enough for our Marge when she went into the religion biz. Her little sermonettes are read across the country, and wherever earnest Americans gather in the wilds of Europe and Asia. She has appeared on TV, where her smile dazzles—"

"Oh, no," Ellie said involuntarily. "Sermonettes . . . You don't mean Marjorie Melody?"

"I do indeed. And I'm glad to see you share my opinion of her. Doesn't she write the most nauseating stuff?"

"Aren't you being a little hard on the woman?" Donald asked. "Her husband is a drunk, permanently unemployed—"

"He was a rising young businessman when he married our Marge," Ted interrupted. "I consider him her greatest achievement. It took her only five years to reduce him to a slobbering wreck."

Ellie agreed with Ted's appraisal of Marjorie Melody's syndicated column—nauseating was too mild a word for the mixture of unctuous prayers, sloppy sentimentality, and back-to-the-kitchen antifeminism—but his last speech, delivered with a viciousness quite unlike his usual expressions of petty resentment, made her protest.

"Don't be so catty, Ted. I think you're trying to change the subject. Maybe I ought to call that number Kate left for me."

"First sensible thing you've said all day," Donald remarked.

"Getting in touch with Kate can be a long, frustrating process," Ted said. "You know she's never where she says she is going to be. Ellie, you aren't really frightened, are you? I find the whole business utterly fascinating. But if it worries you . . ."

"Well?" Donald demanded, as Ted stopped speaking. He was watching the older man suspiciously. "What do you suggest?"

"The logical thing for her to do is get out of the house, at least at night," Ted said promptly. "I've offered to come and stay with her, and I needn't say that she's welcome to sleep at my place. Whatever she wants, whatever will make her more comfortable."

"That makes sense," Donald said, more affably; and Ellie, ashamed of the suspicions that had apparently come to Donald's mind as well as her own, patted Ted's long, fine-boned hand.

"I know you offered, and I really appreciate it. But of course I'm not frightened. The whole thing is just a silly hoax. It can't be aimed at me, since I've done nothing to annoy anyone; so why should I worry?"

Ted shook his head. "You're right, Ellie, there is nothing to worry about. But I would feel better if you'd accept my company."

"No; thanks again. Let's drop it."

"Okay. Tell you what. I'll give you a little present."

Ted fumbled with both hands at the back of his neck, under his collar, while the others watched curiously. Eventually he unfastened a delicate chain that had been concealed by his shirt, and held it out to Ellie. Hanging from it was a golden cross. It was about three quarters of an inch long and intricately carved.

"Lovely thing, isn't it?" Ted said, eyeing the cross admiringly as it dangled from his fingers. "One of Omo's pieces; I picked it up in New York. He is an absolute master at this technique. At most angles the carving appears completely abstract; you have to see it from just the right distance to realize what it is."

The workmanship of the small jewel was as amazing as he claimed. When Ellie moved it to the proper distance the tiny, limp Figure on the cross sprang into view, as if it had been hidden in the metal.

"Good Lord, Ted, I can't take anything as valuable as this," she exclaimed. "It must be worth a fortune."

Donald was more acute than she, perhaps because he was less bemused by the sheer loveliness of the jewel.

"What the hell are you trying to suggest, Ted?" he demanded angrily. "Next thing you'll be wanting to sprinkle the place with holy water—or do you favor garlic around the doors and windows? I have no particular religious prejudices, but—"

"Oh," Ellie said blankly. "Oh, I didn't realize ... Honest, Ted, I don't think—"

But Ted had taken the ornament from her hand; rising, he leaned forward and hung it around her neck. The entire clientele of the restaurant watched with avid interest as he fastened the clasp. Ted turned.

"We're engaged," he announced, in a piercing voice. "I'm so glad you were all here to share this lovely moment with us."

The watchers hastily returned to their meals and their luncheon partners. Ted sat down.

"Nosy ghouls," he said loudly.

Ellie had both hands over her mouth trying to stifle her laughter, and even Donald was grinning.

"You are too much, Ted," he said. "I don't know why the hell we put up with you."

"I add a little spice to your dull lives," Ted said complacently. "Ellie, darling, I want you to have the crucifix because I love you, and because you appreciate it. You may not believe in its efficacy; I don't know that I believe, either; but I'm sure that while you are wearing it you will be safe from harm. Wear it to please me, if for no other reason."

It was impossible to refuse the gift after that, and Ellie knew she would cherish it as an expression of affection as much as for its beauty.

II

The coming of darkness only lowered the temperature a few degrees. The weather reporter on television announced cheerfully that the entire East Coast was in the beginning of what would probably be the worst heat wave of the summer, accompanied by humidity and smog. This information made Ellie feel even hotter. She was tempted to set the thermostat down a few degrees, but decided to leave it at 78. Kate's bills must be astronomical as it was.

The heat and the varied annoyances of the day had worn her out; at least that was her excuse for going to bed early. It had nothing to do with the fact that the lower regions of the house felt too quiet and too empty at night.

It was even warmer upstairs. Ellie decided to dispense with a nightgown. It was not until she had gotten into bed that the tug at her throat reminded her of Ted's crucifix. With a faint smile she unfastened the chain and put the ornament carefully on her bedside table. Even if she had believed in the efficacy of the crucifix she wouldn't have chosen to wear it to bed; it might get twisted and broken during the night. Besides, the town would really get a thrill if she appeared next day with a thin red line around her throat. Someone would be sure to come up with a story about an earlier inhabitant who had been hanged or decapitated.

Roger the rat paid his usual courtesy call and then departed for whatever activities filled his nightly hours. The cats, sprawled languidly across the bed, gave off heat like little individual stoves. Franklin, who had trouble with his adenoids, snored on the sea chest.

Before she turned out the light, Ellie went to the window. Nothing stirred on the wide, moon-washed lawn. Then there was a flicker of movement on the grass. Involuntarily Ellie stepped back, pulling the curtain around her body. Moving with a queer hopping movement, the creature came out onto the lawn; and Ellie's pent breath came out in a soft laugh. It was the big buck rabbit, the patriarch of the tribe that lived somewhere in the woods. In spite of Kate's best efforts, the cats and dogs occasionally caught a young rabbit, though most of them had learned not to bring their catch home for approval. But the patriarch was immune; for all his age—and he had been around longer than any rabbit might be expected to survive—he was the quickest, wiliest, and biggest of his tribe. Now he sat up, wriggled his ears, and looked around, with a comical air of nonchalance. He knew that the house animals were locked up for the night.

Reassured by the bucolic normalcy of the scene, Ellie went to bed and fell asleep at once.

She never knew what awakened her several hours later. It might have been a sound, or it might have been the cold. She was shivering when she came up out of the depths of slumber. The room felt like a refrigerator. It was pitch-black except for the faint starlight from the windows. The hall light was out—

and from the darkness there came the sound of slow, ponderous footsteps.

Wide awake and covered with goose bumps, Ellie tried to do two things at once—pull the sheet over her cold body and turn on the light. As the footsteps came closer she forgot about the first need and concentrated on the second; light was more necessary than warmth. But when her stiffened fingers finally found the switch of her bedside lamp, it clicked and clicked again without result. Squinting into the darkness, Ellie realized that she could now make out the outline of the doorway. It was beginning to fill with light—not normal electric light, but a faint, greenish-white luminescence like the rotten glow of fungi that grow in lightless cellars.

The episode could not have taken more than a minute at the outside, but it seemed to stretch on forever. Ellie's senses, quickened by fear, took in a jumbled variety of impressions. She could hear the animals stirring uneasily. The sheet, twisted around their bodies and her own, resisted her frantic efforts to pull it up. It was not modesty that motivated her, but the primitive equation of nakedness with helplessness.

Franklin began to growl. It was a quiet, uncertain growl, barely audible; but it made those few hairs that were not already quivering rise up along Ellie's neck. The light strengthened. The footsteps stopped. A figure stood in the doorway.

The light seemed to come from its own breast. It shone upward, illumining the white bearded face, the snowy hair of the man she had seen that afternoon in the portrait at the library. But this face was not at all saintly. Ellie was too far gone to grope through her vocabulary for a suitable description; later, she produced "leer" and "lascivious," which were in themselves symptomatic, because they were words she had never used except jokingly. If she had been able to think rationally she would have known that the creature could not see her, except as an indistinct shape against the white sheets; but she could have sworn that the glowing eyes inspected her naked body feature by feature, that the dreadful smile broadened, that the hands lifted in an incipient and unspeakable embrace.

Up to that point she had not thought of screaming. Now she did; and that was the worst moment of all, when her straining vocal cords produced only a voiceless gasp. Her hands flew to her throat.

The figure in the doorway recoiled. The face changed from lechery to furious rage. The snarling noise might have come from its throat—or it might have come from Franklin; Ellie was never certain. Suddenly the intruder was gone—blown out like a candle flame. At first Ellie thought she heard the sound of rapid footsteps; then she realized it was the sound of the pulse hammering in her ears.

She didn't faint, but she was quite incapable of movement for some time. Her first move was to fall out of bed, on the side away from the door. Kneeling, she snatched at the sheet and gave it a tug that sent cats flying like rubber balls. Their angry exclamations, couched in all ranges of feline complaint, restored Ellie's composure slightly; they didn't sound as if they were frightened, only annoyed.

Her eyes had adjusted to the darkness as much as they were going to. As she stood by the bed, trying to drape the sheet around herself, she could see the shapes of the furniture and the darker, gaping oblong of the doorway. There seemed to be nothing there; but it took more courage than Ellie had known she possessed to go to the door and slam it.

She thrust the bolt home, even though she knew that was illogical; wooden panels and iron bars were no hindrance to spirits, if the literature on the subject was to be believed. Even so, she felt safer—calm enough to remember that Kate kept candles in all the rooms in case of a power failure. After some fumbling, for her fingers still felt numb with cold, she located candles and matches.

In the feeble yellow light the room appeared normal enough. Two of the cats had returned to their places on the bed. The Siamese was sitting by the door staring fixedly at the panels. Franklin was gone.

Ellie sat down on the edge of the bed and reached for the telephone. She had to call the operator to get the number, but there was no delay. Donald answered on the second ring.

"I'll be right over," he said, cutting short an incoherent explanation. "Come down and let me in, will you?"

"I wouldn't go down those stairs alone for a million dollars," said Ellie. Her teeth started chattering at the very idea.

"Then how do you propose that I get in?" Donald inquired patiently.

"You can come in my window."

"Oh, for— All right. There's a long ladder in the shed. I suppose I can manage. Of all the damn-fool ideas—"

On her way to the window Ellie tripped over the sheet. This reminded her that she might be more conventionally attired; it also reminded her that she was freezing. She put on her robe, wrapped a blanket around her shoulders, and opened the window.

The warm, sticky air felt wonderful. Throwing the screened panel wide, she leaned out and let the heat soak into her bones. She was still in that position when Donald appeared.

He came straight across the lawn to the house and stood looking up. He had dressed in a hurry; the tails of his shirt were half in and half out of his jeans, and his sneakered feet were stockingless.

"Are you all right?" he called.

"Yes."

"Feel like coming downstairs?"

"No."

"All right, hang on," Donald said resignedly. "I'll get the ladder. And I'll let the dogs out. They might pick up someone's scent."

He was back in a few minutes, wavering under the awkward weight of the ladder, and accompanied by two delighted dogs, whose gambols were an added hazard to his balance. Despite their enthusiastic interference he managed to get the ladder in position. The German shepherd immediately started up it. Donald grabbed him by the collar.

"Damn furry clown," he shouted. "What do you think this is, a circus? Go guard the grounds or something."

A short wrestling match ensued, the dog evidently assuming that this was a new and delightful game. The ladder fell over. Donald finally got the dogs away and the ladder back up. Breathing hard, he stared at Ellie.

"If you are through horsing around," she remarked, "why don't you come up?"

Donald's reply was unintelligible. He started up the ladder. Ellie moved back from the window and he climbed in.

They contemplated one another in silence for a second or two. Ellie still clutched her blanket; Donald was sweating and disheveled after his romp with the dogs. Still in silence, Donald crossed the room and flicked the light switch.

The overhead light, a charming miniature chandelier, immediately went on. Ellie blinked.

"Do you prefer candlelight for these encounters?" Donald inquired. "More romantic, I admit, but—"

"The lights were out," Ellie said indignantly. "I always leave the one in the hall on when I go to bed, but it was out when I woke up. I tried my bedside lamp half a dozen times, and nothing hap——"

The rest of the word was lost in a gulp as Donald switched on the bedside lamp. He unbolted the door and after an almost imperceptible moment of hesitation threw it open.

The hall light burned steadily. Franklin, who had been sitting outside the door, got up off his haunches and trotted in. His plumy tail waving, he leaped up onto the chest and lay down.

"There's nobody in the hall," Donald reported, peering out.

"If you're so brave, why don't you go out and make sure?" Ellie snarled.

Donald appeared to be in no hurry to leave the room.

"Why have you got that blanket wrapped around you? Your thinly clad charms may be devastating, but I think I've got enough willpower not to ravish you on the spot—"

"Oh, Lord." Ellie sat down on the bed and stared palely at him. "Don't talk about ravishing, will you please? I have seen a leer or two in my time, but I have never seen a look like that on any man's face. And to see it on *that* face—"

"You're sure that's who it was? Old Man Lockwood?"

"Oh, yes. I couldn't see his clothing too clearly, but it looked like the same outfit he was wearing in the portrait—one of those old-fashioned dark suits, with a vest and high collar. And the beard was the same."

Donald put his arm around her, tentatively at first, and then more tightly as she pressed closer to him.

"You're cold," he said gently. "Shock, I suppose."

"It wasn't shock when I first woke up. The room was absolutely icy, Donald. It may have been the cold that woke me."

"It isn't cold now. But you've had that window open for some time. . . ."

He gave her shoulders a comforting squeeze and went across the room to examine the thermostat next to the door.

"Seventy-eight. These rooms are separately controlled, aren't they?"

"Yes. Kate says it saves fuel bills in the long run; she can shut off parts of the house when it's very cold or very hot."

"Then it's theoretically possible that someone could have turned the switch way down after you fell asleep and waited till the temperature dropped into the sixties before he played his little drama. Could he have flipped the switch back, just before he left?"

Ellie tried to think.

"He could have been peeling bananas with his toes; I wouldn't have noticed. All I saw was that awful face, and a general shape. The light seemed to come from just under the face—"

"A flashlight, masked in some sickly color, and hidden in his clothes," Donald said promptly.

"How do you know?"

Donald scowled hideously.

"I suppose it's natural that you should suspect me. I would only like to make a few minor points. One: I am taking your word for what a lot of people might consider a very questionable story. Two: I suppose I could have run like a bat out of hell in order to get home before you called, but if you think about the probabilities—"

"I'm sorry," Ellie said pathetically. "I didn't mean it."

"Well, you should have. You should suspect everybody. I don't suppose you had sense enough to call a few other people to see if they had alibis?"

"Who?"

"Ted, for one," Donald said. "Far be it from me to cast aspersions—"

"It couldn't have been Ted. He gave me— Donald! The crucifix he gave me. I wonder if . . ."

"Oh, come on," Donald said. "Don't tell me that.

Don't tell me. You thrust your crucifix in the face of the horror and it recoiled, shrieking—"

"I don't remember that I did," Ellie admitted. "But the crucifix is there—on the bedside table. I might have touched it. I was groping around, trying to turn on the light."

"Forget it." Donald made a wide gesture of dismissal. "I will not, repeat, *not* be seduced into contemplating the remotest possibility of the supernatural. Ellie, why don't you try to get in touch with Kate? You owe it to her to let her know what's been going on."

"I don't know whether I can reach her. She gave me a number, but it was only for emergencies."

"If this isn't an emergency, I don't know how you define the word." Donald rubbed his forehead. "I need some coffee. Come on."

"I don't—"

"You have to face it sometime. It's all right, Ellie. Look at the animals."

Four cats lay sprawled across the bed, relaxed and unconscious. Franklin, nose on his outstretched paws, seemed to be chewing on something.

They had not gone more than a few steps along the hall before Donald stopped with a muffled exclamation and bent over to pick up something from the floor. He held it out for Ellie's inspection.

"Dirt," she said, staring. "A little ball of dirt. What—"

Donald had gone on a few steps.

"Here's another patch. Queer-looking stuff—dark, almost black. Damp, too; that's funny, it hasn't rained for two days. Now where—"

The idea hit both of them simultaneously, perhaps because their minds were tuned to horrors. But neither said it aloud; they followed the evidence on down the hall until it finally disappeared—little clumps of moldy, damp, black soil, with a rotten leaf or two crumpled in it. Rich black soil like mulch, or—

"Graveyard dirt," Ellie said, on a quick intake of breath. She turned and bolted for the bedroom.

It was not sanctuary she sought, but more evidence—the evidence Franklin was demolishing. She pried it from his jaws and, after one quick glance, flung it away and began wiping her fingers on her robe. But it was not filthy or contaminated. It was just a bone, a small bone, part of a small animal—or a human hand.

CHAPTER
SIX

"It is not a human bone," the doctor said, for the
third or fourth time. "I don't claim to be an expert
in animal anatomy, but I would say it came from
some variety of rodent—a squirrel or rabbit, perhaps." He flung the grisly little object down on the
table and glared at Ellie and Donald. "I'm disgusted
with both of you, letting your imaginations run away
with you like this."

It was late afternoon of the following day. They
had been unable to consult Doctor Gold before this
time, since he had left for Richmond at dawn to
check on a patient who was undergoing a dangerous
operation. Donald had spent the remainder of the
night in the room next to Ellie's; he did not explain,
nor did she ask, why his father did not worry about
his absence. Ellie drew the logical conclusions. Not
that she cared about Donald's morals, or lack of
them. . . . By mutual consent they had left the lights
on all night. What the Beaseleys thought of the entire proceeding they never knew; the house had been
clean, and deserted, by the time they got up late in
the morning.

Donald returned his father's frown.

"That dirt on the floor wasn't imagination. Dad,
you know I'm not voting for the supernatural bit; all

I'm saying is that this joker is going to considerable lengths to carry out his plot. I can think of ways in which all these stunts could have been rigged, but the psychological effects have been damnably well thought out."

At Donald's suggestion they were meeting in Kate's workroom. He had asked his father to join him in a thorough search of the house after they finished talking. The room was cool and shadowy; Ellie had drawn the curtains to keep out some of the sunlight that poured in through the wide bay windows. The temperature outside was high in the nineties; the heat wave was in its second day and going strong.

Dr. Gold shook his head perplexedly.

"I can't figure out why anyone would go to such lengths. I'll certainly search the house with you, Donald, but I doubt that we'll gain anything by it. You say you've already looked in a cursory fashion. If the Beaseleys were here, they would have tidied away any clue—assuming there was a clue."

"The dirt was gone when we got up," Donald said. "I don't know how they ran the vacuum without waking us, but they did."

"It's the motive that bothers me," the doctor persisted, running his finger through his gray hair. "Nothing has been touched or damaged—"

"Only the azaleas." And, as the others looked at him in surprise, Donald went on, "I noticed it this morning—a place in the bushes where some heavy body had crashed through. Kate will yell about that, but it was probably one of her precious hounds. I heard the dogs barking outside, sometime in the wee hours. I was too groggy to get up even if I'd been inclined to do so, but the barking didn't last long. They must have been after a rabbit or something."

"I hope they didn't catch old granddad rabbit," Ellie said. "I saw him last night on the lawn. That's why Kate doesn't let the dogs out at night."

"There's not much point to letting them out," the

doctor said. "They aren't trained watchdogs; they are apt to run off in pursuit of game or a friendly female."

Donald's face was studiously bland; it must have been ESP that made Ellie exclaim, "They haven't come home, have they? Donald, you took care of the animals this morning; did Duke and Cumberland ever come home?"

"They'll be back," Donald said. "They are trained to come home to be fed at night. I suppose their freedom went to their heads. Don't take on, Ellie, they both have ID tags; you'd have heard if anything happened to them. They're big, grown-up dogs."

"I wonder if they could have been chasing someone," the doctor said.

"But that was hours after Ellie's admirer left," Donald protested.

"We'll have a look at the grounds, all the same. And tonight—if you won't come to us, Ellie, Donald will stay here. Your generation doesn't worry about the conventions, and in this case—"

"I don't care about the conventions," Ellie began. She didn't have to finish the sentence.

"If it's Donald you object to, I don't blame you," the doctor said cheerfully. "I only offer him because he's the most available candidate. We don't want to spread this story any farther than it has already spread. But—I'm forgetting. You have a fiancé in Washington—didn't you say that? Perhaps he—"

"Oh, God," Ellie said, clapping her hand to her mouth. "No, no, it's not what you're thinking, Dr. Gold. It's just that—the last time I talked to Henry he was—he was not feeling too well. I meant to call back to see how he was, and then I forgot."

"Dear me, I am sorry to hear that," said the doctor politely. "That he is ill, I mean. Of course if he *is* ill, he wouldn't be able to come, would he?"

"He couldn't come anyway. He's a very busy and successful lawyer."

"I see."

Donald didn't look much like his father; but at this moment the older man's face had the same blandly courteous expression Ellie had seen so often on Donald's face. She had no doubt that the doctor had read all sorts of unspoken meanings into her comments and had drawn several unwarrantable conclusions about her and Henry. Ellie reminded herself to be sure and call that evening.

"I guess I'll have to put up with Donald," she said ungraciously.

"Gee, thanks," said Donald.

They toured the house, finding nothing; which was not surprising, since none of them knew what they were looking for. Then they went out to inspect the broken azalea bushes Donald had mentioned.

The sun was low in the west, but it was hotter than ever. Cats and dogs were scattered over the lawn wherever there was a patch of shade. Ambrose, the big Maine Coon, was stretched at full length across the steps, like a long, bushy, orange mat. He did not offer to move, so they had to go around him.

The gap in the azaleas was certainly man-sized. But, as Donald pointed out, several of the dogs were man-sized, too. Ellie was distressed at the damage to Kate's cherished shrubs; they were thirty years old, six feet high, and were solid masses of blazing color in the spring.

"It does look as if some large object went through here in a hurry," Dr. Gold admitted.

"If this were a proper Gothic," Donald said, kneeling to look at the ground, "there would be a scrap of fabric caught on a twig. We need clues."

"Gothics don't have clues," Ellie said. "They have lots of horrible happenings instead. Werewolves howling, bloodstains on the floor, murders—"

This extravagant description was interrupted by Donald's exclamation. He was on all fours, his nose almost touching the ground.

"A footprint!"

The soil under the thick bushes was still damp. Unfortunately it had been mulched with the pine bark those acid-loving plants require, and neither Ellie nor Dr. Gold would admit that the faint impression was that of a human foot, much less the large, booted, size-thirteen foot Donald claimed to see. Donald continued to cast about, barking occasionally to encourage himself. The barking may have been his undoing. He was suddenly flattened by a large dun-colored shape that came hurtling over the bushes and landed squarely on his back.

Ellie ran up and grabbed the dog by its collar. It relinquished Donald's shirt and faced Ellie with a broad, embarrassed canine grin. One ear hung down in a fashion no German shepherd breeder would approve.

"Duke!" Ellie crooned. "Bad dog! Where have you been all this time, sweetums? Ellie was worried about you."

Donald sat up and spat out a mouthful of mulch. The spectacle of Ellie and Duke embracing, with cries of mutual rapture, appeared to disgust him. He spat again.

"No wonder those dogs act like spoiled children instead of animals. For God's sake, stop talking baby talk to him, Ellie."

The doctor, who had been watching with amusement, sobered.

"Ellie, he's got something in his mouth."

Ellie fell over backwards, rolling like a tumbler.

"If it's another bone . . ." she began, grimacing.

"No." The doctor pried Duke's jaws apart. Duke was not cooperative, but when the doctor had freed the object that had been caught between his back teeth, he gave an almost human sigh of relief and lay down.

"Here's your scrap of fabric," the doctor said. "Not on a twig, however."

Donald took the damp strand of cloth from his father. He began to laugh softly.

"This case is turning into a farce, Watson. The great detective falls flat on his face, and now this."

"What is it?" Ellie asked, making no attempt to inspect the object more closely. It was not aesthetically pleasing after its sojourn in Duke's mouth.

"A scrap of white cotton knit," Donald answered. "The sort of fabric that is often, though not exclusively, used in making gentlemen's underdrawers."

II

"I don't believe it," Ellie said. "It's too farcical. Duke grabbing a burglar by the seat of the pants—it isn't even Charlie Chaplin, it's the Three Stooges."

"It is also inconclusive," the doctor said. "Duke may have raided some innocent householder's laundry line. And, as Donald says, underwear isn't the only thing this material is used for."

"I shall keep it, nonetheless," Donald announced. "An envelope, Watson. This exhibit must be labeled and filed."

"There are envelopes in the library," said Ellie, assuming, correctly, that the role of Watson had been assigned to her.

They started toward the house, reaching the porch just in time to see a car come out of the woods. It was a dark, unostentatious vehicle; Ellie, who was not a car buff, didn't recognize the genre until she saw the Mercedes insignia. Driven with a deliberation that verged on demureness, the automobile purred around the circular drive and came to a stop. A woman got out.

Ellie took an instant dislike to her. She insisted on

this initial impression long after she had learned to
know and dislike the lady even better.

She was immaculate. That was enough to be irritating on such a sticky, hot day. Her bouffant blond
hair curled around her high forehead in little carefully planted ringlets. Her dress was raw silk—
ridiculous, for a casual call on a neighbor on such a
steaming day—and was carefully tailored to conceal
a slight affluence of hip and thigh—though it did not
conceal this from Ellie's critical eye.

"Hi, there." The newcomer raised a plump white
hand. Her teeth were white, too. Capped, Ellie decided. Her gums showed when she smiled.

"You must be little Ellen." Gums shining pinkly,
the woman caught Ellie by the shoulders and exuded
charm. "Darling Kate has spoken of you so often. I
meant to call earlier, but life is so—so— And now
I'm in search of an absentminded cavalier. Don,
sweet, did you forget our tennis date?"

Affability oozed from her like a sticky stream of
molasses. Ellie felt as if invisible viscous strands had
glued her to the spot and closed her mouth. Overdone as it was, the performance was effective; she
felt like a grubby urchin of twelve—as if she were
wearing pigtails.

"Tennis on a day like this?" Donald demanded.
"You must be nuts, Marge. Anyway we didn't have a
date. Just a casual possibility."

"Isn't that just like him?" Marge made a cute little
grimace at Ellie.

"You must excuse me," Ellie said stiffly. "I'm
afraid I don't remember—"

The doctor started, as if he too had felt the paral-
ysis of sticky sweetness.

"Sorry, Ellie. This is our famous author-columnist-
lecturer . . ."

"You are Marjorie Melody?" Ellie stared.

The older woman lowered mascaraed lashes.

"People usually are surprised," she murmured. "I

can't imagine why. Of course, I'm not as young as I look. . . ."

Ellie was not amused, as she usually was by women of Marjorie's type. She interpreted Donald's blank expression as bemused fascination, and was irrationally exasperated by it. Any man who was fool enough to fall for a haggard fake at least ten years his senior, with an ego the size of Mount Everest and a literary style that combined the worst of Edgar A. Guest, Dale Evans, and Kathryn Kuhlman. . . . This she wanted to see more of. Besides, she had little choice; rudimentary courtesy demanded that she invite her visitor in.

Marjorie accepted the invitation with a little squeal of pleasure.

"Darling, how sweet of you. I did promise Kate I'd look in on you now and then."

Seething, Ellie led the way into the house. She couldn't imagine Kate tolerating Marjorie, much less asking her to check up on Ellie, as if she were a child. She escorted her guest into the kitchen instead of one of the more formal rooms, wishing it weren't so elegant. It had been remodeled when Kate bought the house and was now a *Better Homes and Gardens* color spread, with an aged-brick fireplace wall complete with iron cranes and oak settles, a central work island bristling with copper pans and bunches of dried herbs overhead—"the works," as Kate had happily explained.

Marjorie sat down at the antique Spanish Colonial Mission table, put her elbows on the table, her chin in her hands, and gave them another view of healthy gums.

"How delightfully casual. Let's do sit here, shall we, like old chums? I adore kitchens. I always say a kitchen is the chummiest place in the house—the core of the friendliness, you know. Don—I'll have my usual, darling."

Ellie stepped back from the refrigerator with an exaggerated bow.

"Do take over, Don, darling," she said sweetly. "You know where everything is."

Donald gave her an expressive look but carried out his duties as bartender smartly. When they were settled—chummily—at the table, Marjorie raised her glass.

"Here's to darling Kate. I do hope she is enjoying her vacation. I don't suppose you've heard from her?"

"I don't expect to." Ellie took a long, vulgar swig of her beer. "You know how she is. You're such good friends. . . ."

"I know something Kate doesn't know," the doctor put in. He seemed peculiarly restless; his face was flushed as if with heat, and his mouth kept twitching.

"What's that?" Ellie asked.

"They are going to broadcast the first preseason game on local TV," the doctor said. "It's not on a national network, so if Kate wants to see it, she'll have to come home sooner than she planned."

Marjorie laughed; a light, tinkling little laugh.

"Football? It's so darling of Kate to pretend to be interested in football, isn't it. She's so cute, with her little affectations."

The doctor pushed his chair back and stood up.

"I must be going. You—er—young people enjoy yourselves. I'll see you—when I see you, eh, Donald?"

"Cold cuts and salad in the fridge," Donald said. "Eat. I'll check up on you later."

"Talk about Jewish mothers," the doctor said, with a smile.

When he opened the kitchen door, three cats streaked in. Finding their food dishes empty they began to prowl, looking for crumbs. Simbel jumped onto the counter and posed with the elegance of a miniature cougar, his yellow eyes fixed steadily on Marjorie. Contrary to the accepted tradition, it was her eyes that shifted away first.

"You're such a good son, Don," she said softly. "I think it's darling of you. In this hard, cynical age—"

"It's his only virtue," Ellie said caustically. "For a grown man to spend his life cutting lawns—not that he cuts them, some of Kate's grass is a foot high."

"You want me to cut it now?" Donald inquired. "The temperature is only about ninety-five out there."

"No, darling, you mustn't take chances," Marjorie exclaimed. "Not in your condition. But—there is one little teenie thing you could do for me; my car has been making the funniest rattling noise. . . ."

"I'll have a look." Donald accepted the car keys and left, with alacrity. Another cat slipped through the swinging door—the old Siamese, who, after the inevitable investigation of the food dishes, climbed arthritically onto Ellie's lap. Marjorie gave it a look of undisguised loathing. Then she looked at Ellie and lowered her voice confidentially.

"Darling, that wasn't a terribly Christian thing to say, now was it? Donald isn't well. Typhoid takes so long to get over, and he was frightfully ill with it."

"Typhoid," Ellie repeated stupidly.

"Of course you know all about it, you two being so close. . . . If he hadn't continued to carry the load after he took sick—but he was the only medically qualified person in that entire stricken village—only a third-year student, but there were no doctors, not in that remote corner of Mexico—why, it was absolutely noble of him. 'Greater love hath no man than this, that a man lay down his life . . .' "

"He's still very much alive," Ellie said. Her voice sounded dry and harsh because she was writhing with self-contempt and unwilling to betray her feelings to Marjorie.

"Ah, but he was willing to die." Marjorie's voice had the revolting oiliness she used for her little sermonettes. "Be more charitable, darling. It's such a lovely world, full of lovable people. Love them and they will love you!"

She never knew how close she came to having the dregs of Ellie's beer poured over her head. As if sensing Ellie's mood, the Siamese put out its claws. They pricked like ten little needles, like penance or punishment. Ellie bit her lip.

Marjorie's mood changed abruptly. She leaned forward. Her self-consciously beatific expression was replaced by one of greedy curiosity.

"What are these peculiar stories I've been hearing about you, darling? Is Ted exercising his well-known talent for exaggeration, or—"

"I expect you know as much about them as I do," Ellie said. "I wish I knew why anyone would want to play such bizarre practical jokes."

"Jokes? On you?" Marjorie lifted her eyebrows. "Oh. Oh, yes, I see. There certainly does seem to be malice involved, doesn't there? Aimed at our old respected families. . . ."

"None of your relatives has turned up yet," Ellie said. "Of course it's early days."

Marjorie gave one of her tinkly little laughs. Her eyes looked like hard brown pebbles.

"Do be careful what you say, dear. Some people might interpret that as a threat."

The opening door saved Ellie from a reply that would have done her no credit. When Donald came in, Ted was with him. So were three cats, and Franklin the Pekingese. Marjorie began to look rattled. She put her feet up on the rungs of her chair.

"Your car sounds okay, Marge," Donald announced. "If you have any more trouble, better take it to the garage."

"It sounded fine to me, too," Ted said. "Marge, you're hearing funny noises again. It's all in your head, dear. One of the dangers of spiritual communication, hearing noises that aren't really there."

"Apparently I'm not the only one who hears, and sees, things that aren't there," Marjorie said shrewishly.

"Don't be catty, darling," Ted said. "It doesn't suit your public image. Ellie, my pet, I hope you don't mind my dropping in. I told you I hate to drink alone."

"Help yourself," Ellie said. She was glad to see Ted, although she knew he had come to find out more about the latest goings-on. He was a gossip, but he was genuinely fond of her—and he seemed to have a unique knack of getting under the thick skin of Marjorie Melody. That alone would guarantee him a welcome from Ellie.

"Of course I didn't mean that the way it sounded," Marjorie exclaimed. "I'm truly concerned for Ellen. Spiritual evil . . . As I was saying to Ellen, it almost seems as if someone has a grudge against our fine old families."

"Then Ellie can't be suspect," Donald said bluntly. "She doesn't even know who the old families are, much less any dirt about them."

"There are books," Marjorie murmured. Then she looked up, wide-eyed and apologetic. "Oh, you know I don't think that, darling. I'm simply trying to prepare you for what certain evil-minded persons might say. Miss Mary was telling me about an old book you bought for Kate—"

"She couldn't have gotten any juicy legends from that book," Ted interrupted. "It's the usual collection of pious lies. Your grandmother is prominently featured, Marge."

"Among the lies?" Marjorie showed her teeth. "Ted, you're such a tease."

"Oh, I am, I am," Ted agreed. "But get one thing clear, Marge. Ellie is not inventing these stories. Something is happening here; something quite out of the ordinary; and when it's finished this town may never be the same."

The words cast a shadow over the sunny kitchen. For a moment no one spoke. Marjorie's face was unmasked; it was hard and lined and a little frightened. The cats, lined up along the counter top, looked like a stiff Egyptian frieze. They were all staring at Marjorie.

The silence was broken by a scrabbling sound outside the door. Ellie got up.

"That must be Roger. I guess it's time I fed everyone."

"Roger McGrath?" Marjorie started. "Oh, God, you mean that horrible rat of Kate's. Don't let him in, Ellie, I'm terrified of rodents."

"Wrong move, Marge," Ted said, grinning. "You should have let Roger enter; then you'd have an excuse for flinging yourself into someone's manly arms."

Marjorie glowered at him. Her brand of cattiness was no match for Ted's battering-ram tactics.

"I'll go out the back way," she said. "I must get home to the kiddies; they'll be wanting dinner."

"I'm sure your cook and nursemaid and butler and parlor maid have that problem under control," Ted said. He winked at Ellie, who was remembering a recent sermonette in which Marjorie Melody had rhapsodized about the joy of preparing wholesome home-cooked meals for one's darling children.

Yet she couldn't help admiring Marjorie's nerve. The woman had been shaken by Ted's jeers and by the animals, which she clearly disliked (though a much-admired, often reprinted series of sermonettes described Marjorie's tenderness toward our Little Furry Four-Footed Brothers). But she paused to strike a pose, her chin lifted (it tightened those nasty sagging neck muscles), and her face turned in the three-quarter view with which readers of her column were familiar.

"Spiritual evil," she repeated musingly. "Yes, I feel it here. Ellen, dear child, remember that you can call on me at any hour. What small influence for good I may possess—in my humble reliance on God's mercy—is at your disposal."

She raised one hand in a gesture that was not quite a formal blessing, and bowed her elegant head. Whether by design or accident, a ray of sunlight struck it so that her hair glowed like a nimbus. Ellie looked hard at the exposed roots, but was disappointed; Marjorie must take excellent care of her hair. Then, timing her move perfectly, she was out the door before Ted could spoil the performance with a caustic comment.

Ted circled the kitchen, dipping his fingers into his martini and flicking little drops of gin around the room.

"Ceremonial fumigation," he explained. "Isn't she revolting? I hate all my friends—present company and their relatives excepted—but I truly believe Marjorie is the utter end. Would you like to hear some stories about her grandam?"

Ellie opened the door for Roger, who deliberately sat down on the threshold and cleaned his whiskers, forcing her to hold the door like an obsequious servant.

"Move, you rat," she told him. "Who was her sainted grannie, Ted? Another of the town's distinguished citizens?"

"She wrote sermonettes too," Ted said dreamily. "She had them published—first in little tracts, to be handed out to the helpless poor—then in a private limited edition bound in limp leather covers. I have a copy. When I'm feeling depressed I read it and laugh myself sick."

Donald began to help Ellie with the animal food for the evening meal. A hubbub outside the back door indicated that the dogs were assembling. They knew the schedule as well as the humans did.

"I have never seen such a display of malicious petty-mindedness," he said, over the whir of the can opener. "All three of you. Shame, oh, shame!"

As he reached for the next can Ellie saw how sharply the tendons stood out on the back of his thin brown hand. She had not forgotten what Marjorie had told her. Naturally, it made her absolutely furious with Donald.

"You should be ashamed, forgetting your date with dear Marge," she said. "Don't let my little problems interfere with your love life."

Donald stared at her. "Do I detect the ring of jealousy?"

"Don't flatter yourself!"

"Children, children," Ted said. "Marjorie isn't worth quarreling about. I guess I won't tell you any stories about her granny after all; I don't know anything too bad. However, she was hand in glove with that old hypocrite Lockwood in his charitable schemes. Maybe they were running a white-slavery ring on the side."

"Have another drink, Ted," Ellie said. She shoved a cat off the counter with her elbow as it nosed at the can of fish.

"No, thanks. I'll run along. You are spending the night, aren't you, Don?"

"Yes."

"Good. I may have a look around myself in the witching hours, so don't be alarmed if you hear the dogs barking."

"I haven't decided yet whether I'll leave them outside," Donald said. He picked up two bowls of dog food. Ted opened the door for him. A chorus of canine rapture arose.

"I'll be off now," he said, as Donald came back for the next round. "Be sure to call, if you need me."

"Thanks," Ellie said abstractedly, setting out bowls of cat food. There were thirteen bowls, one for each, but there was a lot of pushing and shoving and some rude remarks before the crowd finally settled down. Roger, sitting upright on the kitchen table, squeaked imperiously, and Ellen gave him his dinner in his own Sevres porcelain bowl.

"That's the most unsanitary thing I ever saw," Donald said.

"He's cleaner than a lot of people I know," Ellie retorted. "Where are you going now?"

"To count the rest of the livestock. And then, boss lady, I will finish mowing the lawn."

III

He did finish the lawn. Wise in the illogical ways of the male, Ellie made no attempt to dissuade him; she knew this would only spur him on to more exhausting demonstrations of virility. She spent the ensuing hours moving from window to window, watching, and alternately cursing herself and Donald.

It was nine o'clock before he finished. The temperature was still in the eighties. Ellie had removed herself, after leaving a temptingly arranged salad plate and a pitcher of iced tea in a prominent place in the refrigerator. She had also made up his bed in the room next to hers and turned the sheets down.

Eventually Donald joined her in the workroom, where she was watching television and working on one of Kate's abandoned pieces of embroidery—a Danish counted cross stitch tablecloth of unbelievable complexity. The pattern was a wreath of poppies, cornflowers, and other summer flora. Kate had finished about half of it before getting bored.

Ellie knew she made a charming domestic picture as she sat with the lamplight shining on her crown of curly hair, her head bent over her busy needle.

She was wearing a ruffled, flowered robe that Henry had picked out for her—his tastes ran to the sweetly charming—and she was surrounded by purring pussycats and devoted dogs.

To her anxious eye Donald looked pale under his tan, but the set of his mouth told her that questions about his health would not be well received. The mouth relaxed fractionally as he took in her pretty tableau; but his first question indicated that they were still in a state of careful truce.

"You wanted me to remind you to call your fiancé."

This was not strictly accurate, but Ellie did not challenge the statement.

"He's in the hospital."

"Oh?"

"He wasn't home, so I called a friend of his, who told me where he was." Ellie finished the edge of a scarlet poppy petal and threaded her needle with rose pink. "They don't know what the problem is exactly. Some kind of rash. It seems to be very painful."

She made three careful stitches and then looked up. Donald's face was contorted hideously as he tried not to laugh. Meeting Ellie's eyes, he lost the battle; both of them laughed till Ellie was breathless and Donald's face had turned a bright, healthy pink.

"I suppose you told him about the shingles," he wheezed. "Kate's bragged about that ever since she came home from your place last year. You shouldn't have done it, Ellie."

Ellie wiped her eyes.

"I don't know why I am behaving so badly. It isn't funny. What do you suppose can be wrong with him?"

"Autosuggestion, probably," Donald said, with an unprofessional snort of leftover laughter. "Is he an impressionable person?"

"I wouldn't have thought he was in the least impressionable," Ellie said, and then realized that her voice had given away more than she wanted to disclose. "But I guess people are suggestible when their health is involved."

"Sophomore syndrome," Donald said. "Med-school students are susceptible to it in their first year or two. My roommate had leprosy one week. His skin even started to peel. It's very common, and damn interesting. We don't know enough about the ways in which the mind affects the body. When an internist fails to find a specific physical cause he ships the patient off to a psychiatrist, who starts digging into childhood traumas. We need a whole new discipline."

Enthusiasm flushed his face and made his eyes shine. Ellie was conscious of a peculiar sensation somewhere in the region of her diaphragm.

"You'll never make any money starting new disciplines," she said critically.

"No. There's a lot of quackery in the area of psychosomatic medicine; the professionals shy away from it. I doubt that we know enough about the brain and nervous system to make any real progress as yet. But it fascinates me."

He seemed to take it for granted that she knew of his medical training, and Ellie was glad no apologies or explanations were necessary.

"About Henry," she began.

"Henry. Oh, well, I guess you tried to warn him about Kate's peculiarities. I sure would, if I were introducing her to my fiancée. He was anxious to make a good impression, and you must admit she's a weird lady. . . . One little itch—one mosquito bite— and he was on the way. His own nervous system did the rest. He'll get over it."

"I'm sure he will."

The TV program, a cops-and-robbers movie, had been rumbling along throughout the conversation.

"You watching that?" Donald asked.

"No. I just needed some . . . noise."

"Yeah. Does the house always seem this—well, this empty at night?"

"Usually it's a very friendly house. Must be my nerves tonight."

"It isn't ever really empty, is it?" Donald glanced around the cluttered room. Recumbent cats strewed the furniture like animals in Sleeping Beauty's castle, piles of gray, orange, tabby, tawny fur.

"What did you decide to do about the dogs?" Ellie asked, after a moment of silence that seemed to stretch on too long.

"I don't see much point in letting them out. They're so stupid they might run off or get hit by a truck. I'm not worried about anybody who is outside the house, so long as nothing gets in."

"The animals haven't been much help so far," Ellie said. "The first . . . person . . . in the hall upstairs; they just sat there yawning."

Another overlong silence followed. Ellie repressed a desire to look over her shoulder. From beyond the closed and curtained window came a faint echo of sound like a far-off wailing. She knew what it was— a dog, less pampered than Kate's, footloose and fancy free, baying at the moon. It was an eerie sound, all the same.

"Want a night cap?" Donald asked.

"No, thanks." Ellie started folding up her work. "I don't mind admitting that I am spooked tonight. I'm going to bed. It's silly, but I feel safer upstairs."

"I'm a little tired myself," Donald said.

He preceded her up the stairs. She didn't debate the issue; so far as she was concerned, there was little to choose between the advance and rear guards. They parted, casually, at their respective doorways.

Ellie's inexplicable nervousness subsided when she was tucked up in bed with pillows behind her and a nice soothing book—and enveloped in her most concealing nightgown. It was not Donald's near presence that prompted her modesty. A shiver ran through her as she looked at the open doorway; her imagination recreated the dreadful figure of the previous night with unpleasant distinctness.

But the lights shone clear and steady. On her bedside table lay candles, matches, and a flashlight. And from the next room came the small reassuring sounds of occupation. After a while she heard a thud and a muffled curse from Donald. Ellie deduced that one of the larger cats had landed on his stomach. Smiling, she surveyed her own bedfellows. They had their own private arrangements about sleeping rights. Tonight her companions were Simbel the Abyssinian, his shadow, George, and the Balinese, Henrietta, a dainty, fine-boned creature with long silky hair and the dark markings of a seal-point Siamese. Franklin was in his usual position on the sea chest. Ellie finished her chapter and then turned out her light.

It was several hours later when she was awakened by Franklin, who was proving to be the exception to the general incompetence of Kate's watchdogs. His threatening growl dragged Ellie out of slumber into pitch-blackness. The hall lights were out. Against the pale shape of the window she could just distinguish Franklin's erect little body. He was sitting upright and growling like a thunderstorm. As Ellie stirred, groping for one of the various sources of light on the bedside table, Franklin let out a shrill bark and jumped down to the floor.

The dog's outburst was like a signal; it set off an unholy racket somewhere in the lower regions. There were crashing sounds, like glass breaking, duller thuds that might have been pieces of furniture falling, thumps and voiceless shouts—the audio accompaniments to a good old-fashioned free-for-all.

Ellie's first thought was for Donald. Had he been fool enough to go downstairs alone to investigate some unusual sound? He had promised to waken her

up, but he was such an idiot. . . . She found the flashlight and was obscurely surprised when it responded to the pressure of her finger on the button.

The noise downstairs had subsided except for
Franklin's excited yelps and a deeper booming bark
from one of the other dogs. It sounded like William.
Usually he hid under the piano or tried to climb into
bed with someone if he was frightened, but Franklin's foolhardy courage sometimes shamed him into
acting like a dog—so long as the Pekingese was
around to protect him.

Donald was in the hall when she came out of her
room. Fully dressed except for his shoes, he also had
a functional flashlight. Ellie ran to him and threw
her arms around him. She was moved, let it be said,
not by a girlish need for male protection, but by the
desire to keep him from rushing headlong into the
melee below.

He didn't seem to be too anxious to proceed.

"Where's the fuse box?" he asked, returning Ellie's embrace with what struck her as inappropriate
enthusiasm.

"In the basement, of course. You think that is
why—"

"Seems logical."

"The downstairs lights may not be turned off."

The switch at the head of the stairs confirmed this
hope; when Donald pressed it, the chandelier in the
hall below went on. The light encouraged Donald. He
squared his shoulders and told Ellie to get behind
him.

"You're twenty years out of date," she said con-
temptuously. "We go shoulder to shoulder or not at
all."

It was not difficult to locate the scene of the disturbance. Franklin's barks led them straight to the
library. Donald delayed only long enough to turn on
every possible light as they passed the switches. The
final switch was to the right of the library door. The

bulbs in the heavy wrought-iron chandeliers blazed into life; and for a few seconds Ellie gaped speechlessly at what the light revealed.

Books had been pulled from the shelves, objects swept off the desk, and chairs overturned. The wide French doors hung open, motionless in the still night air. One of the panes had been smashed.

It was not the disarray of Kate's handsome library that made Ellie gasp. Face down in the middle of the floor, surrounded by the rucked folds of Kate's prize rose-and-gold Kirman, was a familiar form. An oozing dark patch disfigured the silver-gray hair. By his head sat Franklin, alert and silent now that the assistance he had summoned had arrived.

"Ted . . ."

Donald pushed her out of the way. With a rush of relief Ellie remembered that he was no amateur, but medically trained. He didn't touch the fallen man except to take his pulse and run a knowledgeable hand over his head and limbs. When he looked up at Ellie his face was grave.

"Call the police. We need an ambulance, fast."

"Is it a fractured skull?" Ellie reached for the phone.

"Heart. It's bad, Ellie."

Ellie gave the message and was cheered by the promise of prompt assistance.

"I didn't go into the details," she said, as she hung up.

"No. We'll leave everything as it is. Too late to catch up with the burglar now; anyway, we might trample on clues. Damn, why didn't I let the dogs out tonight!"

Ellie opened her mouth and then closed it without speaking. She had been too thunderstruck to think logically. Now she realized that the condition of the room indicated the presence of at least two people. Ted wouldn't have made such a mess; he had his own key, no need to break windows. Unless he had been trying to create the impression of an ordinary burglar. . . .

She felt ashamed as she looked at Ted's unconscious body. How could she have leaped to the conclusion that Ted had been responsible for this? He certainly hadn't hit himself on the back of the head. Earlier he had mentioned that he meant to take a stroll around the grounds during the night. Presumably he had seen the burglar enter, or had found the broken window.

"Isn't there anything we can do for him?" she asked.

"A blanket might be a good idea."

Ellie rubbed her bare arms. She felt cold herself. Shock, no doubt.

"I'll get one," she said, and went quickly into the corridor.

It did not strike her as strange, then, that the animals were conspicuous by their absence. Usually they were inconveniently underfoot when anything was going on. Even through her worry about Ted she was vaguely aware that the house seemed chilly. But it was not until she reached the end of the corridor, where it entered the great beamed hall, that she realized something was badly wrong.

The cold collected in an invisible barrier, solid and icy as a glacier. Coming to a sudden stop, Ellie stared in horrified disbelief at the stairway. Her lips were so numb she could scarcely move them, but she managed to shape them into Donald's name. The word issued as a croaking gasp; but he heard her.

She felt his hands close hard on her arms. She didn't turn. She couldn't move, or take her eyes from the stairs.

On the landing, shadowed by the darkness above, something was taking shape.

It was a rounded pillar of ice, emitting frigid air. Or an obscene, giant white candle, crowned with a dim flame. No heat came from it, only those paralyz-

ing waves of cold. Slowly, or so it seemed to the
watchers, the shape took human form—still icy
white, robed in a snowy fabric that gleamed dully
like satin. A woman fiery-haired, with eyes the color
and intensity of blue-white diamonds. The other features were indistinct. Ellie was grateful for that; she
had no desire to see them more clearly. She could
hear Donald's harsh breathing behind her, could feel
the painful pressure of his fingers.

Then the tall form began to move slowly down the
stairs.

"I'm going to faint," Ellie announced firmly, and
did so.

CHAPTER
SEVEN

She was not allowed to luxuriate in unconsciousness for long. When she came to, Donald was shaking her till her teeth rattled. A piercing wail reached her ears.

"The ambulance is here," Donald said. "Wake up. It's all right. She—it—whatever—is gone."

When she received this news Ellie opened her eyes. She, it, whatever, was certainly gone. Not even a lingering wisp of fog remained, and the temperature was a comfortable 78 degrees.

As soon as her eyes opened, Donald dropped her unceremoniously back to the floor, from which he had partially raised her, and went to the door. Ellie scrambled to her feet.

Later, when she tried to recall the events of the succeeding hour, she felt as if she had been watching some tightly wound-up doll move mechanically through a set of programmed responses. After Ted had been removed, still unconscious, she answered the questions of a state trooper while another trooper searched the room. She could not have described either one of them.

When the taillights of the police car finally disappeared, the treetops to the east were black against the first flush of dawn. The air felt like that of a tepid Turkish bath. Ellie turned to Donald.

"What did I say?" she asked blankly.

"You did fine," Donald said. "Come on, let's have some breakfast."

The sun was fully up by the time they finished eating and Donald decided they were strong enough to discuss the night's events.

"You did fine," he said again. "Not that either of us needed to say anything; the room spoke for itself. A nice normal ordinary burglary, that's what we had."

"I didn't say anything because I was stupefied," Ellie said wryly. "You don't think we should have told them about—about the other things?"

"Why confuse the law? These boys were state troopers, not local cops, so they won't have heard the gossip. I told them I was sleeping in while Kate was out of town, to protect you and the house, but I suppose they drew the obvious conclusions."

Ellie shook her head impatiently.

"I don't care about that. How did you explain Ted's being here? A ménage a trois?"

"I didn't try to explain it. They figured he must have been taking a walk or coming home from a late date when he saw someone behaving suspiciously; but no one will really know until he is able to be questioned. If I know Ted he'll think up a good story."

"Donald—he will be all right, won't he?"

"I hope so, honey. We'll call the hospital in a little while."

"You don't think he saw—her, do you?"

"In an earlier, preview appearance? I doubt it. He isn't a young man; overexertion could have brought on an attack."

"Who was she, Donald?"

"I'm not sure, but I can guess."

"Marjorie's granny?"

"I have heard she had red hair," Donald said. "Damn it, Ellie, don't you see how coincidental this is? First you see the portrait in the library, then old man Lockwood appears, slavering with lust. This afternoon we were talking about Marge's grandmother—now she turns up, and if she wasn't slavering she was not exactly exuding warmth and goodwill. There were four of us here today when the subject came up. Obviously Marge has no reason to perpetrate a stunt like this. Quite the contrary. You and I were together—"

Ellie interrupted with a rude, raucous noise.

"Stunt, he says. If that—that awful thing was a stage illusion, it was arranged by a genius; and a genius could have arranged it to go off automatically, to give him an alibi. I mean, if you don't know how it was done—"

"You think I'm the joker," Donald said.

"No. I don't think you're that smart."

"Thanks. I'll return the compliment. I don't think you did it either."

"Me! Why would I—"

"This is the first time you've had a witness," Donald pointed out. "A fiendishly clever, malignant villainess would make sure the plot didn't rest solely on her unsupported word. Stop making horrible faces at me, Ellie; I know you're as innocent as a babe in arms. I hate to say it, with Ted so sick and all, but till tonight he was my prime suspect. Did you see the gleam in his eye when Marge was talking about dear old granny? I was rather expecting something to happen tonight, and it wouldn't have surprised me to find granny the star act. But what did happen was not what I was expecting. A burglar! It's so crude."

"It's a mess," Ellie said despairingly. "What am I going to do?"

"Send for Kate. You have to, Ellie."

"Oh, I agree. She'll want to know about Ted anyway. But what can she do? She can't explain this incredible business any more than we can."

"She may be able to explain more than you think," Donald said.

II

By noon Ellie was forced to admit that she was not going to be able to reach Kate by telephone. The number she had been given did not answer. When she suggested a telegram, Donald pointed out that this had no more chance of reaching the recipient than a phone call. Yet Ellie was reluctant to set the complex apparatus of police search in motion. A call to the hospital where Ted had been taken produced only the bland assurance that the patient was "about the same." After that Donald got on the phone, trying to reach his father. As is always the case when one is in a desperate hurry, he kept missing him by five minutes. It was midmorning before the doctor called back from his office in town. He had not heard of Ted's illness, and was horrified at the bad news Donald tossed him, but he refused to leave his patients until his morning office hours were over. He promised to visit Ted immediately thereafter, and report back. When Dr. Gold finally called, his voice had the false cheeriness that poorly conceals anxiety.

"He's in intensive care, honey; it's routine, in these cases, but I think he'll make it. Of course it's impossible to question him, or even let him talk about anything that might worry him. He's semiconscious and in no pain, I promise you. No, there is nothing you can do. Dr. Koch is the best cardiac specialist in the area, I wouldn't attempt to interfere even if I wanted to. This is turning out to be a busy day. It must be the heat; my patients seem to be dropping like flies. So I won't be able to get to you until late this afternoon. I'll come straight out as soon as I finish my calls, okay? You two hang on; I'll keep in touch with Dr. Koch and let you know the moment there's any change."

After that Ellie agreed to call the state police in Vermont.

That call, like all the others, took some time; explanations were tedious; but finally Ellie hung up the phone, which was hot from so much handling, and said limply, "They'll send someone to the lodge. And let us know."

Donald, who was looking as haggard as she felt, nodded. They were sitting in Kate's workroom, which was even more cluttered than usual. Neither of them had had the heart to do any housework.

"The Beaseleys," Ellie said suddenly. "Donald, the Beaseleys haven't shown up today."

"How do you know?"

"You don't often see them," Ellie admitted. "But you can usually tell they've been around."

"Let's look."

The Beaseleys had not been around. Breakfast dishes still cluttered the table, the egg-stained plates and crumb-covered mats looking as dissolute as such objects do by midday. The library had not been touched.

Automatically Ellie began tidying the room, replacing furniture, straightening the rug, collecting the objects that had stood on the desk.

"Maybe you shouldn't disturb anything," Donald said.

"The police have already seen it. I have to do something, I'm so nervous. Come on, Donald, help me. Do you suppose—"

"Yes," Donald said. "I do suppose. People like the Beaseleys have a kind of sixth sense for abnormality. I don't mean ghosts; the fact that the police had been here would be enough to send them into hiding for a while. Like all semiliterates they are extremely suspicious of authority."

"But how would they know—"

"My dear girl, the entire town probably knows by now."

With the neat contrivance of a stage direction, the telephone chose that moment to ring. Donald looked inquiringly at Ellie, who nodded. He picked up the instrument. The expression on his face told Ellie who was calling even before he spoke.

"Oh, yes. No, no, nothing like that; you know how these stories get exaggerated. . . . Well, he's in intensive care, but they seem to think he'll recover. . . . A burglar, we suppose. There was a struggle, and the door to the library was forced. . . ." A long pause followed; Ellie could hear the voice at the other end of the wire as a tiny, wordless noise that went on and on and on. Donald glanced at her; he was chewing his lower lip in a fashion that indicated indecision. Then, abruptly, he seemed to make up his mind. "Well," he said finally, "I don't know how you found out, but something did happen. Yes, something like that. Look, I don't want to discuss it over the phone. Why don't you come out here this evening? Maybe a conference is in order. About eight?" He cocked an eyebrow at Ellie, who shook her head vigorously; with a grin, Donald went on, "Ellie says that would be fine. See you then, Marge."

"Donald—" Ellie began.

Donald hung up the phone.

"She'll come, invited or uninvited, if I know Marge. Better to have it on our terms. Besides, I think some straight speaking is in order. I can support your story now. You have proof that an outside influence is at work. Maybe we can learn something by getting all these people together and letting them talk. Somebody might get careless and make a slip."

"You mean—invite the whole crowd?"

"The old families," Donald said, with a wry twist of his lips. "They are all involved in this somehow. Maybe we can find out how."

"You mean—call them up and invite them—"

"Quit saying, 'You mean,'" Donald said irritably. "I'll bet you a moderate sum of money we won't have to cal them. If the word hasn't already spread, Marge will spread it."

He was right. They were eating a makeshift lunch of sandwiches and beer when the second phone call came, from Roger McGrath.

Donald had taken over the telephone duties, with Ellie's tacit consent; she was glad of it when she heard the high-pitched shriek from the telephone and saw Donald's face harden. Donald dealt with McGrath effectively, and hung up.

"Number two," he said. His voice was calm, but there were spots of color on his cheekbones, evidence of controlled anger. "What a mean little creep that guy is.... I know how you feel, Ellie, but it's better to have him under our eye than squirming around the outskirts telling lies. He's going to call the others."

"Eight o'clock?"

"Yes, I think it's the best way, Ellie."

"I suppose you're right. Where the hell do you suppose Kate is?"

They found out, not long afterward, where Kate wasn't. The Vermont police reported that the lodge where Kate had been staying was closed and deserted. A sign on the front door read simply, "Gone. Back eventually." Kate's friends shared some of her habits. The police were broadcasting an appeal for Kate to get in touch with them, or with her home. More than that they could not do.

This news came close to breaking Ellie down.

"Something has happened to her," she mumbled, hanging up the phone. "It's the last straw, Donald; if Kate is hurt, or—or—"

"Don't be silly," Donald interrupted, in his nastiest voice. "This is perfectly normal behavior for Kate. If we had been able to locate her right away, you'd have had cause to worry about her. She'll turn up in her own sweet time. Look, Ellie, you're exhausted, that's part of the trouble. Let's get some sleep. I could do with a few hours myself."

Ellie raised her face from her hands and looked at him; something in her expression made a faint color come into Donald's cheeks. He went on, quickly, before she could speak.

"After we've had a nap, I suggest we sit down and write out a coherent account of what has happened. Who knows, we might see some pattern that has eluded us so far. Dad will be along later; we'll have time to talk it over with him before the crowd arrives. How does that strike you?"

"Fine," Ellie said meekly.

A few hours' rest made her feel a little better, but not much. As she said to Donald, the situation hadn't changed. There was no word from Kate, no sign of the mysterious Beaseleys, no information about Ted's condition, and no explanation for what had been going on.

"Ah," said Donald—who appeared to be one of those irritating people who are fully restored by two hours of sleep—"that last is what we are about to tackle. Sit down, take pen in hand, and prepare to write."

They were in the kitchen. Although neither would admit it, the picture-book modernity of that room was more spiritually comfortable than the period atmosphere of the remainder of the house. An eighteenth- or nineteenth-century apparition would have been quite at home in the library or parlor, but Ellie felt, illogically, that they wouldn't have the nerve to materialize among blenders and microwave ovens. Kate's workroom was getting too messy. The accu-

mulation of cat hairs had reached monstrous pro-
portions.

Donald had placed two pads of legal-sized paper
and several pens on the table. He now presented Ellie with a mug of black coffee and poured one for
himself.

"I'd rather have beer," Ellie said.

"You have to keep a clear head."

"It will take more than coffee to clear my head,"
Ellie said darkly.

"Stop griping and get to work."

Amid considerable debate—the least acrimonious
sections of which are reproduced here—they produced the following document.

SUMMARY OF EVENTS

I. *The apparition in the hall.*
   When: the first night; approx. 11 P.M.
   Appearance: young male, middle- or late-18th-
century costume, bearing striking physical resem-
blance to Donald P. Gold.
   (Ellie: "What does the *P.* stand for?"
   Donald: "None of your business.")
   Where seen: upper hall, slightly to left of
stairs.
   General comments: Transparent. Search (next
day) revealed no sign of wires, switches, etc.
   Note: animals displayed no reaction.
   Tentative identification: Francis Morrison,
died, 1777.

II. *The apparitions on the lawn.*
   When: the second night; approx. 3 A.M.
   Appearance: Apparition A. Female, young(?)—
   (Ellie: "Why the question mark?"
   Donald: "You didn't see her face, did you?"
   Ellie: "No, but she moved like—"
   Donald: "I cannot admit conjecture.")—late-

19th-century costume (long, full skirts) and hair style. Hair color blond or white

Apparition B: presumably young male; except for long dark hair, costume and other details hidden by woman's body and wide skirts.

Apparition C: male, middle-aged, late 19th-century costume (dark suit, vest, white shirt with stiff collar); bearded; expression of extreme malevolence.

(Donald: "That last is conjecture too."

Ellie: "What do you mean, conjecture? I saw it. It was malevolent."

Donald made a rude comment.)

Apparition C followed A and B after approx. 5-minute interval.

Where seen: lawn, near old footpath through woods, northeast of house.

General comments: Apparitions A and B moving swiftly as if running. Apparition C stopped long enough to make gesture toward house.

(Donald: "I know, I know, it was a malevolent gesture."

Ellie: "Menacing.")

Tentative identification: Frederick Fraser, Anne McGrath, died 1875; Jeremiah McGrath, died 1902.)

III. *The apparition in Ellie's room.*

When: the fourth night, approx. 3 A.M.

Appearance: elderly man, white hair and beard, late-19th-century costume (dark suit and vest, white shirt with high collar).

Where seen: doorway of Ellie's room.

General comments: lights out, switches inoperative (later found in normal working order by Donald P. Gold).

(Ellie: "You do love the sound of your own name, don't you?")

Apparition wore expression of leering lust.

(Donald: "That's extremely subjective, but I suppose you'll complain if I leave it out."

Ellie: "Correct.") Apparition displayed agitation, recoiled, vanished when subject moved. (Crucifix? Very doubtful.) Later search revealed clumps of damp soil, resembling—

(Donald: "Damn it, I refuse to put that in."

Ellie: "Sure, just leave out everything you don't like to face."

Donald snarled.)—resembling graveyard dirt, along upper hall. Another item, a small bone (probably rodent) found in mouth of dog, may have come from hall also.

Tentative identification: Albert J. Lockwood IV, died 1912.

IV. *The apparition on the stairs.*

When: the fifth night, approx. 2:30 A.M.

Appearance: female, long white robe or formal dress, red hair, features blurred.

Where seen: landing of front stairs.

General comments: first visible as white shape, gradually becoming more distinct. Accompanied by sensation of extreme cold. Began to descend stairs, faded at sound of siren of ambulance. Apparition followed fight in library between Ted and unknown intruder who entered by breaking glass in French doors. *Note:* When investigated by Donald P. Gold, fuses governing lights on second floor of west wing were found to be switched off. Query: is this the explanation of the darkness accompanying Apparition III? On that occasion intruder had time to restore switches to "on" position before leaving.

When Ellie read this document over, she was forced to admire its neat arrangement and semilegal phrasing, but she couldn't see that it got them any farther and she said so.

"I haven't even begun to study it yet," Donald retorted. "Besides, we aren't the only ones who will be
bringing our wits to bear on this masterpiece. It may
suggest something to Dad."

His elbows on the table, he studied the neatly written pages. Ellie fidgeted. She couldn't concentrate on
anything, much less the implacable, black-and-white
account of a series of outrageous events.

"It's getting darker," she said after a while.
"There's a big pile of purple clouds over there, to
the west."

"A good thunderstorm may break the heat wave,"
Donald said, without looking up.

"It may break me, too. Donald, if I have to stay
here tonight with the weather thundering and lightning and blowing outside. . . . I don't think I can do
it."

Donald looked up.

"You mean you're ready to cop out?"

"Yes, I am. I've had it. What are you looking so
glum about? Your dad said I could stay at your
place, and you seemed to agree. . . ."

"It seemed like a good idea at the time."

"So what's changed your mind?"

"Marjorie's granny."

"Well, well," Ellie said. "Donald P. Gold, professional scoffer, has had his comeuppance. You think
that was a genuine honest-to-God ghost, don't you?
Just wait till I tell your father."

"A logical person considers all possibilities," Donald said stubbornly. "It makes a certain amount of
sense, you know. You could be the catalyst. Some
students of psychic phenomena claim that the presence of a young person of a certain age . . . I don't
know how to put it without making you mad."

"I'm mad already," Ellie snapped. "I know the theory you're referring to, and the word is 'puberty.'
In case it has escaped your attention, I'm long past
that stage."

"It has not escaped my attention. Damn it, Ellie, I'm trying to apologize. I admit I didn't take you too seriously before; thought you had been fooled by stage-magician-type tricks. But if what you've been seeing was anything like what I saw tonight . . ."

"In some ways this was unique," Ellie said thoughtfully. "The others frightened me—more or less—but this is the first time I've ever passed out cold from sheer terror. Oh, look here, Donald, there has to be some rational explanation for all this, including Marge's granny. Think."

"Hmm. An idea did pass rapidly in and out of my overworked brain when I saw that mess in the library. I couldn't pin it down then. What do you think of when I say 'library' ?"

"Books," Ellie said, humoring him. "Magazines. Card—".

"Books. We assumed the books on the floor were knocked off the shelves during the struggle. But those are deep shelves, deep and solid. Suppose the burglar was disturbed while he was looking through the books—looking in such a frantic hurry that he dislodged some of them, threw them on the floor when he failed to find what he wanted?"

Ellie's mind remained blank. Her face registered this emotion, or lack of it. Donald exclaimed in disgust.

"That book you brought for Kate. Where is it? Not in the library, I hope. Because if it was—"

"No, it's in Kate's workroom, somewhere. You don't think—"

"It is the only thing that has been brought into this house, aside from your charming self," Donald said. "Let's have a look at it."

It took them some time to find the volume. Ellie finally located it under a pile of unfinished embroidery, from which she had selected the piece she was working on. Donald snatched it from her hands.

"I think you're crazy," Ellie said. "What could

there be about that book to cause all this commotion? There are other copies of it around; Miss Mary has one."

Turning pages, Donald dropped into a chair. The cat that was occupying it—the Siamese—got out just in time, but not without protest. Donald jumped a little when the claws sank into his ankle, but went on reading.

"Offhand it looks like a perfectly ordinary book," he muttered. "Incredibly dull, too. I wonder if I'm going to have to read every word of this tripe. Tell you what, I'll tear it in two and you can read—"

"Don't you dare! That's Kate's present. She hasn't even seen it."

Donald, who was nothing if not thorough in his enthusiasms, had taken the thin volume between his hands in the grip required for the vandalism he planned. Ellie's cry stopped him just in time, but his first quick twist had already had its effect. Ellie let out another exclamation as Donald inspected the inner front cover.

"You've torn it. The cover is split. Damn it, Donald—"

The expression on Donald's face stopped her.

"It's not torn," he said, in a queer voice. "It's come loose. There's something under it—between the leather and the paper that was pasted over the inside of the cover. I don't suppose there's such a thing as a letter opener in this chaos."

"There undoubtedly is. The question is, where?"

Prolonged search produced, not a letter opener, but a penknife, which Kate used for whittling. Ellie leaned over Donald's shoulder as he began working carefully at the book.

The paper that had been glued on to the inside of the cover, in order to conceal the rough edges of the outer leather binding, was a handsome colored sheet, printed in gold and green. The ease with which it loosened along the outer edge suggested that it had been glued by an amateur, and that the old glue had dried and become brittle. When the paper was lifted along three of the four edges, Donald was able to extract the thing that had been hidden beneath it.

It was a single sheet of a substance that was not paper, but something thicker and more pliable. At first glance it resembled a page from an ancient illuminated manuscript, with an oversized initial letter twined with miniature devices in gilt and scarlet and green. The rich black ink of the text was unfaded. At the bottom of the sheet were other words, less regularly spaced; these had faded almost to invisibility.

"It's a *P*," Ellie said, breathing heavily on the back of Donald's neck.

"And an *a*," Donald said. He started to beat time with a finger. "Gimme a *t*, gimme an *e*, gimme a *p-a-t.* . . ."

"You are hopelessly frivolous."

"This is Latin, Ellie."

"Do you know Latin?"

"Just enough to write indecipherable prescriptions. Shut up a minute and let me think. *Pater noster . . . qui erat in caelis.* . . ."

" 'Our Father,' " Ellie said. "I know that much Latin. It's the Lord's Prayer, Donald."

"I guess you're right. Looks like a page out of a medieval manuscript."

They looked blankly at one another.

"Why hide it in a book?" Donald asked finally.

"Is it valuable?"

"Damned if I know. I suppose it could be. But I've seen old parchment pages on sale in antique shops for—oh, a few bucks. They aren't that rare. Now if it were a page of some lost play by Aristophanes, or an unknown dialogue of Plato's—"

"Then," said Ellie, unable to resist, "it would be in Greek."

Donald burst out laughing.

"Got me that time. Would you believe it if I said that many Greek masterpieces survive only in Latin copies?"

"I probably would. Is it true?"

"Damned if I know."

"The fact is, neither of us knows much. We need an expert."

"Then you agree that this little bit of piety has something to do with our problem?" Donald asked, waving it high in the air.

"I don't see how it could. What could be more harmless than the Lord's Prayer? If all that psychic stuff is true, then this should be a protection against evil spirits, shouldn't it? Not something to summon them up."

"True." Donald looked chagrined. "It's peculiar all the same, Ellie. Finding something like this carefully concealed in the cover of a book, I mean. And what has been happening here is also peculiar. Two peculiar things ought to be connected."

"We could drive over to the University tomorrow and find ourselves a medieval specialist," Ellie suggested.

"Good idea. Anyway, we'll have something interesting to show Dad when he gets here. What are you planning to give us for dinner?"

They had the meal well underway when the doctor finally arrived. Donald was deeply involved in an au gratin sauce that refused to thicken, so Ellie went to the door. She was shocked at the doctor's appearance; his shoulders sagged and his face was drawn with fatigue.

"Ted!" she exclaimed. "Is he—"

"No, no." The doctor smiled at her. "If I weren't trained to professional caution I'd say he was a little better. It's been a hard day, that's all."

"The weather is enough to wear anyone out." As she drew him into the house she glanced at the sky. The cloud bank she had seen earlier was larger and more threatening; a streak of lightning crossed the swollen purple mass. "I wish it would rain."

"There's not a breath of air." The doctor mopped his forehead. "Where's Donald?"

"Cooking. You've really got him well trained. No, you come into the parlor, those chairs are more comfortable. Take off your shoes and put your feet up and I'll get you a drink."

"Sounds great." The doctor collapsed with a sigh.

Donald came in as Ellie was removing the doctor's shoes, over his embarrassed objections. He gave his father a tall glass and a long calculating appraisal.

"Damn it, Dad, you look like death warmed over. How many times have I told you—"

"I'm perfectly all right. Just a little tired."

"Back in a minute," Donald said, and left the room.

Ellie followed him to the kitchen, where he was heaping a tray with crackers and cheese and other snacks.

"Take this in and make him eat something," he snapped, handing Ellie the tray.

"He works too hard," Ellie said. "Can't you persuade him to hire an assistant, or take a partner?"

"Why do you think I feel so damn guilty? He won't hire anybody, he's waiting for me. And I've added another year to the waiting period by my stupid behavior—"

"That's not the adjective I'd choose."

"I had no right to take the chance. Playing hero, making like Saint Donald among the lepers—but it's Dad who has to pay for my little ego trip. He's not getting any younger."

"You sound to me as if you're on another ego trip," Ellie said. "Enjoying your guilt feelings? They don't do him any good."

Donald's brows drew together. After a moment he relaxed and gave her a faint smile.

"Whatever happened to sweet female sympathy? Go on, I'll bring your drink."

The words were ungracious, but he didn't sound angry. As Ellie carried the tray toward the parlor she couldn't help wondering how Henry would have responded to such a caustic criticism. No, she didn't wonder; she knew.

At first Donald was reluctant to discuss the "problem," as they referred to it, until his father had relaxed and had had something to eat. But Dr. Gold's interest could not be restrained. After all, Ellie thought, the "problem" probably seemed less tragic than the life-and-death issues he dealt with daily, and its outré nature was an intellectual challenge to a logical man.

"Well," he said, when Donald had finished bringing him up to date, "you two have certainly been busy, haven't you? And now we can look forward to an evening of heated debate. Some of your guests are going to be nasty; you realize that, don't you?"

He had said "we." Feeling as if she had acquired an army of allies, Ellie said calmly,

"Mr. McGrath, you mean? There isn't much he can do except yell."

"Not only McGrath," the doctor said. "Miss Mary can be quite a handful when she gets her back up; so can Marjorie, in a different way. Actually, my dear, the only person you can count on to behave in a relatively civilized fashion is Senator Grant."

"It's interesting that you should say that," Ellie said. "I was looking over our outline, and it struck me that Grant's family is the only one that hasn't been represented yet—ghost-wise, I mean."

"Ghost-wise," Donald repeated. "Is that Washington bureaucratese?"

The doctor waved this objection away with an impatient hand.

"A good point, Ellie. Several other points have occurred to me. Can I see your outline?"

"In the kitchen." Donald rose. "Everything is ready

but the steaks; you two can sit at the table and cogitate while I cook."

"I want to see that manuscript sheet, too," the doctor said.

Ellie went to fetch it and the book. When she returned she saw that the enticing odors had attracted others. A mob of furry bodies jostled and mewed at the kitchen door.

"We forgot to feed the animals," she said, opening the door and trying to keep her feet as the mob poured past her.

"So we did." Donald glanced out the window. "I'd better get it over with. It's going to rain like hell before long. Ten minutes. You two have another drink."

Turning off the broiler, he set to work. Throughout her conversation with the doctor Ellie was conscious of his movements—neat, quick, economical—as he passed back and forth, in and out of the house. When he opened the back door, a blast of steamy air came in, and Ellie saw that the topmost branches of the trees were beginning to sway in a rising wind. The sunset was a masterpiece of angry color, blood-red and purple and somber black split by streaks of coppery sunlight, and by an occasional lightning flash. Thunder echoed distantly.

With the hot air from outside came William, a quivering mass of jelly covered by fur. Ellie hadn't realized that he was outside, with the terrible dangerous lightning; she had to soothe him and apologize to him before he finally settled down under the table with his huge head on her feet.

The doctor was a fast reader. He skimmed through their outline and then glanced at the page of manuscript.

"I'm not a Latinist," he admitted. "Looks like the Lord's Prayer to me, and I don't know what to make of it either. What are these marks at the bottom of the page?"

"They're so faded I can't decipher them," Ellie said. "They were written in a different kind of ink from the body of the text."

"I wonder why they didn't use the same India ink," the doctor murmured. "You know what this reminds me of?—the different kinds of ink, not the form—old Egyptian manuscripts I've seen in museums. The main text was written in black ink, which has held up incredibly well for thousands of years. But sometimes special words—what would correspond to paragraph headings in our texts—were written in red ink, to make them more conspicuous. Rubrics, I think that's what they were called. The red ink has often faded, just as this has."

Donald, on his way to the door with two bowls of dog food, came to a stop. He put the bowls on the counter and leaned over his father's shoulder.

"Something occur to you?" Dr. Gold asked.

"I was just thinking," Donald said slowly. "But I can't really believe. . . . Something about the arrangement of those words; faded as they are, I get an impression of—names. Like at the bottom of a contract."

The doctor held the parchment at an angle, trying to get the maximum amount of light on the surface. After a while he shook his head.

"Possible, I suppose, but I really can't see enough to be sure. Don't they have methods for bringing out faded writing? Ultraviolet light, or chemicals of some kind?"

"That's an idea," Ellie said. "We could ask about that at the University too."

"Has Kate got a Latin dictionary?" Donald asked.

"Probably. She has everything else. But why a dictionary? We know what the text says, and we can't even see the other words."

"Mmm," said Donald. A plaintive whine from the patio reminded him of his duties as waiter. He picked up the bowls and went out.

"I don't think we can get anything more out of the manuscript," Dr. Gold said, laying it to one side. "Now for your outline. I get a couple of ideas from that."

"What?" Ellie looked hopefully at him. He smiled at her.

"I'm afraid my ideas aren't very startling, Ellie. The first point is the one you made. To date, five of the old families of the county have been represented by your apparitions. Why not the sixth?"

"To date," Ellie repeated. "I hate to think it, much less say it; but the performance may not be over."

"I'm afraid I came to the same conclusion. It appears, then, that someone is playing a series of practical jokes aimed at the founding families. I know, I know; the word 'jokes' seems inappropriate. But with one obvious exception these episodes have done no damage, except to your nerves. They don't even threaten the members of the families involved, except with a certain amount of embarrassment."

"I don't agree, Dad." Donald had come back for the final round of dog food. "Suppose these stories were widely disseminated—like, suppose some news service printed them. Could they do any of our friends serious damage—reputation-wise?"

He winked at Ellie, who made a rude face at him. The doctor ignored this byplay; he looked thoughtful.

"I don't see how, Donald. Nobody cares about the minor peccadilloes of a century ago."

"Miss Mary cares," Donald said. "She's a little cracked on the subject of her family. She would regard an attack on Granddaddy's reputation as a personal threat. And Marge's popularity—and income—depends on the fact that a lot of imbeciles think of her as sweet and noble."

"I'll give you Miss Mary," the doctor said slowly. "A thing like this could hurt her—not materially or financially, but emotionally. But Marjorie? Her admirers are—well, let us be kind and say that they are not particularly logical people. No, I don't see how it could hurt her even if it turns out that her grandmother was—er—a woman of ill repute."

"What about Mr. McGrath?" Ellie asked. "He's another nut on the subject of family."

The doctor smiled tolerantly.

"In popular parlance, Roger is a trifle paranoid. He tends to interpret any criticism as a personal attack. You see what you're doing, don't you, Ellie? Miss Mary and Roger are beginning to look like the victims of the jokes. I insist on that word; the worst these things can do is annoy and distress some people."

"Except Ted." Ellie shifted her feet; they were getting numb from the weight of William's head. He moaned pathetically and licked her shoes.

"Yes," the doctor said soberly. "Except Ted. That was obviously an accident, Ellie, but that one episode is strikingly different from the others—an anomaly in an otherwise consistent series. It was a purely physical event—one might even say ordinary or commonplace, in these days of rising crime. Was there anything about the library, or about Ted himself, to suggest that he had encountered an—well, let's say apparition, for the time being—such as you saw on all the other occasions?"

"No, nothing. The police said it was quite clearcut. The burglar broke the glass, got his hand in, and unbolted the door. So far as I could tell, nothing was taken, but of course we assume the burglar was interrupted before he found what he was after."

"This book?" The doctor held it up.

"Yes. That was how we happened to find the parchment. But I can't imagine why anyone would commit burglary to get it."

Donald came back in time to hear the last speech. He slammed the door and locked it.

"All the livestock is set for the night, Dad, there's

one point that didn't occur to the police. The burglar was someone who knew the house."

"Why do you say that?"

"For one thing, that's the only set of doors that could be jimmied so easily. I've spoken to Kate about it several times. Sure, he could have prowled around the house till he found the best place to break in. But that would have taken a lot of time, and I can't believe the dogs wouldn't have heard something. They are incredibly stupid, but they wouldn't let a stranger crash around in the shrubbery for half an hour without commenting."

He moved as he talked, finishing the cooking; the steaks needed only a final touch of the broiler flame. Ellie shifted her elbows as he slapped a plate down in front of her. Manlike, he had served from the stove; why get all those bowls dirty? he would have asked if she had commented.

She was pleased to see that the doctor looked perfectly relaxed and at home; his elbows stuck out jauntily as he carved his meat and he continued to talk animatedly, sometimes with his mouth full.

Ellie offered to clear off the table, and Donald didn't argue with her. He wandered off, mumbling something about the library. In spite of Ellie's objections the doctor helped her scrape dishes, his sleeves rolled up and his hair rumpled. The cats hung around until the last scrap was disposed of, and then departed.

They had barely finished when Ellie heard the doorbell. Kate had had a set of particularly revolting chimes installed; they played the first few bars of the choral section of Beethoven's *Ninth*.

"It can't be them yet," Ellie said, glancing at the clock. "It's only seven thirty."

But it was.

"We came early, to avoid the storm," Senator Grant explained. "I hope you don't mind."

He was the only one who spoke. For a few uncomfortable seconds Ellie stood motionless, confronting the silent group. She knew how a householder of a less tolerant era must have felt when he opened his front door to find a delegation of neighbors who had come to complain about some transgression—failing to come to church, perhaps, or working on the Sabbath. The same hard, critical faces, the same sense of a mob much larger than the actual numbers. . . .

"Come in," she said, fighting an irrational urge to slam the door and run. "No, of course, I don't mind. The sky does look dreadful, doesn't it?"

Normally at this hour on a summer afternoon it was still full daylight outside; the sun did not drop below the horizon until close to nine. But today it was almost as dark as night. Rolling clouds covered most of the sky. Only a few bars of sullen scarlet showed in the east; the rest of the sky was a study in shades of gray and black and purple, boiling like a caldron of some unspeakable liquid. Lightning flashed and thunder rumbled, but so far only a few large drops had fallen, leaving damp spots the size of dimes on the steps.

"I hate this weather," Anne Grant muttered. "It's like radiation or something. My skin feels all prickly."

Ellie led them into the library. There was a long, directors'-size table in the room, and plenty of chairs. She was hoping Donald was still there and was relieved to find both Golds waiting.

Senator Grant was the only one of the guests who seemed to find the situation embarrassing. He began to apologize—Ellie wasn't quite sure what for, and doubted that he knew, either—but he was cut short by Miss Mary.

"Don't waste time, Alan," she said and closed her lips like a trap on the end of the sentence.

The Golds did all they could to relieve the tension. The doctor's very presence radiated calm; he seemed to be respected by all his neighbors, even by Miss

Mary—which was a tribute to his personality, for Ellie suspected that the marriage of Donald's mother had been regarded as something of a mésalliance. Donald offered drinks all around, and this also improved the atmosphere. Miss Mary, of course, did not drink. She accepted a cup of tea. They finally settled down around the table, and Ellie realized, with an uncomfortable sinking sensation, that all eyes were focused on her.

She cleared her throat.

"I appreciate your coming," she began in a thin little voice. Then she caught Donald's eye, saw the amusement in it, and rallied. "I really don't know what is going to come out of this meeting," she said, more briskly. "But I guess you have a right to know what has happened. It all began—"

She broke off as William—who was, of course, under the table—let out a yelp. From the look on Donald's face she deduced that he had tried to kick her in the shin and had kicked William instead.

"Would you care to narrate the events that have transpired?" she inquired formally.

"Yes," said Donald.

He was better organized than she would have been, she had to admit that. Probably he had also anticipated that there would be comment, and felt himself better equipped to deal with it. She would not have been able to squelch Roger McGrath as neatly as he did. The others did not interrupt. Miss Mary sat with a face like stone, even when Donald described her grandfather Lockwood's leer.

He finished by displaying the sheet of parchment. It passed from hand to hand around the table. So far as Ellie could tell, no one gave it more than a cursory glance except Miss Mary.

"You're the scholar among us, Miss Mary," the doctor said, as she held the sheet up to the light and peered myopically at it. "What do you make of the text?"

"It is certainly the Lord's Prayer," Miss Mary said. "Beyond that there is little anyone can make of it."

"I'm hoping some expert at the University can tell us more," Donald said. "They may even be able to read the writing at the bottom of the text. I'll take it over to Charlottesville tomorrow."

Miss Mary grunted and passed the sheet to Senator Grant on her left. Ellie wondered whether the old woman could read Latin. She hadn't told them anything they didn't already know.

"How about another round before we begin the debate?" Donald asked hospitably.

Miss Mary rose ponderously to her feet. "No. I should not have permitted any indulgence of that nature. Alcohol has a most unfortunate effect on communication."

Ellie was so aggravated at the old woman's assumption of authority that the meaning of the speech eluded her for a moment. The others, who knew Miss Mary well, were quicker. The doctor was the first to speak.

"Miss Mary, I cannot permit any such thing. It is childish and dangerous."

His voice was mild; he was an unimposing figure as he sat slouched in his chair, his hair unkempt and his tie loosened. But Miss Mary sat down. For the first time in Ellie's experience of her, she sounded defensive as she continued,

"I assure you, Doctor, I know how to deal with dangerous entities. I am not totally inexperienced—"

"That was not the danger I referred to," the doctor interrupted. "Kate would have my hide nailed to the door if I allowed such goings-on in her house."

"Now there you are mistaken," Miss Mary said triumphantly. "Kate and I have conducted several séances in this house. She has a frivolous mind, but it is not closed."

"Hey," Ellie said, "just a minute, Miss Mary. I don't want any more ghosts. We're trying to get rid of the ones we've got, not call up—"

The remainder of her protest was drowned by a babble of voices. Donald's rose over the rest.

"What results did you and Kate get from your séances?" he asked interestedly.

Miss Mary's iron control cracked for an instant.

"I prefer not to discuss it."

A broad grin spread over Donald's face. He glanced at Ellie and she grinned back at him. Like Donald, she had some idea of what Kate could do to a séance when she was in a whimsical mood. It was becoming a little unnerving, the way she and Donald were communicating, with only an exchange of glances. Ellie's eyes dropped.

Finally the doctor pounded on the table for order.

"This is a waste of time. Has anyone got a useful suggestion? I think," he added dryly, "that we must return to the primary-school method of raising hands to gain the floor, or we'll all be talking at once."

The Senator's hand was the first to rise. An indulgent little smile played around his lips as he made the childish gesture, and when the doctor nodded at him he rose with the graceful deliberation he displayed in his TV debates.

"Ladies and gentlemen . . ."

He talked for several minutes. His voice was that of a trained speaker, smooth and well modulated. One platitude followed another: We must all keep our heads, discretion is certainly called for under such unusual circumstances. . . . The speech could have been summarized in a single phrase: Let's keep this quiet.

Roger McGrath may not have been the first to comprehend this, but he was the first to speak.

"It's all very well for you," he said shrilly. "Your family has not been traduced—insulted, slandered. What about me? Don't you realize that this sort of talk could lose the election for me?"

"You exaggerate," the Senator said. His voice was less smooth. The interruption had annoyed him.

"Oh, no, I don't. I'm being made a laughingstock! It's hard enough to get any decent legislation through in this county, with all the new people moving in—radical do-gooders, strangers who don't understand our problems—rebels striking at the very fabric of all that has made America great—"

"Time's up," Donald said loudly. He nodded at Marjorie, who had raised a graceful arm and was wriggling her fingers daintily.

"We are rather wasting time, aren't we?" she asked, and twinkled at the audience, each in turn. "I'd like to know who is responsible for all this."

"Have you any ideas?" the doctor asked.

"Well . . . I hate to put my little ideas forward, with all these clever men present; but sometimes a woman's intuition . . ." The twinkle vanished; the sweet voice hardened. "Ted, of course. Who else could it be?"

"My dear," the Senator said reproachfully. "It is rude, if nothing more, to speak ill of—"

"Ted isn't dead," Marjorie said. The girlish charm was gone; she was all hard-voiced, hardheaded business woman, and Ellie had to admit that she was displaying more intelligence than most of the men. "The tricks are precisely the sort of thing his childish mind would invent. You all know how he loves to dress up and play games—"

"Women's clothes," McGrath said. "Disgusting. People like that should be drummed out of town."

"Never mind that," Marjorie said. "Ted has always been interested in amateur theatricals; he played several roles with that summer-stock group two years ago. You remember, Donald, you were in one of the plays too, weren't you?"

"Uh-huh," Donald said.

His voice sounded so peculiar that Ellie gave him a sharp look. He was careful to avoid her eyes.

Marjorie continued. "As for the so-called burglary, that could have been a trick that went wrong. Think about it. Is there any proof that there was a second person in that room?"

A blank silence followed. Marjorie was a skilled speaker; she waited for several seconds, giving them time to assimilate the idea.

"We all know Ted had a weak heart," she continued, more assuredly, as the circle of faces showed a dawning conviction. "Suppose he had entered the house in order to set up some new trick. He broke the window, he tossed the furniture around; then his heart failed, with exertion or excitement. Now admit it, Dr. Gold, could not his injuries have been self-inflicted?"

"He was hit on the back of the head," Ellie said hotly. "You can't say that was—"

Slowly, reluctantly, the doctor shook his head.

"I'm afraid Marjorie is right, Ellie. It's quite probable that Ted hit his head when he fell, on some sharp object in the room. The corner of the mantel, or the desk, perhaps."

"Has anybody bothered to look?" Ellie had never realized how fond she was of Ted. Although she had entertained doubts herself, Marjorie's attack made her rush to his defense. "He's helpless, he can't defend himself; you have no right to accuse—"

"Cool it, Ellie." Donald interrupted. "Ted doesn't need to defend himself. The circumstances do that. Sorry, Marge. Your theory won't wash. Ted was flat out and unconscious when Ellie and I saw the woman on the stairs. If you can tell me how he could have arranged that, I'll consider your theory."

"If I'm not mistaken, he has an alibi for another of the tricks," the doctor said. "The figures on the lawn, Ellie; didn't you say you saw two, a man and a woman?"

"That's right," Ellie said quickly. "There were two. And when the third figure appeared—the man in black—I was actually talking to Ted on the phone."

Marjorie said a word that made several of them

jump. She was obviously too shaken to maintain her public face.

"That means two people, then," the Senator said. "I hadn't thought of that. At least two. I suppose Ted could have been one of them—"

Marjorie's face brightened. Before she could speak, Donald said,

"Even if that were true, you'd still have to figure out the identity of the second person. Ted is too smart to *hire* a confederate; can you think of anyone who would assist him in a stunt like that?"

"I can," McGrath said.

"Who?" Ellie asked innocently.

Anne's sudden laugh made her jump. She had almost forgotten Anne was present; now she realized that the Senator's wife must have had several drinks before she arrived. When she leaned forward across the table, her eyes were bright and her smile was very broad.

"Oh, Ellie, he means Kate. And I've got to admit—"

"Anne," her husband said sharply.

"Don't be such a damn hypocrite." The face she turned toward him was ugly with anger. "You don't dare say anything for fear of offending some constituent. You wouldn't say it was Thursday if some old fool told you it was Sunday. Why can't you be honest for once? These people all know you, you don't have to put on an act for them. Kate would love a stunt like this. She has no respect for sacred cows, she loves to puncture them. And of all the fat, sacred cows in the world, this town has more—"

"Stop it." Miss Mary did not raise her voice, but it cracked like a whip. "Ted is not the only one who despises this community and the values it represents. I would sooner suspect that person than Kate, who has, despite an occasional display of frivolity which I cannot help but deplore—"

Then they were all shouting; the Senator was red-faced with anger, his dignity forgotten. The doctor had to pound for order again, and he was some time in obtaining it.

"I think we'd better end this discussion. It isn't getting us anywhere."

"It seems to be airing a lot of private hatreds," Donald said dryly.

Some of the tension in the air was due to the approaching storm. Slowly and ponderously it was coming closer. A flash of lightning whitened the windows, and the thunder that followed rattled objects on the desk.

"I'm not going home in this," Anne muttered. "I'm terrified of storms."

A moan from William, at Ellie's feet, echoed the sentiment.

"I refuse to leave until we have tried my experiment," Miss Mary said, and as the doctor started to object, she raised a firm hand. "No, Doctor Gold, you shan't deter me. You have all debated—somewhat ineffectively—the possibilities inherent in the assumption that these tricks, as you call them, have been perpetrated by human agency. You are deliberately ignoring the second possibility, despite the fact that, to an unprejudiced mind, the weight of the evidence is on that side. Donald. The visitant on the stairs—Marjorie's grandmother—no, Marjorie, do not interrupt me—can you honestly look me in the face and tell me that you believe it was a stage illusion, a shoddy creation of cheesecloth and luminous paint? Oh, yes," she added dryly. "I know the tricks false mediums use. You must think me totally devoid of intelligence if you believe I have investigated this subject for years without realizing that ninety-eight percent of the phenomena are produced by trickery. But there is that two percent, young man. It cannot be denied. In all fairness to me, you must allow me to do what should be done."

"But—" Ellie began.

The hard gray eyes turned to her.

"The simplest way of dealing with a disturbance of this nature, my dear, is to ascertain what has caused it. If I can reach one of the troubled earth-bound spirits, I may be able to free it."

"I'm in favor," Anne said suddenly. She glared at Miss Mary. "Maybe one of your damned spooks will speak a good word for me. If the ghosts are real, nobody can accuse me of planning this."

"Mr. McGrath?" The librarian turned to him.

Roger McGrath's face had never more closely resembled that of his namesake. A kind of guilty, greedy curiosity struggled with dignity.

"Well," he said finally, "I don't see why we shouldn't try—"

"That makes three in favor," said the Senator. "Marjorie, what do you—"

"Just a bloody minute, here," Donald interrupted hotly. "This is not a town meeting. While Kate is away, the house is in Ellie's charge. It's up to her to decide what is to be done."

"Of course the decision must be hers," Marjorie said sweetly. "But I do think, Don, that she should consider the feelings of others. You need not fear spiritual danger; the pure of heart are in God's hands, and in my own small way—"

"All right, all right," Ellie broke in, not because she was convinced, but because she knew she could not stand another word of sanctimonious hypocrisy without spitting or doing something equally vulgar. "I think it's dumb. Dumb and useless. But I'll go along if Dr. Gold says it's all right."

All eyes turned toward the doctor.

He sat in silence for a while, staring at his hands, which were folded on the tabletop. Then he glanced at his son. Neither spoke, but a silent message of some kind passed between them. Donald, who had been sitting on the edge of his chair, tense with indignation, leaned back and relaxed.

"I agree with Ellie," the doctor said shortly. "It's dumb. But I guess it can't do any harm."

Imperturbable as ever, Miss Mary rose and began to make the necessary preparations. Now that the decision had been made, the others seemed uneasy; they avoided one another's eyes, and no one spoke. Ellie was silent too. She was trying to figure out what had made the doctor change his mind. Perhaps he hoped that someone in the group might be sufficiently unnerved by the eerie trappings of a séance to betray some information.

By the time Miss Mary finished her preparations, Ellie felt that she would be moved to confess, if there had been anything on her mind. The setting could not have been more appropriate if it had been designed by Hitchcock in his heyday—the Gothic gloom of the library, with its high, shadowy ceiling, and the gaping black hole of the great fireplace; the electrical influence of the gathering storm, which lashed at the windows with windblown branches and sounded an occasional kettledrum roll of thunder. Miss Mary completed the eerie atmosphere by insisting that all the lights be turned out. A single candelabrum, with six branches, gave the only illumination; in its flickering light the faces looked like those of criminals in Madame Tussauds', waxen and dead. The groans of William, under the table, lent the final, uncanny touch. Ellie planted her feet firmly on the warm, furry head, and William wriggled gratefully.

They could not hold hands; the table was too large. As Miss Mary pointed out, in response to the doctor's objection, it was not really necessary to resort to this device to protect against trickery. The table was too heavy to be moved by a single pair of hands.

"We will adopt one of the conventional means of communication," she explained. "If we are fortunate enough to make contact, we will ask the spirit to answer questions by tapping out the letters of the alphabet—one rap for *A*, two for *B*, and so on. One rap for yes, two for no. Is that clear? Now I beg you, put aside all frivolous or hostile thoughts. Concentrate. Do not speak to one another; address the spirits only if you have a question. Do not interrupt. Do not move."

For a long time nothing happened. Time seemed to stretch out, as it always does when the mind is without occupation and the nerves are taut. There was no sound except for the creak of branches outside, the ever-nearing sound of thunder, and William's loud, asthmatic panting. He had shifted his head so that it was on Ellie's feet. He was drooling nervously.

Then Miss Mary spoke.

"Is there a spirit present? Signify your presence by moving the table, or by rapping, if you please."

Ellie suppressed a sudden hysterical desire to laugh. The old woman sounded like a stern schoolmistress. Any spirit who disregarded that order had a lot of nerve.

Apparently no spirit was present. Another period of silence ensued—silence from the human participants. Nature was becoming noisy. The first hard spatter of rain hit the windows, and the draperies billowed out in a gust of wind. Ellie remembered that in the confusion of the day she had forgotten to have the French doors fixed. The rain would ruin Kate's draperies. She must get a piece of cardboard or something to cover the hole—

She was slightly distracted by these prosaic domestic worries. Miss Mary repeated the question.

"Is there a spirit present?"

Three loud, reverberating raps followed.

Ellie felt the hair on the nape of her neck stand straight up. Simultaneously the storm broke in all its fury. Lightning brightened the windows, even through the closed draperies, and was followed by a crash that deafened her. Several hundred pounds of solid oak table shifted like plywood under her hands.

CHAPTER EIGHT

Only once, in the years to come, when he had, uncharacteristically, taken a drop too much, did Donald admit that the moment was almost the worst of the entire affair. For five full seconds he believed in hellfire and brimstone, a devil in red tights, and the powers of the pit.

Ellie was more fortunate. She had felt William move out from under her feet, and even her dazzled brain could make the connection between the movement of the table and that of the terrified dog. When the raps were repeated—half a dozen of them this time—she was the first to regain her senses.

"It's someone at the door," she gasped. "Someone knocking."

Doctor Gold was on his feet; she heard him stumbling across the room, and then she heard the ineffectual click-click as he tried to turn on the lights.

"The lightning must have hit a wire," he said. "Sit still. I'll go—"

"You'd better stay here," Ellie said, as someone's chair fell over and the sound of a shrill voice rose in hysteria. "I'll go."

She wrenched one of the candles from its socket and started along the hall. The house was solidly built; the candle flame burned steadily, although the battering of wind and rain outside had risen to a crescendo. Ellie heard footsteps behind her and whirled, imperiling the fragile flame.

"It's me," Donald said unnecessarily.

The knocking had become a fusillade of sharp raps.

"Go on," Donald said. "It's not a night to leave someone standing outside."

It was, certainly, a human hand that was wielding the heavy knocker. With the electrical circuits out, the chimes would not operate. All the same, Ellie was glad Donald was behind her when she opened the door and saw the hooded figure outside. It was a dark shape, featureless, muffled; the folds of the garment that enshrouded it streamed out in the wind like a long cloak. She had only a second's glimpse before the blast of wind and rain extinguished the candle. Then lightning split the sky apart; the cloaked form pushed forward; and a familiar voice said irritably,

"Close the door before the cats get out."

"Kate!" Ellie fell on her neck.

After a moment Kate asked mildly, "Couldn't we do this inside? I'm rather wet."

Donald put out an arm and dragged them both over the threshold. He closed the door. Ellie continued to clutch Kate, who stood motionless while Donald fumbled for matches.

"I'm glad you're so happy to see me," Kate said, when the flame finally sprang up. "What's going on around here? Yes, yes, I know the lights are out; they always go out when it rains. I mean, what are all those cars doing outside? Are you having a party?"

She put Ellie's arms aside, gently but firmly, and began divesting herself of the long hooded rain cape she was wearing.

"How did you get here?" Ellie asked.

"Taxi from the airport."

"But, Kate! The airport is fifty miles from here."

Kate's face took on an expression Ellie knew well—a look of cunning, shifty defensiveness. She would spend a hundred thousand dollars on a painting without blinking an eye, but she was parsimonious about minor expenditures. With her damp, tumbled curls, and the soft light blotting out the lines in her face, she looked like an urchin who had been caught with his hand in the cookie jar.

"I didn't want to bother you to come and get me," she mumbled. "I knew you weren't expecting me, and the weather looked bad—"

"Expecting you? I've been praying you—Kate. Didn't you get my message? Didn't the police call you?"

"Police?" Kate's face changed. "What's wrong, honey?"

"That," said Donald, "is not a question to be answered in a word, or even a sentence. Where is your luggage, Kate?"

"Outside." Kate made a vague gesture, her eyes still riveted on Ellie's face. She threw the rain cape onto the floor. "Jack's," she explained, gesturing at the garment. "I lost mine someplace. Ellie, what—"

"Tell her," Donald said. "A brief synopsis only, if you please."

He opened the door and plunged out into the rain. When he returned with Kate's dripping suitcases, Ellie had barely begun her recital. Kate listened in silence. She had the enviable knack of knowing when to keep quiet and when to ask pertinent questions. She had gone a little pale when Ellie told her about Ted, but she made no other sign of distress, except for a quick, sharp intake of breath when Ellie described the figures out on the lawn.

"Amazing," she said, when Ellie had finished. "Absolutely amazing . . . Who's in there?"

Ellie glanced over her shoulder. Sounds of minor riot were issuing from the library.

"The whole crowd," Donald said. "We called a

conference. Some conference! Miss Mary insisted on holding a séance, and all hell broke loose when that last bolt of lightning knocked out the electricity. We thought your pounding at the door was the answer from the spirit world—"

"And then poor William got all upset," Ellie added. "He was under the table; when the lightning struck, he took off like a bat, and the whole table shook."

"Was that what shook the table?" Donald pursed his lips in a long, soft whistle. "I don't mind admitting I'm relieved to hear it."

Kate's grin faded. "William! Poor baby, he's terrified of storms. I'd better go and see if—"

"Later," Donald said firmly, catching Kate's arm as she turned. "Damn it, Kate, we've got more serious problems on our hands right now. William is probably under somebody's bed."

William was not. The familiar voice had finally reached him, through the fog of panic. Kate staggered back, pinned to the wall by a hundred and fifty pounds of upright Saint Bernard. His huge paws on her shoulders, William licked her face and then collapsed at her feet, whining.

"Poor baby," Kate crooned, bending over him.

"Kate!" Donald pulled her to her feet. "Will you try to concentrate? The first thing is to get rid of that mob in the library. Will you do it or shall I?"

"I think I'd better," Kate said thoughtfully. "Yes. I would like to exchange a few words with the group. William, darling, get off Mama's feet; she can't walk."

Singularly impeded by William, they walked down the hall to the library. Someone had found and lighted more candles. The doctor was bending over McGrath, who was slumped in his chair, his head thrown back. Ellie realized that the frantic screams she had heard were McGrath's. The women were all quiet, although Anne's face was the color of tallow. Marjorie's head was bent over her folded hands.

The doctor was the first to see the newcomer.

"Kate," he said, straightening up. His voice was quiet; but he seemed to shed ten years in an instant.

"Hello, Frank," Kate said calmly. "I see you have things under control, as usual."

"Roger got a little upset," the doctor said. "Come on, Roger; you're all right. Nothing happened except in your mind."

McGrath sat up and mopped at his face with a handkerchief.

"Weak heart," he mumbled. "Shock to anyone . . ."

"You'd better get home and get to bed," the doctor said shortly. "The rest of us had better go, too."

"Without wishing to appear inhospitable, I am forced to agree," Kate said. "It seems that I have a lot of catching up to do before I can talk sensibly to you. I'll telephone you all tomorrow."

The tone was pleasant but final. Even Anne, who had expressed her fear of thunderstorms, made no demur, and the others rose. They had begun to straggle toward the doorway when Donald said suddenly,

"Wait a minute. The parchment. It was on the table. It's gone."

"Probably got knocked off in the confusion," the doctor said, looking around as if he expected to see the missing document suspended in midair.

"It will turn up," someone said.

"Oh, no." Donald spread his arms across the open doorway. "Nobody leaves this room till that parchment is found."

"Well!" McGrath exclaimed indignantly. "Of all the outrageous remarks! Are you seriously suggesting, Donald, that one of us—"

"Who would want a dirty old thing like that?" Anne demanded.

"I don't know. But I mean to find out. Ellie, you and Kate can search the women. Dad and I—"

A howl of outrage arose. Even the Senator, who

had been subdued and silent since Miss Mary had accused his wife, roused himself enough to protest.

"You have no right to do that, Don," he said. "Let's search the room. The damn thing must be here somewhere."

He had the habit of authority; the others spread out, looking under the table, in the shadowy corners. Kate stood back. She looked disappointed, and Ellie deduced that she had been looking forward to playing lady detective.

Finally one of the searchers straightened up with an exclamation of triumph.

"Here it is. I told you it must be somewhere."

The speaker was Senator Grant. Donald took the sheet from him and subjected it to a searching scrutiny. He nodded grudgingly.

"Okay. You can go now."

"Well, of all the nerve," McGrath squeaked.

"Forgive him," Marjorie said softly. "We must not judge others without charity, Roger—all of you—perhaps a brief prayer—"

"Pray on your own time," Kate said. "Scoot, Marge. Your four-footed friends and your kiddies are waiting."

The group filed out. Donald, clutching the parchment to his chest with both hands, went with them. The last to leave was Miss Mary. Her schooled face gave no hint of the emotions that lay within, but Ellie knew she must be disturbed; she had not spoken since the collapse of her séance. As the doctor prepared to follow the others, Kate put out her hand.

"Please stay, Frank. I won't keep you long, I promise; but I want to know about Ted. Ellie just told me."

"Of course I'll stay, Kate, as long as you like." The doctor's singularly sweet smile lighted up his face. Then he looked surprised. "Ellie just—didn't you get the word from the police in Vermont? The kids sent out an SOS hours ago. But if you didn't . . . Why did you come home?"

Kate's eyes widened. In their blue depths miniature candle flames, reflected, danced briskly.

"Of course I had to come home. I should have realized before, but I'm so disorganized— There's a football game tomorrow."

II

Kate might claim to be disorganized—and in certain crucial areas she undoubtedly was—but no one was more efficient in a crisis, not even Donald. The house had its own emergency generator, which the rest of them had forgotten in the stress of the moment; Kate reminded them. In a surprisingly short time they had restored order to the house, brought Kate up to date on what had been going on, and were sitting in the brightly lighted kitchen, with the air conditioner purring and food on the table. They would have reached this stage even earlier if Kate had not insisted on checking all the animals before she sat down. Kate was eating like a construction worker after a long day; she had been on the road, by one means of transportation or another, since dawn. She had one cat on her lap while she ate, three others squatting beside her waiting for tidbits, and William on her feet. The rest of the cats sat on the counter, in a neat line; Roger sat on his chair, at Kate's left. From time to time he squeaked imperatively and she reached out to tickle his whiskers.

"My, it's good to be back," Kate said, smiling fatuously at the assembled throng. "I don't know why I go away. I love it here."

"It's too bad Ellie can't say the same," Donald said grumpily.

Not at all put out by his critical tone, Kate transferred her affectionate smile from Roger to him. She had changed into a particularly impractical caftan of trailing chiffon adorned by gold thread and bright embroidery. Ellie deduced from this that she was feeling sentimental.

"Well, I'm sorry about that," Kate said, in the tone of a hostess regretting a minor inconvenience, such as an inadequate supply of hot water. "But I'm sure we can straighten it all out in no time."

The doctor laughed out loud, and Donald, who had been on the verge of a rude reply, produced a sour smile.

"Kate, you are too much. You can't settle this one by calling the governor or one of your buddies in the UN."

"Really, Kate, the situation is no joke," the doctor added gently.

"I know." Kate pushed her empty plate away and rested her chin on her hand. "Believe me, darlings, I'm not taking this lightly. I am—I am concerned about Ted." Her face, which reflected every passing mood, looked suddenly old and gray; and Ellie, who had been a little exasperated at Kate's debonair air, melted like a candle.

"He'll be all right, Kate."

"I hope so. The point is that everything is being done for him that can be done. We can't do any more—except find out what happened to him." In spite of her obvious distress, Kate's eyes took on a faint sparkle. "Really, this is the most extraordinary story! All these years I've hoped for a haunted house, and now—"

"Come on, Kate, you don't believe that," Donald said.

"I wish I could." Kate looked sad. "But I'm afraid there are several unmistakable signs of human inventiveness—careless, too."

Accustomed as they were to Kate, the other three

gaped at her for a moment. The doctor was the first to get his voice back.

"What do you mean? Damn it, Kate, we've been over this time and time again—"

"You've been awfully rushed," Kate said charitably. "You really haven't had time to think sensibly." She broke off a piece of cheese, offered a chunk of it to Roger, who refused it with a shake of his whiskers, and absentmindedly ate it herself. She reached for the papers on which Donald and Ellie had written their account. "First of all," she began, and then paused to swallow. "Excuse me. First of all, look at this second—er—visitation. Your description of the woman's clothing."

Ellie took the sheet, while Kate fed Roger a chunk of pâté. He accepted this.

"Full, flowing skirts," Ellie read aloud. "Shawl or cloak around the shoulders. . . . What's wrong with that?"

"The period," Kate said. "You deduce that these people were the protagonists in our little domestic tragedy of about 1875; and the clothing of the third personage, the man, fits that date. But women weren't wearing full, flowing skirts in the 1870's. The bustle had come in by then. Skirts were fairly tight and close-fitting, except for that bump in the back. A fashionable woman of that era could barely toddle, much less run. Mrs. McGrath was a lady of fashion, not a farm girl."

"So," the doctor said, after a moment of apoplectic silence, "you're right again, darn it. What conclusion do you draw from that, Mrs. Sherlock?"

"Ms. Sherlock," Kate corrected. She licked her fingers. "It's obvious, isn't it? Either your trickster is abominably careless—an assumption which does not fit his ingenuity in other aspects of the affair—or he needed a particular type of garment for a certain effect, and counted on your being too distraught to notice the discrepancy." She smiled at Ellie. "It must have been a frightening sight; I doubt that I would have been cool enough to spot something like that under those circumstances.''

"Thanks," Ellie said wryly. "But why? What effect could—"

"I've got an idea," Donald interrupted. "Full skirts have one conspicuous virtue. They conceal. Either something about the person who is wearing them— or something behind the skirts."

"Good," Kate said crisply. "Your description of the second person—the presumed young man—is very vague, Ellie. How much did you actually see?"

"Not much," Ellie admitted. "Only the upper part of his body; his legs were completely concealed by—" It struck her then; the others had already caught on, to judge by their expressions. "A dummy?" she demanded, her voice rising with excitement. "A kind of half-scarecrow on a pole, carried along by—"

"That would explain the point that's been worrying me," Donald exclaimed. "I have never liked the idea of a group conspiracy. If we eliminate that second figure, everything could have been done by one person."

"Precisely." Kate dropped a chunk of pâté into Simbel's open mouth. He spat it out at his feet; George ate it. Kate gave Simbel another piece. "I don't believe in a group conspiracy either. Although . . ."

The others waited expectantly. After a moment Kate gave herself a little shake.

"Never mind. The inaccuracy about the costume proves something else. Ghosts don't make mistakes like that. A human agency is implied."

She sounded genuinely regretful.

"What else?" the doctor asked eagerly. He was watching Kate like a disciple awaiting the words of the guru. Kate shrugged modestly.

"The library episode is obviously nonsupernatural. Somebody wanted something in the house. I can't believe in the coincidence of a professional burglar; the intruder must have been connected with the other events. There's just one more thing—" She turned suddenly to Donald, who sat up straight, removing his elbows from the table. His smile had vanished. "I think Donald knows what I only suspect," Kate continued calmly. "Out with it, Donald."

"You're an awful woman," Donald growled. "All right, if you're so smart; what is it you suspect? No fair waiting till I tell you and then claiming you knew it all along."

"But if I tell first, you'll claim you knew," Kate protested.

They eyed one another warily.

"Okay," Donald said. "How about this? It has to do with the parchment—"

"With a certain word on the parchment?" Kate's eyes twinkled.

"And the implications of that word—"

"Which suggest a possible motive—"

"For a burglar. And the word—"

"Is in the past tense."

The other two had followed this insane dialogue in stupefied silence. As soon as it was concluded, the speakers burst into whoops of laughter, exchanged cries of mutual congratulation, and went through a complex ritual of handshaking, which ended with each of them slapping the other's hand as hard as possible. Ellie looked at Dr. Gold. He shook his head.

"If we didn't love them—" he said.

"I'll explain," Donald said. Kate, who had gotten a little carried away by the ritual, was rubbing her stinging palm. "Here's the parchment. I looked the word up in the library earlier this evening."

"You'd better let me explain," Kate broke in. She produced a pair of glasses from amid the voluminous folds of the caftan, perched them crookedly on the end of her nose, and squinted through them. "*'Pater noster qui erat in caelis ...'* The Lord's

Prayer, as you correctly identified it. But listen to the precise translation. 'Our Father who *was* in heaven.' A trifle unorthodox, surely.'' She removed the glasses; her expression had lost all traces of humor. "It is, however, a quite orthodox version of another kind of prayer. Lucifer, the fallen angel, who was once in heaven with the other angels, was the god of the witches. Perversions of Christian prayers were popular with devotees of what Margaret Murray has called the Old Religion. The worship of Satan. This is a Satanist prayer; and the person who concealed it in the cover of that book was a devil worshiper. Possibly the leader of a local coven.''

III

Kate was quite in earnest, but she had been unable to resist making the announcement in her most dramatic voice; and the statement itself was sufficiently startling. The doctor refused to believe it. His cool skepticism did not prevent Kate and Donald from rushing headlong down jungly paths of conjecture.

"Motive," Kate exclaimed, with a wide, sweeping gesture. "If the names on the parchment are those of local worthies who were practicing witchcraft under their veneer of respectability . . . sacrificing babies . . . sexual orgies . . .''

"Wait, wait," Ellie pleaded. "Kate, you don't know—"

"Blood!" Donald shouted. They all jumped. "The names are written in blood. When Dad mentioned those papyri with the red rubrics, that gave me the idea, and then I checked the Latin to see if there was any peculiarity in the text. They always signed contracts with the devil in their own blood—''

"Donald," Ellie said plaintively. "Won't you please stop doing that?"

"Thank God for someone with a little common sense," the doctor growled. He and Ellie exchanged glances of mutual approval and commiseration. Then he continued, "Listen here, you two. You don't know that those names are written in—in—good God, I can't bring myself to say it. Ridiculous! You don't even know that they *are* names. And if they are names, you don't know *whose* names!"

"Oh, we'll check it out," Donald said airily. "I'm for Charlottesville first thing in the morning. Want to ride along, Ellie?"

"I think I'd better," Ellie said.

"Of course we'll check it," Kate said indignantly. "Really, Frank, you act as if I had no sense at all." Her expression softened as she looked at the doctor. "You're exhausted. Go home and get some sleep. There's nothing more to be done tonight."

"I'm going to get some sleep, but not at home," Dr. Gold retorted. "You girls can't stay here alone."

Ellie heartily concurred with this sentiment, but Kate was furious at the suggestion that she couldn't handle any emergency single-handed. Ellie suspected she was hoping for something to happen; a burglar or a ghost, she would welcome either with pleasure. Finally she was reluctantly persuaded to accept Donald's company, provided Dr. Gold went home and got a good night's sleep. They all went to the door with him.

"It's stopped raining," Ellie said. "Look—there's a star."

"Storm didn't do much good," the doctor said. "Hot as ever. Well—you promise you'll call if anything—"

"Nothing will happen," Kate said firmly. "If it does, I have my gun. My Mauser."

The Golds exchanged glances.

"I'll get it away from her," Donald assured his father. "Good night, Dad; don't worry."

After the doctor had gone, Ellie was conscious of a distinct change in the atmosphere. She didn't know what had caused it, but she rather thought Kate was looking shifty again.

"I'm bushed," Kate announced, stretching elaborately. "I'm going to bed. Would you two young, strong, healthy people mind—"

"Of course," Ellie said. "We'll lock up and everything."

"Don't forget to count cats."

"Naturally."

"Thank you, honey." Kate patted her cheek. "I'll see you both in the morning."

She moved languidly toward the stairs. Donald turned to Ellie.

"How about making some coffee? I've got to get that gun away from Kate."

"Good idea."

It had been a reasonable suggestion. Ellie was halfway to the kitchen when the unworthy suspicion struck her mind. She did not hesitate but tiptoed quickly back into the hall.

Kate and Donald were trying to keep their voices down, but they were standing in the upper hall, not far from the top of the stairs, and Ellie caught just enough to assure her that her suspicions had been justified. She took off her shoes and started up the stairs. The first sentence she heard clearly was spoken by Kate, and it was, in its way, quite characteristic.

"None of your business!"

"What do you mean, it's none of my business? You used my picture, didn't you? I want to know how, and I want to know why."

"How did you know—I mean, what makes you think it was your—"

"I recognized Ellie's description of the costume,"

Donald snapped. "I wore it in that silly damn costume drama the summer theater did two years ago. You were studying photography that year and you were all over the place snapping pictures. Come on, Kate, quit stalling. Where did you hide the projector? There must be a secret panel in this wall—"

From the muffled thuds that followed, Ellie realized he was pounding on the wall.

"Don't do that; Ellie will hear you," Kate hissed.

"I'll tell Ellie the whole thing if you don't come clean."

"Ellie knows!" said that young woman, making a dramatic appearance. The two whirled around, looking as guilty as a pair caught in adultery. Ellie leaned against the wall, folded her arms, and spoke out of the corner of her mouth.

"The jig is up, Kate. Confess."

Kate was seldom at a loss for long. She studied her niece speculatively.

"How much did you hear?"

"I know you planted the first ghost. I think I even know why...." To her fury—for she had thought herself completely in control of her emotions, and the situation—she felt herself blushing. She realized that Donald had turned red, too. Reading her mind again ... Really, he was less sophisticated than she had believed.

Kate was regarding both of them with a fond, maternal smile. Her expression snapped the last threads of Ellie's self-control.

"Don't think it worked, either," she snapped. "Really, Kate, you are the most outrageous combination of arrogance and naiveté. Just because you don't like Henry, that doesn't give you any right to meddle in my private life. And why you should think that a silly adolescent trick like that would make me susceptible ... would make me fall in ... I mean ..."

"We had better drop that," Donald said hastily. "Except that I want to go on record as agreeing with

Ellie one hundred percent. How did you work it, Kate?"

Kate's face was as smug as that of one of the cats. "There's a hiding place in the paneling," she said gaily, and demonstrated. A section of wood slid aside; in the cavity was a neat miniature projector. "You don't notice the hole," Kate went on. "It looks like a part of the thermostat. The wires go down inside the wall. I rigged it myself."

"With a trip switch under the stair carpeting?" Donald asked.

"Yes. I had a terrible time with that part of it," Kate said, frowning. "I kept blowing fuses."

"But I looked," Ellie said. "Ted and I looked the next day. . . ." Her voice trailed off. Kate nodded.

"I had to let Ted in on it. I figured you would be too distracted to look for wires that night. He came in next day—he has his own key—and disconnected the visible part of the apparatus."

"But how did you have the time?" Ellie asked. She was conscious of a horrified fascination—an emotion Kate often induced in her friends. "You didn't know Henry till that day—at least I assume you—"

"Oh, I had taken a violent dislike to Henry before I ever met him," Kate explained easily. "The things you said about him in your letters . . . I had the apparatus set up a long time ago, however. I've used it on several people." A wicked, reminiscent smile curved her soft lips. "At first I thought I'd set up some nice little vision for Henry, but when I met him I realized that he was far too stupid and pigheaded to be affected by something like that. He would simply have wiped the experience out of his mind. Then I got my inspiration."

She smiled widely at Ellie.

They were getting back to the part of the problem they had all agreed to avoid. Donald, still slightly flushed, said firmly,

"Never mind that, Kate. Did you arrange anything else?"

"No, of course not." Kate looked startled. "You don't think I would—honest, Ellie . . . Donald. You believe me, don't you?"

Oddly enough, both of them did.

"Then someone else must have used your initial offering as the springboard for his own tricks," Donald said.

"Obviously. But who? And why? I know what you're thinking; and it's true that Ted was the only one I told. But you've proved that Ted can't be the villain. I only wish I could be sure. . . ."

Her self-reproach was obvious, and obviously sincere. And her infuriating charm was so overpowering that the others had forgotten their outrage; they both joined in reassuring her.

"You can't blame yourself for what happened to Ted, Kate," Donald said, patting her shoulder. "Get some sleep and forget about it for tonight. We'll tackle the problem again in the morning."

If Kate had had an ulterior motive in arousing their sympathy, it did not work. Donald had not forgotten the gun. Snarling, Kate finally produced it from under her pillow. The color left Donald's cheeks as he examined the weapon.

"The safety," he said, choking. "You sleep with it under . . . and the safety isn't . . ."

"Of course I don't sleep with it under my pillow," Kate said. "Really, Donald. I put it on the bedside table."

Donald and Ellie hovered in the hall until Kate's light went out and they heard the sounds of peaceful breathing.

"I feel like a nurse in charge of a disturbed child," Donald whispered.

Ellie was inclined to agree.

She thought she would not close her eyes all night, but she was very tired; she fell asleep the minute her head hit the pillow. Subconsciously, however, she must have been expecting a disturbance. After all, since her arrival she had only twice had a full night's sleep in the house; a pattern had been established. She sat up, fully awake, when the noise began.

At least the lights were still working. She switched on her bedside lamp and ran to the window. The sounds were coming from outside. Roused rudely from sleep, Franklin sat up and began to bark shrilly.

"Shut up," Ellie said. The sounds were coming closer, the sounds of pounding hooves.

Kate ran in. "Ellie, are you all right? What's happening?"

"Sssh." Ellie gestured for silence. She had flung the window and the screen open. There was something odd about the hoofbeats. They were clear and distinct, with a ringing echo, as if the horse galloped on a hard-packed path or a road. But there was no such surface close to the house—particularly not in the thickly overgrown woods to the west, the direction from which the noise seemed to emanate.

"Oh, wow," Kate said, breathing heavily on her neck. "Isn't this great? I was afraid the tricks were— Ellie, where's Donald?"

Ellie, who had been about to make a rude retort in response to Kate's girlish enthusiasm, felt as if a fist had struck her in the stomach.

"He wouldn't," she gasped. "He wouldn't be so dumb—"

She turned from the window, stumbled over a cat, and almost fell. Kate caught her arm in a grip that left bruises.

"Look."

At first it was a shimmer of phosphorescence among the trees. It came quickly—though not, as Ellie later realized, as quickly as the galloping hooves should have brought it. A great black horse, muzzle and hooves dripping with infernal fire, the eyes rings of light. The rider . . .

The moon was out, full and bright; the storm was blowing away to the east in wisps of abandoned cloud. The rider was a hunched, cloaked figure, sitting low on the saddle, but his face was uncannily distinct. As if he were giving them ample opportunity to observe, he reined in the horse and lifted his face to the moonlight.

Ellie knew she had seen it somewhere before; surely she had been familiar with that lean, pale countenance long before she came to Kate's. The black moustache was long and drooping, the face was framed by lank black locks. The black cloak had a high collar. The whole effect was theatrical, and yet there was a false note somewhere. . . . She had no time to think about it. The apparition had made her forget Donald for a moment; when she saw him run out from the bushes near the house, she was as surprised as the ghostly rider.

He gave a wholly human start. An uncontrolled movement of his hands on the reins made the great horse rear. Ellie drew in her breath and thought about screaming. She knew what was going to happen, as surely as if she had already seen it, and there was nothing she could do to prevent it. Screaming would do no good. A movement behind her, followed by the rapid retreat of Kate's running footsteps, told her that her aunt was trying to get to the scene. She would, of course, be too late. Ellie couldn't move.

Donald was running like a track star, although the soggy, saturated ground impeded his progress slightly. The horse was fighting his rider. But what happened was not an accident. Donald was still several yards away when the rider jerked his dancing mount around in a half-circle, gathered him in, and set him straight at the running man.

Donald tried to veer off. The damp ground betrayed him. He slipped and fell. To Ellie's horrified eyes the great hooves seemed to strike squarely on his body. The horse thundered on, plunging at dangerous speed into the thick woods, and Donald lay still where he had fallen, his white face upturned to the silent moon.

Ellie had no conscious memory of descending the stairs. She must have tripped and fallen at least once; her knees were bruised and discolored the next day. She might have tripped over Franklin, for the Pekingese was with her when she fled across the soggy lawn.

Kate was already on her knees beside Donald. She looked up as Ellie flung herself forward; her small hands caught the girl in a grip of surprising strength.

"Don't touch him. Go call— No. First let the dogs out. Hurry."

"They're out," Ellie said. She was vaguely aware of Franklin barking and running around in agitated circles. In fact, the lawn seemed to be alive with animals. She must have left the front door open. This violation of one of Kate's strongest taboos barely brushed the surface of her mind. She was only aware of Donald. He lay in a twisted, uncomfortable position, one leg at an odd angle. His eyes were closed. Blood trickled down his face from under his ruffled hair, and the front of his torn, wet shirt was disfigured by a great dark stain. It looked like a hoofprint.

Kate slapped her hard across the face.

"The dogs in the kennel. Let them out, this instant. Run!"

Ellie obeyed.

The dogs were awake and disturbed. She hadn't realized it before, she had been too preoccupied, but as she approached the kennel she heard the mournful baying of the bloodhound rising over a cacophony of barks and movement. The dogs poured out when she opened the door. They were delighted to see her, and they followed as she ran back to Kate.

"How is—"

"Broken ribs, I think." Kate sat back on her heels

and brushed her hair back from her face, leaving a smear of some suspicious dark substance on her forehead. Her face was calm, but for once she looked her full age. "Listen carefully. Take Toby"— she nodded at the bloodhound, who sat down on his haunches and stared at her, his tongue lolling— "and go telephone Frank Gold. Tell him what has happened, and try to break it gently. Tell him *not to come on foot*. Make him promise. Use the phone in the hall. Don't go anywhere else in the house, understand? There's an afghan in the chest by the suit of armor. Bring it and get back here on the double."

Ellie almost saluted.

As she left she heard Kate giving instructions to the other dogs. One of them went loping off into the woods; she did not linger to see what the others did.

Kate had always maintained the animals understood her perfectly. Her friends took this claim with more than a grain of salt, but this night Ellie was inclined to believe her. Toby stuck to her like a burr, and she was grateful for the big dog's companionship when she reentered the silent house.

Kate had had presence of mind enough to turn on lights as she went, but the house had a strange aura—a sense of something waiting, as if an alien presence hovered. The cats seemed to have taken advantage of the open door, but Ellie fancied that Roger must be somewhere about. At least she hoped the rustling sounds she heard were made by the rat, and not by something else. Roger had better sense than to go outside. There were too many predators out there in the dark.

The doctor answered the phone on the first ring. He didn't ask questions, or allow Ellie to explain at length. "I'll be there," he said, and hung up.

Ellie followed suit. She was glad to get out of the

house, but she realized that Kate had had to choose between two unknown dangers when she remained with Donald. Neither knew what further peril the night might hold, nor from which direction it might come. The only defense they had were the dogs, and it had been eminently sensible of Kate to see to that first, even though it meant delay in reaching help.

Kate was sitting cross-legged on the grass when Ellie got back to her. The skirt of her pale-blue silk negligee lay around her in damp folds. A dog stood on guard on either side of her. The contrast between Franklin, who was smaller than several of the larger cats, and the German shepherd was more amusing than impressive. She watched impassively while Ellie spread the blanket over Donald's limp body. He was still unconscious.

"I don't think it's as bad as it looks," Kate said coolly. "Something is damaged in the rib area, and he got a glancing blow on the head. Maybe a slight concussion, but no skull fracture. His arms and legs are sound. The only thing that worries me is the possibility of internal injuries. No sign of them; but I don't dare move him." She hesitated for a moment, and then added, in a gentler voice, "You can hold his hand if you want to."

Ellie did so. The long, limp fingers felt so pathetic; she had always seen them moving with quick competence.

"Donald," she said, "please wake up, Donald."

"That's silly," her aunt said. "He'll be in pain if he wakes up. Tell him to stay unconscious."

She began groping around in the front of her negligee. Kate's clothes, like her house, were all constructed with hidden pockets and panels. From some such place she produced a pack of cigarettes and a book of matches.

"I thought you quit smoking," Ellie said, unreasonably annoyed at the calm air with which Kate flicked her match away and blew out rings.

"You can't expect me to stop smoking when I'm so nervous," Kate said. Ellie was about to make a nasty comment when she realized that the fingers holding the cigarette were shaking visibly, and that Kate's mouth was drawn in at the corners.

"You *are* upset, aren't you?" she asked.

"I am not wholly without feelings," said Kate. "But there is no sense in making the situation worse by leaking tears or bleating out sentiments I may regret later. I am very fond of that boy."

"So am I," Ellie said.

And she could have sworn—though she did not for a moment doubt that Kate's concern was as profound as her own—that a flash of smug satisfaction momentarily lightened the somber blue of Kate's eyes.

The doctor had followed Kate's instructions; he did not come through the woods, but drove. The car skidded on the wet gravel and slued halfway around when he slammed on the brakes.

"That's bright," Kate said nastily, as he came running up. "Get yourself smashed up in a crash, that's all we need."

The doctor did not reply; either he understood the reason for Kate's harshness, or he simply didn't hear her at all. After several long, horrible minutes, he looked up, and Ellie started to cry with sheer relief before he spoke.

"I can't find anything serious. I want him in for X rays, though."

"I'll go call the ambulance," Ellie gurgled, weeping.

"I'll do it. I can get faster action." The doctor stood up. So did Kate. She put out one hand. It was a strangely tentative movement; there was an expression on her face that Ellie had never seen before. At first she thought Dr. Gold wouldn't notice the small movement. Then he took Kate's hand in both his.

"It's all right, dear," he said, and smiled at her before he ran toward the house.

Much later they found the chaos in the library. Every book was off the shelf; every drawer had been emptied onto the floor.

CHAPTER NINE

Perched on the edge of her chair, Kate leaned forward tense with expectation. A cigarette dangled out of the corner of her mouth; the ashes, almost an inch long, menaced the lovely old Bokhara. She paid it no heed. Brows drawn together, eyes blazing, she suddenly shouted,

"Screen pass! Screen pass, you bloody blithering—oh, damn!"

The ashes dropped. Kate pounded on the arm of the chair.

"Third down and five yards to go and he tries to run the ball! The Colts had the best defense against the run in the NFL last year, he hasn't got a running back over two hundred pounds, and he tries to run the ball on third and—"

"They're ahead by ten," the doctor said.

"That's how they lost all their games last year, sitting on a ten-point lead," Kate said bitterly.

Ellie stared balefully at the twenty-seven-inch screen and a row of Redskins lining up in punt formation. She had already expressed her astonishment that Kate meant to spend three hours watching a football game—and a preseason game at that—when the universe was breaking up around them. Her words had fallen on deaf ears, to put it mildly. The doctor, for once, was no help. No longer concerned about his son, he was as intent on the game as Kate.

Somebody kicked the ball, which bobbled around at the other end of the field while a crowd of hulking players danced nervously around it.

"Coffin corner," Kate exclaimed triumphantly. "Now if that butter-fingered quarterback will just fumble the ball—"

"I wish you would stop making stupid comments about a subject you do not understand," the doctor snapped. "Why should he fumble the ball? Of all the times when he will be careful not to—"

An unseemly scramble ensued on the screen, accompanied by grunts and thuds. From Kate's shriek of rapture Ellie deduced that the quarterback had indeed fumbled the ball. Baltimore recovered, however; Kate settled back looking disgusted, and the doctor mopped his forehead.

Ellie could have followed the progress of the game by watching the faces of the two spectators. The doctor brightened visibly when Baltimore made the first down, but to Ellie's uneducated eye that team still seemed to be rather close to its own end of the field. Suddenly Kate rose to her feet as if propelled by a spring. The doctor emitted a moaning cry that sounded like William forecasting rain; and the football, soaring high and long, smacked firmly into the waiting arms of a receiver who jumped two opponents, kicked another neatly in the stomach, and sauntered in for the touchdown.

The doctor was shrieking insanely.

"The bomb! The bomb! Right on the numbers! Right on the numbers!"

Ellie was surprised to find herself on her feet jumping up and down and yelling.

Kate glowered at her. "Whose side are you on anyhow?"

"I'm not on anybody's side," Ellie said. "I just love those—what did you call them? Bombs?"

"Beautiful," the doctor crooned. His eyes were glued to the screen where the touchdown pass was being repeated in instant replay and slow motion, from the front, from the rear, from the side, and backwards.

"Not bad," Kate admitted grudgingly. "Of course, once you've seen a virtuoso—"

The doctor could afford to be generous.

"Oh, yes, Sonny was the master, no question about it. Remember the Dallas game in sixty-five?"

"And the Philadelphia game in 1974," Kate said, her eyes glistening with sentimental fondness. "When he came off the bench in the third quarter, when the 'Skins were behind by twenty-one points, and won the game?"

"Well, Larry Brown helped a little," the doctor said.

The conversation became too technical for Ellie; she sat watching hopefully for another bomb. She was disappointed. Washington ran the clock out, accompanied by a stream of vitriolic criticism from Kate, and the half ended.

"It's kind of interesting," Ellie said, as a group of hearty men in hard hats began singing about beer. "What's the score now?"

"Seventeen to fourteen," the doctor said. "But the game's only half over. Wait till the second half."

"Shut up," Kate snarled.

Ellie didn't understand why she was in such a bad mood. The Redskins were winning, weren't they? She wanted to request enlightenment but decided maybe she had better not. She was beginning to understand why Kate liked football. It was an awfully silly occupation for a bunch of grown men, but it was rather relaxing. Watching other people bang each other around took one's mind off one's private worries.

The half-time activities were not as distracting as bombs and thudding bodies, however; and Ellie's private worries were far from minor. At least Donald's injuries weren't as serious as they had feared. He had a broken rib and a magnificent bruise; as the doctor said, he wouldn't be able to play golf for a long time. The cut on his forehead was superficial. He had been incredibly lucky. Ellie was sure the rider had deliberately set his living weapon at Donald in order to maim or kill.

The rider had been human, and clumsy, at that. It was the first of the "apparitions" that had been so badly stage-managed. The unknown miscreant must be losing his touch, or else he was getting panicky.

It had been Donald who identified the rider's face. They had been allowed to see him for a few minutes before driving home in the gray dawn. Ted was still not allowed visitors, but Dr. Gold had checked on his progress, and that, too, was cheering.

Encased in a plaster corset, groggy from pain and painkillers, Donald had not appeared particularly happy to see them—especially Ellie. She hung back, feeling strangely shy. The pale, romantic invalid, with the theatrical white bandage on his brow, looked like a stranger, and he had given her a stare of active dislike before turning his head painfully toward Kate.

"Booth," he said, slurring the word. "Did you recognize him, Kate?"

"Ah." Kate nodded. "I wasn't sure."

"I've seen pictures." Donald's eyelids dropped. He opened them halfway and blinked. "Damn, this stuff is knocking me out. Just—like pictures. John Wilkes Booth."

"Okay." Kate patted his arm. "Get some rest. The night is over, no need to worry. Anything else you noticed?"

"No. Can't think. Too groggy . . ."

"The parchment," Kate said. "What did you do with it?"

Donald's eyes opened wide.

"Go away," he said distinctly.

They went.

"There's no need to snuffle in that maudlin fashion," Kate said, as they pulled out of the hospital parking lot. "He's not damaged. If I know Donald, that corset won't prevent him from—"

"Oh, you're disgusting," Ellie said, knowing what she was about to say. Kate had moments of extreme vulgarity when she was tired. She was obviously very tired indeed; the lines around her mouth were like grooves, but her head was high and she drove with her usual élan. Most people refused to ride with her. Ellie simply closed her eyes and braced her feet.

"Macho," Kate went on, "plain old machismo, that's why he was so rude; he hated having you see him down and out. Men are such egotists. That's why I won't remarry; I haven't got the time or energy to spend the rest of my life coddling some man's childish image of himself."

"What about Dr. Gold?" Ellie asked.

"Oh, well, Frank . . ." Kate's voice softened. "Don't get any romantic ideas, though. He's a wonderful—uh—friend, but I wouldn't marry him either. Even if he asked me," she added.

It was after they returned home that they discovered what had happened in the library. Ellie had a strange feeling that Kate had expected some such development.

The mess made her swear with an inventiveness that surpassed her usual gift for invective. She started picking up books, mingling commentary with curses as she worked.

"The performance was meant as a distraction, of course—to get us out of the house and keep us busy. I suspected it, but there really was no choice; Donald came first. Anyway, the burglar didn't find what he was after."

Ellie was suddenly sick with exhaustion. She could hardly stand, much less move.

"The parchment, you think? Where is it?"

"I don't know." Kate dumped an armful of books onto the shelf and began sorting them with nimble fingers. "But Donald does; and he isn't talking. Didn't you get that byplay?"

"Oh. But—I wanted to take it to the University."

"Yes, the sooner we do that, the safer we'll be. I'm sure there is something on that sheet of parchment that someone is desperate to keep quiet. But Donald has taken it into his stupid head that he can protect us by being the only one who knows its hiding place. I wonder . . ." Kate paused, holding another armful of books. She chewed her lower lip thoughtfully. "Oh, no, he wouldn't be *that* stupid. Anyhow, he should be out of this world for the rest of the day. I told Frank to dope him to the gills."

In the stupor of weariness Ellie failed to follow this semisoliloquy. With infinite labor she restored a pair of bookends to the top of the desk.

"What was all that about John Wilkes Booth?" she asked. "He was Lincoln's assassin, wasn't he?"

"Stupid," Kate repeated, with relish. "A stupid performance throughout. Yes, of course he was, and he had nothing to do with this area; he was born in Maryland and he was caught and killed—popular rumor to the contrary—in a barn in Maryland. But the plotter counted on our recognizing Booth—he gave us plenty of time to do so—and he knew we would be reminded of the old slander that the Grant family was involved in that assassination plot. Nothing was ever proved, but . . . So now we have all six families represented."

She glanced at Ellie.

"Go to bed, you're out on your feet. I'll deal with this."

"But you're tired, too," Ellie protested. "And Marian Beaseley—"

"She'll be back. Not till after this business is cleared up, but eventually. The Beaseleys always go into hiding when anything unusual happens."

"Marian said—all that about Francis Morrison—"

Kate chuckled. She was a quick worker; most of the books were back in place now.

"Marian loves to startle people," she said tolerantly. "Go to bed, Ellie."

So Ellie did. It was not until she was halfway down the lovely dark path that led to sleep that she realized Kate's explanation of Marian's knowledgeability had been somewhat enigmatic.

Apparently Kate had had no sleep at all. At some point during the early morning, Ellie had been dimly aware of Kate's voice calling cats. She had succeeded in collecting them all by the time Ellie came down to a very late breakfast. Ellie got a long animated lecture on football with her bacon and eggs. Now as she watched the Redskins perform, Kate looked as bright-eyed and cool as if she had had eight solid hours of rest, and she was wearing one of her most businesslike outfits—severely tailored blue slacks, a man's work shirt, and a pair of dangling silver earrings that jingled when she tossed her head.

The gesture occurred frequently in the second half of the game. During the last ten minutes the earrings rang a continual chime of distress and agitation. The final score was 24 to 17 in favor of Baltimore. Kate stuck it out till the whistle blew, mumbling about fumbles and interceptions; then she stormed out of the room. The only intelligible word in her parting tirade sounded like "Sonny."

The doctor leaned back with a sigh of satisfaction.

"Good game," he said.

"Not enough bombs," Ellie said.

II

Kate returned after a while, with drinks and canapés; she looked quite pleasant, but there was a glint in her eye that warned Ellie not to ask any questions about football. After all, it was high time they got down to business.

Before they could start talking, the telephone rang and Kate crossed the room to answer it.

"I'm surprised we haven't heard from our friends before this," Ellie said.

"Oh, they know better than to call when there's a game on," the doctor said. "Kate always unplugs all the phones. We'll be getting a barrage of questions now, though. I imagine the news has spread. Many of the staff people at the hospital have friends and relatives in town."

The room was large, and Kate had turned her back. They were unable to make out what she was saying, although both of them unashamedly tried to eavesdrop. She did not talk long.

"That was Grant," she said, when she returned to her chair. "He's heard the news."

"Is he mad?" Ellie asked.

"Annoyed. Very cool and dignified, of course. He wouldn't be so dignified if he knew about the coven."

"How much damage could that news do, really?" the doctor demanded. "Even if it is true—which we don't know yet—"

"I don't know, and I doubt that anyone else does," Kate said thoughtfully. "Politics is a tricky business. In spite of all the smug pollsters and analysts, it is sometimes impossible to predict how the voters are going to react to an issue. Oh, I agree, it's absurd to consider what someone's grandfather or great-grandfather did; but just think for a minute how the voters in this state would react to the news that Grant's granddaddy had been a slave? And that's an even more irrelevant fact than possible insanity in the family. If I were he, I think I might go to considerable lengths to keep such a story quiet."

The doctor ran his fingers through his tumbled hair.

"Damn it, Kate, we ought to have enough information now to make at least an educated guess as to the identity of our friend. And we've got to act soon. He is becoming dangerous."

"I know. Ted's heart attack might have been an accident, but last night . . . I don't think he had murder in mind," she added. "It would be a singularly inefficient method. But he meant to cripple, or injure, to distract us from his main purpose. That argues a high degree of ruthlessness—or of panic."

"The horse," Ellie said. "Isn't there some way of identifying the horse?"

"This is horse country," Kate answered, with a shake of her head. "Everybody owns horses—except me; I'm scared of them."

"You, scared?" Dr. Gold interrupted, grinning. "I thought you weren't frightened of anything."

"Their backs are too wide," Kate said, frowning. "Or else my legs are too short. . . . And don't tell me about jockeys. Anyway I don't believe in *using* animals."

This was obviously a long-standing debate, and Kate had no intention of reviving it. Before the doctor could shape a retort, she hurried on.

"Everybody rides, and most of them hunt—not on my land, you may be sure!"

"Even Miss Mary?" Ellie asked.

"Like a Cyclops," Kate said, and smiled at Ellie, who was also a devotee of *Little Women*. "It's part of county mystique. The villain could borrow any one of fifty horses. There are several blacks. Ted owns a black gelding—"

"And there's that black mare of Grant's," the doctor broke in.

"Besides," Kate added, "I couldn't swear to the

color. It might have been brown or even dark gray. Distinctive marks, such as stars or blazes, could be painted over temporarily. The villain used some sort of phosphorescent paint—water-soluble, no doubt— around the eyes and muzzle. Very sloppy job; I've never seen such an unconvincing spectral horse. I suspect the man dismounted in the woods and sent the horse home before he sneaked back and broke in. He could clean off the paint and have the horse grazing peacefully before daybreak."

"Then what are we going to do?" Ellie demanded. "We have to do something—"

The telephone rang again before Kate could reply. Ellie did not doubt that she had an idea; her face had a familiar look of smug satisfaction.

But the phone call put an end to that mood. After a moment Kate's voice rose in a most unfeminine bellow.

"What? He told you— When? When was this? Oh, damn, damn, damn. No, of course it isn't true. It's a lie. The damned thing is in my safe-deposit box. You call the others back right this minute and tell them so."

She flung the phone in the general direction of the cradle and spun around to face the others. Her eyes were blazing blue.

"Do you know what that cretin son of yours has done?" she demanded of the doctor. "I thought I told you to keep him doped."

The doctor bounced to his feet.

"Doped, hell; I told them to keep him sedated, of course, but I can't— What is it, Kate?"

Kate had scooped up a cat, which she often did when she was disturbed; she had once said it was the equivalent of a comfort blanket, only better, because it was warmer and furrier. The cat happened to be Jenny, the old Siamese, who did not appreciate being cuddled. She immediately turned into a bundle of bony angles.

"Well, you didn't keep him sedated enough. He made a series of phone calls—must have started about an hour ago—telling all our suspects that he had hidden the parchment, and he was the only one who knew where it was."

"Good Lord," the doctor groaned. "Silly quixotic young—"

"Oh, it was very noble," Kate said bitingly. "He's trying to set a trap, with himself as bait. The instant he moves—"

Her jaw dropped. Releasing the uncooperative cat, she grabbed for the telephone.

They were all half prepared for the news, but it came as a shock all the same. Kate reported it in fragments, as she received it, her voice flat and hard.

"He's gone. Clothes, too. . . . In the last hour; he had lunch at one, and the girl who came for the tray says he was asleep then. . . . The woman at the desk saw a man answering his description leave the hospital. She didn't know him; assumed he was a visitor. . . ."

There was nothing more to be learned, unless prolonged interrogation turned up a witness who had seen Donald getting into a car. The doctor snatched up the telephone and demanded that such an investigation be carried out, but when he hung up he was gray with worry and his hair was standing up like a comic wig.

"They couldn't stop him anyway if he wanted to leave," he groaned. "He's of legal age—"

"He's acting like a sixteen-year-old," Kate said angrily. She had replaced the Siamese with Henrietta, the long-haired Balinese, who adored affection. Draped over Kate's shoulder like a fawn-and-brown fur piece, dainty feet dangling, she was purring hysterically.

"Where do you suppose he's gone?" Ellie asked. "We've got to find him before—"

"Now calm down," said Kate, who was stroking

the amiable Henrietta the wrong way in her agitation. "Be calm. There is nothing to be gained by losing our heads."

"Maybe he's gone home," Ellie suggested. She was calm; she felt half dead.

"No, that's the first place we would look," the doctor said. "He must have called one of his friends. Someone with a car and no sense of responsibility. Randy? John?"

"Think of something sensible," Kate snarled. "You can't start calling all his friends, as if he were ten years old. They'll all be out at this time of day. . . ."

"You weren't much help," the doctor retorted angrily. "Couldn't you have thought of a more plausible alternative? This is Saturday; the bank's closed. You couldn't have gotten into your safe-deposit box since last night."

"Oh, God, that's right," Kate said wretchedly. "Frank, I'm sorry; I said the first thing that came into my head. . . ."

The doctor put his arm around her, and around Henrietta, who squeaked with rapture.

"That's all right, honey; I'm sorry I yelled at you. I doubt that it would have mattered anyway. The villain will have to follow Donald; he can't take any chances. Really, we're getting unnecessarily alarmed. Donald is in no danger until he produces the parchment. It's here in the house somewhere, isn't it?"

"Must be." Kate brightened a little. "He didn't have the opportunity to take it anywhere. Unless he had it on him—"

"No." Dr. Gold shook his head. "Then it's here. He'll have to come here for it, and until he does he's as safe as a baby in a cradle."

Ellie hated to say it, but she couldn't face the idea alone.

"Kidnapping," she whispered. "They might catch him. . . ."

"No, child." The doctor put his other arm around Ellie, so that they stood in a warm touching group—all four of them, including Henrietta. "Don't let your imagination run away with you. We're not dealing with the Mafia, or with organized criminals. Our friend doesn't have a hideout, where a kidnap victim could be hidden; nor does he dare risk being identified. Besides, Ellie, can you seriously visualize any of our suspects— I know, some of them are disturbed, selfish people, but they wouldn't—"

"Certainly not," Kate said briskly. The therapy had worked; she put Henrietta down and straightened up. But Ellie knew she had sown a horrible little fear in all their minds. The idea was fantastic, impossible—but she couldn't rid herself of it. Donald was injured, unable to defend himself. . . .

"I guess we'd better get going," Kate said. She smiled at Ellie, but the girl saw the faintest shadow of buried horror in the blue eyes.

"Where?" the doctor asked.

"Ted's house. No, I won't tell you; I'll show you. If I'm right . . ."

They took the doctor's battered old car; even in the depths of his alarm Dr. Gold refused to let Kate drive.

Ted had a daily housekeeper, who kept his charming little house in immaculate order; he was so neat that one elderly woman could manage without difficulty. Presumably Saturday was Mrs. Moran's day off, for the house was locked and no one answered the bell.

"I've got a key," Kate said, and produced it from the pocket of her shirt.

The house was shadowy and still. Only the soft purr of the air conditioning broke the silence. Kate led the way; the house was almost as familiar to her as her own. It was much smaller—a neat Georgian square, with drawing room and library flanking the entrance hall, and four bedrooms upstairs. Kate went down.

The basement looked cluttered only by comparison to the finicky neatness that prevailed upstairs. Even a man as fussy as Ted could not carry on carpentry and papier-mâché work without making some mess, but his tools were shining, arranged in order of size—everything in its place—and the carpeted floor had not even a trace of sawdust.

Ellie took it all in in one quick glance; and then she saw the masks.

They hung in a neat row along one paneled wall— so lifelike, so accurately done, that for a breathless instant she thought of severed heads hanging—a woman's head, with long blond locks; a bearded Cavalier, a grizzled old man—and, most shocking of all, the familiar ratlike face of Roger McGrath.

Kate removed this last head from the bracket that had been cunningly designed to support it. It collapsed in her hands, unnervingly, like a human face dissolving under the blast of some weird science-fiction ray gun.

"He was going to do all his friends," Kate said. "And enemies . . ." She put her hand inside the mask and bounced it up and down, like a puppet master. "You've seen the flexible plastic masks they sell at Halloween—some kid came by last year dressed up as a gorilla and scared poor old William into fits. They're amazingly lifelike. This is a new process; you can mold it, like wax, before it hardens. Ted is a fairly decent amateur sculptor."

"Yes," the doctor said quietly. "He did a lovely little head of my wife. I should have thought . . . So this is how the faces of Ellie's apparitions were done."

"Yes." Kate put the mask of McGrath back on its stand and turned to Ellie. "Please, honey, don't be angry with Ted. He's pretty childlike in some ways; and over the years he has had to take a lot of insults from some of these people. It was my fault, for starting the whole thing. Ted couldn't resist going on with it. You won't think too badly of him?"

"I guess not. . . ." Ellie looked away from the row of masks; the empty-eyed stare of Roger McGrath was disconcerting. "Anyway, the scheme backfired on him. We still have a villain to identify."

"I don't like to hurry you, Kate," the doctor began.

"Yes, I know; we must get back to the house. But first I want to see if I can find any of the masks Ted used." She began pulling out drawers, and the others scattered to help her search. There were dozens of drawers and cupboards to investigate.

"The John Wilkes Booth mask won't be here," Kate went on. "If our villain has any sense, he will have destroyed it by now. I wonder if Ted used that woman's head for his eloping lady?"

Ellie looked again at the hanging masks.

"That might have been the young man," she said, pointing at a smiling boy's face.

"Then," said the doctor, rummaging in drawers with a careless haste that would have horrified Ted, "we're missing old Mr. Lockwood and Marge's grandmother."

"And the murderous husband," Ellie said, returning to the search. "I'd recognize that face, all right. Grim."

"You're the only one who would recognize it," Kate said. "Frank, if you find any mask at all, let Ellie see it."

But the search was fruitless. If the masks were in the house, they were not in this room, and the doctor flatly refused to look any farther.

"It would take us all evening," he said. "I think Donald will come to your house, Kate. And if he does—"

He didn't need to finish the sentence.

"Frank, how long will it be before we can talk to Ted?" Kate asked, as they got into the car.

"A couple of days, if he continues to improve." The doctor frowned. "Dr. Koch tells me that Ted seems uneasy about something. He's asked for you several times, Kate. But at the moment it would be most ill advised."

"Unless Ted got a look at his assailant, he can't tell us anything we don't already know," Ellie said.

"I doubt that he did," Kate said. "We may not need to bother him. I hope we can have this silly business cleared up before he's able to talk."

"How?" The doctor expressed his feelings by a vicious twist of the wheel as they turned into Kate's driveway. "Stop showing off, Kate. If you have any ideas, this is the time to talk."

But Kate refused to do so until after the animals had been fed. The others helped—if the doctor had not had something to do, he would have been chewing his nails—so it was not long before they were settled in the parlor with cocktails. It was light outside, but the shadows were long across the lawn. Night was coming, and they still didn't know where Donald was.

"You knew, as soon as you heard about the tricks, that Ted was responsible for them," Dr. Gold said, looking accusingly at Kate. "Why didn't you say so before?"

"Because Ted wasn't responsible for all the tricks," Kate retorted. "His motives were harmless, he just wanted to annoy some pompous people. The practical jokes didn't become dangerous until a second person got involved, and I don't have any idea who that person is. But his—or her—motive becomes comprehensible if Donald's ideas about the parchment are correct. It's the charter of a secret society, signed by local dignitaries who were behaving in a very undignified manner. The descendant of one of those people is very anxious to suppress that information. Don't ask me how he, or she, learned about the parchment. That's one of the things I haven't figured out—yet.

"The villain came here looking for the parchment and ran into Ted—or vice versa. Even before that encounter the unknown must have strongly suspected that Ted was manipulating the apparitions. He may have thought Ted knew more about his horrible secret than was actually the case. At any rate, he broke into Ted's house, saw the masks, and realized that he could use the plan for his own purposes. Maybe he even found a written scenario. Ted is compulsively well organized, and there was no reason why he shouldn't commit the plan to paper. It was just a joke, after all."

She paused, stroked the cat in her lap, and looked complacently at the other two.

"It's possible," the doctor said, after a moment. "It's even plausible. But it doesn't get us much farther, Kate. We still have five suspects, if you include Anne Grant. Can we rule any of them out?"

"Oh, we could draw up one of those lists they used to have in the good old British detective stories," Kate said casually. "With columns for motive and opportunity and so on. But it wouldn't tell us anything. How can you calculate the strength of someone else's motives? I'd buy space in a newspaper and tell the world if I had a relative who was headmaster of a coven. But Roger McGrath would pay thousands to suppress a fact like that. So would Miss Mary."

"We can't eliminate Grant," the doctor said heavily. "As you say, it is difficult to calculate what effect such news might have on the voters. And Anne might be after the parchment for another reason. To publish it."

"You're forgetting Marjorie Melody," Ellie said. "I think she's got the best motive of all. Why, she'd be a laughingstock if that information got out. Not only would she lose her livelihood, that big fat ego of hers would never recover."

"Don't you like Marjorie?" Kate asked innocently.

"This isn't getting us anywhere," the doctor said, before Ellie could reply. "Theoretically any one of these people might be considered to have a motive. Ellie, think. Did you see anything—any detail at all—that might enable you to recognize the masquerader?"

"No," Ellie said. "Besides, we know Ted played most of the ghosts. I'm sure he was Lockwood, even if we didn't find the mask. That business with the crucifix, at lunch, was Ted's nutty way of telling me not to be afraid. He thought I'd feel protected when I wore it, and—yes, that's right, it was when I put my hands up, toward my throat, that he pretended to recoil and run. He couldn't see that I wasn't wearing it. What a performance that was! He terrified me."

"He's not a bad actor," Kate said. "I remember him in *The Importance of Being Earnest*, in the summer-stock company; he was excellent. But he never meant to frighten you, Ellie. Like all hams, he got a little carried away by his own performance. He thinks of you as young and tough, and I'm sure he assumed you would be more intrigued than frightened."

"I'm not mad at him," Ellie said. "If I were inclined to resent any particular part of this whole affair, there is someone I might mention who is more—"

"The fourth apparition is the most interesting," Kate said in a loud voice. "The white lady on the stairs. What a title for a Gothic novel! I wish I'd seen her."

"She was sensational," Ellie admitted. The memory of that ice-white pillar still made her shiver.

"So I gathered. What is so interesting is that the white lady was quite well done, on a par with, if not superior to, Ted's other performances. Yet the lady could not have been Ted, who was lying unconscious in the library. We must attribute that apparition, as well as the John Wilkes Booth performance, to our unknown second villain. Yet the Booth business was so badly done as to be almost ludicrous, if it had not been for its unpleasant and completely material consequences—''

The doctor interrupted with a wordless sound, halfway between shout and groan, and got to his feet.

''I know what you're trying to do, Kate, and I appreciate it,'' he said, pacing. ''But you can't keep my mind off Donald any longer, and if I have to sit here, doing nothing, I will go nuts.''

''What are you going to do? What can we do?'' Ellie asked. Kate had settled back in her chair.

''Call the police,'' the doctor said grimly. ''I will tell them that Donald left the hospital, against medical advice; that his injuries and the drugs he has been given make him dangerous to himself and to others. I want him picked up, by any means necessary.''

''You can't do that,'' Kate protested.

''Yes, I can. And I will.''

Before he could get to the telephone, that instrument began to ring. The doctor snatched it up. The hope faded from his face as he listened, to be replaced by a puzzled frown. Then he held out the instrument to Ellie.

''It's your fiancé,'' he said, giving her a strange look.

Ellie suspected the truth almost immediately. In her haste she dropped the receiver; while she was untangling it she heard the doctor say softly to Kate, ''I didn't realize Ellie's young man was Hungarian,'' and then she was sure.

''Hello,'' she gasped. ''Hello. Who is this?''

''If you say one word, one syllable that will give me away, I'll hang up,'' said Donald.

He sounded slightly drunk.

"Are you all right?" Ellie demanded. "Where are you?"

"Yes to the first question, never mind the second. Listen, Ellie, I know you can't talk; I'll talk, you just say yes and no. I want you to—"

"No," Ellie said.

"But all I want you to do is—"

"No."

Donald sighed. "I suppose everybody is pretty mad?"

"Yes. And," Ellie added, "suspicious."

She turned around. The doctor had resumed his seat. He was pretending to leaf through a magazine, but Ellie could almost see his ears twitching. Kate had disappeared.

"I've got a plan," Donald said ingratiatingly.

"So I gather."

"If you would just let me tell you what it is. . . ."

"All right." Ellie leaned against the table. The doctor glanced at her; she smiled at him.

"See, I figured that if I set up a trap, with myself as bait," Donald began.

"That was obvious from the first," Ellie said. "Even to me."

"Oh. Okay. Then you know about my calling all our suspects?"

"Uh-huh!"

"Did any of them call you?"

"Oh, yes. Yes, indeed."

"That's great." Donald was slurring his words just a bit; otherwise he sounded as cheerful and cocky as ever. "It's working. I thought it was." His voice dropped several octaves. "I'm being followed," he whispered loudly.

Since the doctor was listening, Ellie did not say the word that came into her mind. There was a peculiar wheezing noise on the other end of the line; at least Ellie thought that was where it came from until Donald asked, "What's the matter with your breathing?"

Ellie had already suspected that Kate was listening on one of the extensions. Perhaps Donald was dopey from the medication he had been given and was not thinking clearly, but even so it had been stupid of him to fake an accent in order to deceive his father. It had not deceived Kate, and she was not the woman to balk at a spot of eavesdropping.

"I have sinus trouble," Ellie said.

"Oh. Well, what I propose to do is this. I'll wait till about midnight before I come to the house. You make sure everybody is in bed before then. And don't you come downstairs. You can watch, from the head of the stairs, if you want to, but don't—"

"Oh, gee, thanks, can I, really?"

"I think you're being sarcastic," Donald said doubtfully. "Quite uncalled for, sarcasm. This is a neat plan. What I'll do is, I'll pretend to find the parchment, see? I won't really find it, I'll leave it where it's safe, but I'll pretend it's in the library. Then I'll leave. Oh, I forgot; if the library door has been repaired, you make sure it's unlocked for me, okay? Where was I?"

"Leaving," Ellie said gently.

"Leaving. Oh. Yeah, then I'll get in the car and head for Charlottesville. See, this guy won't know for sure that I haven't gotten some guy to agree to see me in the middle of the night, or first thing in the morning; he can't risk my reaching the University, so he'll follow me and—"

"Force you off the road," Ellie said. "Into a tree. Or over a cliff." The doctor had risen slowly to his feet. He was clutching the magazine in a grip that had twisted it into scrap paper, and the look on his face, the mingled hope and weariness, was too much for Ellie. Her voice rose to a shriek. "Where are you, you selfish pig? You tell me where you are, right this second, or I—"

"I know where he is," said Kate's voice. "Don't hang up, Donald; I've already telephoned Mr. Blanchard, at the Silver Fox, and told him to hold you there at gunpoint if he has to."

"How did you call if I'm on the line?" Donald demanded.

"Ha, ha," Kate said coyly.

"I suppose you have half a dozen telephone lines going into that place," Donald said resignedly. "Or carrier pigeons?"

Ellie didn't wait to hear any more. She held out the phone to the doctor, who took it gingerly, as if he were afraid it might be hot to the touch. She heard him say, "Donald?" in a voice that brought tears to her eyes before she left the room.

The tears were tears of rage. She had to pace up and down the hall for a few seconds before she was calm enough to hear Donald's voice again without screaming epithets at him. Then she went to the library.

Kate was on that phone. Ellie went to the kitchen and picked up that extension.

". . . don't see why you're acting so peculiarly," Donald was saying. His voice sounded petulant. "It's a great plan. Kate, you tell Blanchard—"

"It is a great plan," Kate agreed. "Absolutely great, Donald, I love it. But something has happened that you don't know about. I want you to come on out here right away, okay? After all, the important part of the plan starts when you leave this house. Isn't that right? If you come in daylight, then the—the villain can follow you more easily. You wouldn't want him to lose you."

"Oh, all right," Donald muttered. "God, you're bossy, Kate. I shudder to think what kind of aunt-in-law you are going to make. I'll come; but it's my plan, and you just let me do it the way I want. Dad?"

"Yes, son," said the doctor.

"You still there?"

"Yes, I—"

"You sound funny."

"I do not feel funny," said the doctor ominously. "I'm coming in to pick you up, Donald. You stay there till I arrive. Understand?"

"Everybody's bossing me around today," said Donald, and hung up.

Ellie met the doctor in the hall. He was fumbling wildly in his pockets.

"Keys," he panted. "Where the hell are my car keys?"

"There's no hurry, you know," said Kate, strolling languidly out of the library. "He can't leave till you get there; I made sure of that. Don't drive like a madman, Frank."

"Keys," said the doctor, still searching. Two of his pockets hung out like limp wind socks.

"Take my car." Kate fished a set of keys out of her pants pocket. "Now, Frank, don't—"

The doctor snatched the keys and jogged toward the door; he paused only long enough to remark,

"Donald is right, Kate. You *are* bossy."

The screen door banged, failed to catch, and Kate made a flying tackle just in time to grab Ambrose as he hurled himself at the door.

"No, baby, it's getting dark, and Momma doesn't want you out," she crooned, flat on the floor, with her face half buried in Ambrose's thick fur. "Better count cats, Ellie; we may as well get the chores done before the fun begins."

"Fun!" Ellie was limp with relief and frustrated anger. "You and that emotionally underdeveloped Donald; both of you ought to be locked up."

Kate rolled over onto her back, hugging Ambrose.

"If Donald had been his normal brilliant self, he wouldn't have called from the phone in the bar of the Fox. I recognized the background noises. I'd sure like to know what kind of drug he's been taking. What a high!"

III

Whatever Donald had been taking, the doctor dealt with it, by means Donald never cared to explain in detail. He was limp and fairly sober by the time the car pulled up in front of the house to find Kate and Ellie waiting on the porch. The doctor was still seething.

"Popping pills," he exploded, hauling his son out of the car. "A man of your age, supposed to have some sense, some training—"

"You're hurting my ribs," Donald said plaintively.

"No, I am not. Get in the house and stop trying to appeal to my sympathy."

Donald started up the stairs, limping ostentatiously. Before he entered the house he stopped and gave Ellie a long, hostile stare.

"Fink," he said bitterly.

"Fink yourself." Ellie followed him, with the others trailing behind. "Of all the dumb, inconsiderate, cruel things to do to us—"

"It seemed like a good idea at the time." Donald lowered himself gingerly onto the carved chest in the hall. "Maybe it wouldn't have seemed so bright if I hadn't been hopped up on pills, but I still think ..." He looked up at Ellie. "Did you say 'us'?"

"Not that I care what becomes of you," Ellie said. "But your father ... No, I didn't say 'us.' I said—"

"You did, too."

"I did not."

"You—"

"Shut up!" shouted Doctor Gold. "Now listen, you young lout, I've had enough of this adolescent tomfoolery. And when I get my hands on the idiot who loaned you his car and his bottle of uppers, I'll break his neck. I can guess who it was, probably Randy or Mike Jackson—"

Kate cleared her throat. It was such a small sound it seemed impossible that anyone could have heard it through the hubbub—for Ellie and Donald were both shouting, too—but it instantly silenced the others. Kate's hands were clasped over her stomach and her head was tilted back.

"Let us all keep our peace," she said in saccharine tones. "Shouting—cruel, hurting words—oh, fie! Do you not know that anger scars the soul with anguish that cannot be retrieved? Do you not remember the words of that sweetest of saints—and although I am not a member of the dear old Mother Church, friends, I am, I hope, sufficiently broadminded to venerate those shining souls who have been a light of inspiration unto the meek—"

"Go on," Ellie urged. She had sat down beside Donald and was listening to the imitation with as much appreciation as the others. "Go on, Kate."

"I can't do it too long," Kate said, in her normal voice. "My brain goes numb. Donald, were you really followed?"

"Was I really . . ." Donald rubbed his forehead. "Kate, you flip around from subject to subject so fast you make me dizzy. Yeah. I think so. From the hospital, I'm not so sure, I was flying a little high then. But I could swear there was someone after us when we left the Fox. Dad lost him when we got out of town. He hit seventy on that stretch by the fair grounds."

He smiled appreciatively at his father, who flushed slightly.

"A gross exaggeration. Anyway, I don't believe that fellow was following us. He just happened to be going the same way. If—"

The chimes burst into Beethoven's *Ninth*, Choral section. Everyone but Kate started nervously. After a moment Donald got up and went to the door, where he stood peering out through the narrow vertical glass panels that flanked the door itself.

"Hey," he exclaimed, in a thrilling whisper. "It's the same car! The one that was following us." He spun around, cracked ribs forgotten, his eyes shining with the light of the chase. "Now's our chance. We've got him now. Come on, everybody, get ready!"

CHAPTER
TEN

Donald looked wildly around the hall. There was no possible weapon—no object, in fact, that weighed less than two hundred pounds; so he darted into the drawing room and came back with a collection of fireplace tools.

"Here," he said, thrusting a poker at Ellie, who recoiled.

"I'll get my Mauser," Kate exclaimed. "Oh, damn, I forgot. You took it. Where did you put my Mauser, Donald?"

"Never mind the gun, we don't want to kill the guy," Donald said. "Have a poker."

"You act as if you plan to kill him." The doctor awoke from the temporary stupor into which his son's activities sometimes sent him. "Now sit down and be quiet, Donald. If the car is the one you mentioned—and I admit, there was one that seemed to be after us when we left town—it was not one that I recognized. Let me open the door. This is probably some stranger who has lost his way."

He advanced purposefully upon the door. The strains of the greatest of all symphonies were beginning again; apparently the visitor was becoming impatient. Kate and Donald exchanged glances. Then they took up their positions on either side of the door, with poker and shovel raised. Ellie stayed where she was. The situation seemed to be getting out of hand. Even the doctor looked a little rattled, but he opened the door with a flourish.

Ellie leaped to her feet as if she had been stung.

"Henry!"

Donald's jaw dropped. So did the fireplace shovel, which narrowly missed his father's arm. The doctor leaped nimbly aside; and Henry, confronting a total stranger—who seemed to be extremely nervous—and unable to see Ellie in the gloom of the hall, rose, figuratively and literally, to his full stature.

"How do you do, sir," he said, extending a hand. "My name is Willoughby. Ellie's fiancé. May I come in?"

"Oh, sure," said the doctor weakly. He stepped back. Henry squared his shoulders and advanced; and Ellie, who had just realized what Kate was doing, shrieked aloud.

"Kate! Don't you dare!"

Kate lowered the poker.

"Eh?" she said, cupping her hand around her ear.

Torn between amusement and outrage, Ellie could not speak for a moment. Henry, forgetting manners in his curiosity, peered around the door. Kate peered out from behind it. For a moment they confronted one another, nose to nose. Kate squinted hideously.

"Oh, dearie me," she said. "Is it you, Mr. Willoughby? I've gotten so hard of hearing lately. . . ."

"It's nice to see you again, Aunt Kate," Henry shouted.

"Eh?" said Kate.

Ellie saw Donald leaning helplessly against the wall, clutching his aching ribs as he tried to keep from laughing. The sight infuriated her.

"Kate, stop it! Henry, what are you doing here?"

"Why, darling, Al—the Senator—called me," Henry said. "We exchanged phone numbers the other night. He said you were having some trouble down here. And when I tried to call and was unable to reach you—"

"Well, of all the busybodies," Kate exclaimed indignantly, forgetting that she was supposed to be hard of hearing. It was not immediately clear whether she was referring to Grant or to Henry, or perhaps both.

No one else spoke. Donald was no longer laughing. He and the others exchanged glances, appalled at this new development. They had not even had time to figure out a way of dealing with the consequences of Donald's cockeyed scheme. The advent of Henry was a complication they could ill afford. Somehow, without a word being spoken, it was tacitly agreed among them that Henry was not to be told of the crisis building up that night. How much of the rest of the story they would be forced to tell, how much Grant had already told, had yet to be ascertained.

As has often been said, Henry was not particularly sensitive; but the prolongation of the damp, uncomfortable silence would have been hard to ignore.

"If I am in the way, I shall, of course, return to town," he said stiffly. "I dislike driving at night; perhaps I can find a room at the inn."

"Oh, boy," Kate said. "That would really do it. Uh—Henry—the inn is always filled up this time of year, you couldn't find an unoccupied closet there. Why don't you go on up—take the room you had last time—you'll want to shower and change before dinner—"

Her voice increased in warmth and amiability as she went on. Henry relaxed, taking this as a demonstration of Kate's goodwill, but Ellie, who had good reason to be suspicious of her aunt's enthusiasms, felt a wave of apprehension pass through her. There was nothing she could do about it, so she remained silent. Before he went upstairs, Henry gave her the long, cool stare that was part of his "I am bitterly hurt but I remain calm" treatment.

As soon as Henry was out of sight, Kate turned to Donald.

"Go get Angela and bring her into the house."

Angela was the mastiff who had taken such a fancy to Henry on his first visit. She was a sucker for new faces.

"You can't do that," Ellie said.

"Do what? Can I help it if Angela sits outside Henry's door? We've got to have some time to talk. What are we going to do with him?"

Donald had already departed on the errand. Angela was delighted to be allowed in; after snuffling around the hall for a while she gave a low whine of pleasure and bounded up the stairs.

"That should hold him for a while," Kate said. "You'll have to wait till tomorrow to break your engagement, Ellie. If you tell him tonight—"

"What makes you think I am going to—"

"If you tell him tonight," Kate went on, raising her voice, "he'll find a room in town, and God knows what he'll hear there. I sure don't know what we are going to do with him, though. I don't suppose I can leave Angela by his door all night."

"Certainly not," the doctor exclaimed. "I don't know what's the matter with you, Kate. He's another able-bodied man, and heaven knows we're short on those. Can't we tell him—perhaps not the whole story, but enough of it to—"

"No, no, no." Kate waved an impatient hand. "The man's hopeless, Frank. You don't know him. He won't be of any use. . . ."

Her face took on an expression Ellie knew and dreaded. Kate turned to Donald and measured him with her eyes, like a casting director inspecting a prospect.

"No, yourself," Ellie said firmly. "You cannot send Henry out as a decoy. Even if he'd go, he doesn't look a bit like Donald."

"Nobody else is going to do my dirty work," Donald said. "Forget it, Kate."

"Really, Kate, that seems—" the doctor began.

"All right! If you're all going to be so uncooperative . . ." Kate stood in deep thought for a while. Then she heaved a sigh. "Oh, hell. Much as I hate to admit it, this is no time for fun. There is only one sane thing to do and we're going to do it. We'll lock this place up like a fort and stay in, all of us. You, too, Frank; if someone is hanging around out there, he might think you were taking the parchment away. Luckily Ellie and I have already fed and watered the livestock. Tomorrow, when it's light, we'll all go to Charlottesville. Danny Wilkes will be able to locate the experts we need, even if it is Sunday."

"I suppose Danny Wilkes is the president of the University," Ellie said.

"Much more important fellow." The doctor smiled. "He gave the University the new stadium. How do you meet these people, Kate?"

"I can't help it." Kate looked as embarrassed as if she had been accustomed to cohabiting with drug pushers. "It's my damn money. You run into all kinds of people in business. . . . Anyhow, they do come in handy sometimes," she added, looking a little more cheerful. "What do you think of my plan?"

"Excellent," the doctor said promptly. "I knew your basic good sense would triumph in the end, Kate. I'll just telephone Jackson Phelps and ask him to take care of our animals tonight. He's done it before."

Donald said nothing. His lower lip protruded like that of an angry baby. Kate patted him lightly on the shoulder.

"This hurts me as much as it does you, Donald. I would absolutely love to unmask a villain singlehanded and drag him off to the police. But not even to make one of my favorite daydreams come true will I see any of you run the slightest risk of being hurt."

Donald appeared to be convinced by the argument and by the unusual sobriety of Kate's voice. He nodded and gave her a sheepish smile; whereupon Kate's face relaxed into a more characteristic expression of malicious speculation, and she said thoughtfully, "Of course if there were any chance of persuading Henry to leave, around midnight or thereabouts . . ."

"You don't mean that," the doctor said affectionately.

"Oh, yes, she does," Ellie muttered.

Kate heard her and flashed her an impudent smile. The doctor appeared not to hear; a startling idea had occurred to him.

"Good Lord, Kate, you're right, you know. If the fellow is as desperate as you and Donald believe, he might attack anyone who left here tonight. Unless we all went, in a body—he would hardly take on the lot of us—"

"But it's dark," Kate said. "Quite dark now. He might lay some trap on the road. That stretch between here and the highway is very lonesome. I'm not even sure I would trust the cars now. He's had time to work on them."

"Aren't you being a little melodramatic?" the doctor asked.

"I'm not talking about probabilities, Frank, I'm talking about one-in-a-thousand chances; but why risk even those odds? This character is unpredictable, and we've already seen that he can be dangerous."

"Makes sense," the doctor admitted.

"Then that's settled," Kate said briskly. "We'll have a nice quiet evening at home. Ellie, you haven't seen my latest toy; I was saving it as a surprise. You haven't been in the basement, have you?"

"No," Ellie said. She was distracted by a mounting uproar from above. The barking of a large dog mingled with thuds and muffled shouts. It was not possible to distinguish whether the thuds were made by Henry or by the dog hurling itself against his door. "I'd better let him out," Ellie said. "What new toy, Kate?"

"I've installed a little movie theater," Kate said. "Just a little *tiny* theater. I got so tired of sitting up all night to watch Leslie Howard and the Marx Brothers; they always show the good old movies after midnight, and there are so many commercials—"

"So naturally you installed your own theater," Ellie said. "Kate, darling, don't look so guilty; it's your money, you can spend it any way you like. But do you really think this is an appropriate moment for the Marx Brothers?"

The doctor's eyes gleamed.

"You don't happen to have *A Night at the Opera*, do you?"

"Certainly. I'll show it to you another evening, Frank. I have some new films, picked them up when I came through D.C. It's taken me the longest time to get prints; I had to blackmail a dozen people."

Ellie looked apprehensively at the ceiling. The noise was getting louder. The others appeared not to hear it.

"You got them?" the doctor asked eagerly. "I didn't think you could. Which ones? The Dallas game, of course—"

Kate nodded. Her expression could only be described as a smug smirk.

"And the Philadelphia game. The 1966 Giants' game, that Sonny won seventy-two to forty-one . . ."

"I must let Henry out," Ellie said.

"Yes, do." Kate nodded. "I'm sure he'll enjoy the films. I'll explain the game strategy and the finer points to him as we go along."

II

When Ellie was with her aunt she spent a good deal of the time trying to figure out Kate's real motives for a proposed course of action. This evening was no exception. Ellie came to the conclusion that, as usual, Kate had several reasons for proposing her plan. There were alternatives they might have considered; once the immediate impact of Kate's forceful personality was removed, Ellie thought of one or two herself.

Not that the plan was a bad one, and she felt sure that Kate's reasons for wanting them to stay in the house had been valid. There was no need for them to take even the slightest chance of being attacked. However, Ellie suspected that a subsidiary motive had been Kate's anxiety to see her new football films. She was like a child when she had a new toy, and she was probably looking forward to heckling Henry.

Henry was certainly very anxious to please. He didn't even complain about Angela, although he was perspiring and furious when Ellie dragged the dog away from his door, and, with Donald's help, shut her in the cellar.

Donald worried him, though. As they sat in the drawing room with their drinks (Henry was sipping abstemiously), he kept glancing at the other man, and finally, in a lull in the conversation, he said,

"Can't help noticing, Don, that you look as if you've been in the wars. Did you fall off a horse?"

Donald's hand went automatically to the bandage on his forehead, which was the only visible reminder of his accident.

"It was a horse, all right," he said ambiguously. "I'm still a little sore around the ribs."

"Thought so, from the way you walked." Henry looked shrewd. "Well, I'm glad to hear it was only an accident. I couldn't help wondering if it had anything to do with what Al was hinting at. Since

you seem to be so—uh—friendly with the family
here—"

Ellie caught Donald's eye and turned hastily away.
Poor old Henry, she thought—and knew, as she
thought it, that she had reached the final stage of
disengagement, that of kindly pity. Lean and brown
and nonchalant, romantically bandaged, Donald was
everything poor old Henry secretly yearned to be
himself.

"What precisely did that old busybody tell you?"
Kate asked sweetly. She offered Henry another
drink. He refused.

"Nothing specific. You know how politicians are."
Henry winked at her. Kate looked at him as if he had
lost his mind. "You know," Henry repeated. "Cau-
tious people. Never say anything outright. Safer that
way; my profession is the same. No, Al just said Ellie
had been having some strange encounters...." He
tried not to look at Donald, and failed.

"I'm surprised you took such vague hints seriously enough to come," Kate said severely.

"Oh, it wasn't all that vague," Henry said; and Ellie, who recognized the tone in his voice, looked
sharply at him. "He said someone had broken into
the house."

He leaned back, smiling, pleased at the effect of his
statement. The others looked blank. Consciously or
unconsciously they had counted on that very professional caution Henry had mentioned to restrain Alan
Grant from giving a detailed description of what had
transpired. He knew the dangers of being mis-
quoted, and he would never have mentioned ghosts
or ghostly visitations. Since they tended to think of
all the events as being connected, they had forgotten
that one particular episode had been purely physical, criminal in nature, and was on record. And it
was a sufficiently frightening episode to justify
Grant's call.

"Ah," Kate said. "Ah. Yes. I wasn't here at the time—"

"Then Ellie was alone? My poor girl—"

"No, I wasn't," Ellie said; and then stopped, seeing the trap. Damn Henry and his lawyer's tricks. . . .

Henry waited. He knew the effectiveness of silence. He looked from Ellie to Donald, who was sitting stiffly upright—the only position in which his ribs didn't ache—and who gave him a look in return that should have made his ears turn red. No one spoke. Ellie was trying to think. She didn't care what Henry thought of her morals, but there were two considerations that made her want to avoid the issue for the present. In the first place she had no intention of ending her engagement and having a loud unpleasant argument in front of other people—particularly Donald. In the second place she was afraid that Henry, provoked, might rush out into the night into—whatever awaited there. She couldn't imagine what she had ever seen in him, but she didn't want to be responsible for his being injured. She looked at Kate, and got no help from that quarter; Kate was studying the ceiling and whistling softly through her teeth.

Then, suddenly, it was as if the last intangible thread had snapped. Ellie laughed aloud.

"Oh, really, this is ridiculous," she said cheerfully. "Henry, you look so silly; like Cotton Mather judging adulterers or something. The truth is, I've been the victim of a series of practical jokes ever since you and Kate left. Someone has been playing ghost. At first they were only pranks, a little frightening, but not dangerous; then we had the burglary, and Ted, who had been keeping an eye on the house since the pranks began, tried to catch the burglar and had a heart attack. He's in the hospital now. . . . Kate, did you call about Ted today?"

"I'm just about to," Kate said; she was smiling. "Go on, Ellie."

"Donald moved in, to protect me," Ellie said. "That's how he got hurt, trying to stop the person who has been playing the tricks. We still don't know who the person is, but we know he wants something that's hidden in the house. Tomorrow we're all going to take this thing—it would take too long to explain what it is, Henry, and you wouldn't understand anyway—we're going to take it to some people who can tell us all about it. Then the danger will be over. It's not over yet. We think he—whoever he is—may be out there right now, waiting for one of us to leave with the thing he wants so badly. We've got the house all locked up, so he can't get in; but none of us is going to leave, not till morning. I think—I think that's everything, isn't it?"

She glanced at the others. They were all smiling, except Henry, who looked dazed, as well he might.

"Very nice," Kate said approvingly. "Nice and simple; I suppose you know how to talk to Henry in terms he can understand, after living with him so long. . . . I'm getting hungry. Let's have a bite to eat, and then we'll go down and see my movies."

"I—I never heard such a pack of nonsense," Henry said weakly.

"Well, these things do happen," Kate said. She extended a hand, and yanked Henry up out of his chair. "Come along, Henry; nobody feels like cooking tonight, so we'll have to forage for ourselves. Sandwiches and coffee. Can you make drinkable coffee? If you can't, it's high time you learned."

Recovering from his shock, Henry tried to fall back so that he could talk to Ellie alone, but Kate gave him no opportunity. She herded him into the kitchen, and put him to work. He managed to break into her chatter long enough to ask one question.

"You did—you did make sure the house is secure?"

"Oh, yes, Frank and I went around while Ellie was

letting—while Ellie was upstairs with you," Kate assured him.

Ellie wondered why she had ever worried about Henry rushing into danger. He was very careful of his precious skin.

"What about the library doors?" she asked. "Kate, I never did have time to put in a new pane of glass."

"We've got a couple of tons of pots and pans strategically arranged," Kate said. "And Franklin is in there. He'll let us know if anyone tries to get in. Donald, I hope the document is not in the library."

"No," Donald said.

"Cheese, ham, bread, mustard, mayonnaise," Kate said, removing these items from the refrigerator. "Get some plates, Ellie. Lettuce, tomatoes, rolls, pâté—"

They sat around the kitchen table reaching for what they wanted and eating hugely. Even Henry seemed to relax—until Donald suddenly took it into his head to discuss the apparitions. The white lady on the stairs was the pièce de résistance; Donald let out all the stops on that description.

"The cold was frightful," he said in a deep throbbing voice. "I felt encased in ice, cold to the depths of my heart and soul. Those eyes—those terrible, frozen eyes seemed to pierce me like a sword. . . ."

"Stop that," Ellie said sharply.

"I guess I shouldn't remind her," Donald said to Henry. "She fainted, you know; passed out cold, in my arms. . . ."

"Oh, indeed," said Henry.

"On the floor," said Ellie.

"That's interesting." Kate had both elbows on the table; the sandwich she had made was so thick it required both hands to keep it together. "Did you really faint, Ellie?"

"I had a hard day," Ellie said.

"It was the ghastly aura of that visitor from another world," Donald added. "Only my well-known courage prevented me, too, from . . ." He stopped, meeting Kate's steady regard; when he went on his voice had lost its mock solemnity. "No kidding, Kate, it really was pretty bad. I'd give a thousand bucks to know how that stunt was rigged. Ellie mentioned the cold that accompanied old man Lockwood's appearance. We discussed how that could have been accomplished, by someone who knows how your house is designed. But that method couldn't have been used with the white lady. I tell you, the cold was piercing; it cut right down into your bones. And it was localized in a very peculiar manner, all in one spot—"

"That's right, it was," Ellie said. "Like a wall of ice."

"Oh," Kate said softly. She put her sandwich down on the table, where it spread out in an unbecoming manner. Her eyes were a smoky blue and her mouth was wistful, yearning. "Oh, wouldn't it be wonderful if there was a real ghost after all? You don't suppose . . ."

"No," Ellie said loudly. "I don't. And it wouldn't be wonderful at all. Really, Kate, we've already got three or four separate subplots already; you can't drag in a ghost to account for everything that's left over. Just wait till we talk to Ted, he'll be able to explain the whole thing."

"I suppose you're right." Kate's mouth drooped; Ellie felt like an adult who has just told a child there is no Santa Claus. "Oh, well, this world is full of disappointments. Speaking of Ted, I think I'll call the hospital."

"I'll call." Doctor Gold rose. "I can pull rank and get more information than you could."

He went to the phone. Kate contemplated the mess on her plate with disgust.

"I knew I shouldn't have let go of it," she said. "I can't eat this. What—"

"Kate." The doctor was standing quite still; he held the receiver in one hand. "The phone is dead."

"What?" Donald jumped to his feet and then doubled over, arms around his chest. "Dad, are you sure?"

"Either a telephone is functioning or it is not," the doctor snapped. "It is hardly a matter for debate."

"Try one of the other lines," Kate said. "He may have missed the one in my workroom, I had it put in later than some of the others."

But no one moved. Henry stared at them, his expression a blend of incredulity, suspicion, and horror.

"This is some sort of sick joke," he said. "I don't think it's particularly clever, I must say."

"I'm afraid it's not a joke," Kate said. "What Ellie told you was true; she didn't tell you the half of it. Donald, are you all right?"

Donald straightened up, still clutching his ribs. He was pale and perspiring, but he produced a weak smile.

"I'll live. Damn it, what a time to be crippled. I don't like this development, Kate."

"Let's keep calm," said the doctor, whose hair was standing straight up on end. "This merely confirms what we suspected—that someone is lying in wait out there. It is a sensible move for him to cut the wires; he doesn't want us calling for help, or checking up on anyone's alibi for the hours to come. Things are no worse than they were before. I—I think I'll just have another look around, make sure all the doors are secure."

"This is disgusting," Donald said angrily. "Here we are, five relatively strong and capable people, acting like a city under siege by howling barbarians. It's only one man—"

"Or woman," Kate said. "That's what we've been assuming. It might be all of them. Did you ever consider that?"

Donald had considered it; he showed no surprise. The idea came as a shock to Ellie and to the doctor, who spun around with a muffled croak of protest.

"Now, Kate—"

"We don't know," Kate insisted. "Several of them have motives. What's to prevent them from banding together to protect their precious names? I tell you, Frank, we don't know what is out there. And we aren't five able-bodied people; one of us is injured—stop looking stalwart, Donald, one clap on the back and you'd be flat on your face—one of us is small and fragile"—it was obvious that she was not talking about herself, but before Ellie could protest, Kate finished, "and one of us is uncommitted. Usually the defenders have the stronger position, but in this case we are at a disadvantage because we don't know what to expect. Now what I propose is—"

"Are you ever at a loss for an idea?" Donald inquired disagreeably.

"Never. We'll check the doors and windows again. I really don't believe anyone can get in—"

"Hey," Ellie interrupted. "What about that secret entrance Marian Beaseley uses? If she could get in when all the other doors were barred and bolted—"

"Now how could you suppose I would be foolish enough to forget that?" Kate demanded. "That door is always locked, and Marian and I are the only ones who have keys. It's not a secret entrance, it's the old cellar door. It's rather overgrown, and most people have forgotten it exists. But we'll check that one, too. As I was saying when I was so rudely interrupted, I don't see how anyone could enter the house; but we'll barricade ourselves into one of the rooms. Then—"

"I don't suppose the room you have in mind could be your new projection room?" Donald inquired gently.

"Well, why not? It's quite solid; soundproof, you know; and we may as well be entertained while we wait for morning." Kate's eyes shone. "We should be able to watch three, maybe four games before it will be light enough to leave."

Even the doctor looked slightly horrified.

"I don't think I can stand four consecutive Redskin games," he said.

"But these are games they *won*," Kate said. "Oh, well, if you're going to be like that, I'll show *A Night at the Opera* in between the Giants game and the Philadelphia game."

The doctor began to laugh. He laughed so hard his knees gave way and he had to lean against the wall.

"Kate, you are impossible," he said finally, wheezing. "Whatever happens tonight, I love you. Will you marry me?"

"No. But I'll live in sin with you," Kate said promptly. "Come on, let's go the rounds. Frank, you and Donald—"

"No, let's not split up." The doctor was entirely serious now. "All for one and one for all."

So they went in a group, albeit a rather straggling group. The house had never seemed larger, more sprawling, more full of moving shadows.

Ellie found the opportunity to exchange a few words with Kate while the men were erecting a barricade across a particularly vulnerable window.

"Look, Kate, no more jokes about real ghosts, okay? I know you're trying to tease Henry, but— you're getting to me, too. You didn't see that thing on the stairs."

"I didn't have to. Donald gave me a very vivid description of it—and of your reaction."

"Kate, I said no more jokes, please."

Kate opened her mouth as if to speak, thought for a moment, and then said mildly,

"Okay. Sorry."

They covered the entire house without encountering anything more dangerous than Roger, although the rat's sudden appearance, on a bust of Keats in the mid-Victorian morning parlor, almost sent Henry into a fit. He recovered himself more quickly than Ellie expected; in fact, he got quite cheerful as the tour neared its end. Apparently it had finally dawned on him that he was the obvious hero of the night, being the only one who was male, young, and healthy. He started patting Kate on the head and making remarks like "Nothing to worry about, girls. We can handle anything that comes along."

"What about taking a little light refreshment?" he inquired jocularly, as they ended the tour where it had begun, in the kitchen.

"There's a bar in the theater, naturally," Kate said. "Quite well stocked, I assure you. But thanks, Henry; you reminded me of something we certainly ought to take with us. Donald, where's the parchment?"

"It's perfectly safe where—"

"The safest place for it is under all our eyes," Kate said. "You're taking a chance if you leave it up here, unguarded. Where is it?"

"Oh, all right. It's in your workroom."

"Good heavens! That's the most open room in the house. Those bay windows—"

"It's also the messiest room," Donald said cuttingly. "*You* can never find anything; a poor burglar wouldn't have a chance."

"Well, let's get it—no, not you, we'll go together."

At that moment they were electrified by a loud crackling noise that seemed to come from the empty air around them. Henry yelped and grabbed at Donald, who echoed the cry in a different tone.

"Thought you might be about to faint, old boy," Henry said weakly. "Uh—what was that?"

"The intercom," Kate said. "It makes noises sometimes. . . . Who turned it on?"

No one remembered having done so. Kate's face grew longer and more pensive as the denials followed one another, but the doctor said impatiently,

"You probably did it yourself, Kate, without

thinking. Or else you've been fooling with the wiring again and messed it up."

Kate didn't deny the charge, but it was clear that she was uneasy.

"Let's get that parchment," she said. "Hurry, can't you?"

She relaxed visibly when they reached her workroom and found no signs of disturbance, although, as several of them pointed out, it would have been difficult to tell whether anyone had been searching; the room was always in a state of chaos.

"Get it," Kate said impatiently. "Hurry up, Donald; let's get out of here."

"I stuck it in one of these magazines," Donald said, indicating the untidy stack of *Ms.*, *Pro Quarterback*, and *Cat Fancy* that spilled over one of the tables. He began looking.

Kate stood tapping her foot nervously, her eyes searching the room. Her nervousness had infected everyone; Ellie felt a crawling sensation, as if unseen eyes were watching them. Suddenly Kate said,

"Why did you move that screen, Ellie? It should be in the library."

The screen, a heavy three-leafed, man-tall structure of carved wood and gilded stamped leather, stood in the corner farthest from the window. It was a comparatively dark corner, since the table lamp at that end of the room had not been lighted, but Ellie recognized the screen.

"I didn't move it," she said. "Donald, did—"

And then she was struck dumb, like all the others, as Ted's last and greatest effect got under way. It began with light—the same sickly greenish glow she had seen once before. At first it was a dim circle hanging unsupported in midair. Gradually it strengthened; and as it did so, the figure took shape, dark as the shadows from which it seemed to draw its substance, but impossibly transparent. The gilt tracery of the screen shone faintly through its body.

Shrouded in black it stood, hands hidden in the wide sleeves of the garment that covered it from crown to floor. The cowled head was lifted, but there was no face under the hood, only an expanse of darkness. Slowly one arm lifted and straightened, as if pointing. The wide hanging sleeve seemed to be empty, but suddenly a blast of cool air ruffled Ellie's curls and a low humming moan began to rise and fall. The tall, faceless figure wavered in that inexplicable wind like something drawn on paper. Abruptly it solidified. The lifted arm gestured and the cold air moved with it like an emanation from an invisible weapon.

The room shook as a heavy body hit the floor. Ellie turned. Henry had fainted.

For some reason, his collapse shook Ellie out of her frozen horror. It was an effective trick—she still couldn't understand how it had been managed, or how the unknown had gotten into the house—but she knew it was only a trick, not a visitation from beyond. And she knew what it wanted. The outstretched hand demanded it. It moved again, and the pages of the magazine Donald was clutching blew wildly in the draft.

It was a copy of *Sports Illustrated*, with a picture of Muhammad Ali on the cover. The bright, one might almost say secular, appearance of the publication contrasted painfully with Donald's set face. Slowly, without speaking, he shook his head.

The doctor had his arms around Kate; he was not protecting her, he was restraining her. She tugged at his prisoning hands, and then burst out,

"What are you all standing there for? Grab him before he gets away!"

"Oh, no," the doctor said, and Donald remarked coolly, "Not till I see what is in his other hand."

"Oh," Kate said, relaxing so suddenly that the doctor lost his grip. She did not move, though; she stood quite still, her eyes fixed on the same object the others were staring at.

It had appeared as if by magic in the figure's right hand. To Ellie it looked like an unusually large gun, but then her eyesight was not at its best. It was pointed at Donald.

"Give it to him," Ellie gasped. "Give him the magazine."

The figure bowed its cowled head as if in agreement. The unknown dared not speak; the muffling garment masked his face and body, but his voice would betray his identity. However, Ellie had a pretty good idea as to who he must be. Only one of their suspects was that tall—as tall as Ted, for whom the garment had presumably been designed. Roger McGrath was only five feet seven or eight. The "monk" had to be Alan Grant. Ellie was sorry. She rather liked Grant; at least she didn't dislike him as much as she did the others.

"Give it to him," she repeated. "Please, Donald."

Donald shook his head.

There was no need for the unknown to speak. He could convey his wants just as effectively without words. The muzzle of the gun moved smoothly away from Donald toward his father.

Kate tried to step in front of the doctor, who gave her a shove that sent her staggering.

"He doesn't care who he shoots," Gold shouted, too angry to care for grammar any more than for chivalry. "If you and Donald don't stop acting like a television melodrama, somebody is going to get hurt. Donald, you do what I tell you. Give it to him."

The black shrouded head nodded emphatically. Donald swore. He flung the magazine away from him. It struck the floor, its pages crumpled; the parchment, which had slipped out while the magazine was in midair, fluttered down more slowly, riding the air currents like a glider. The "monk," forgetting caution, stepped forward; and Ellie made a futile snatch at Donald, who was crouching stiffly as if to spring.

She needn't have bothered. The "monk" never reached his goal.

The lights in the room burned blue, and a cold wind howled around them, making the earlier breeze seem like a balmy breath of spring. The shadowy corner behind the screen was shadowy no longer. A ghostly conflagration burned there, giving off light, and cold instead of heat. Crimson flames boiled and billowed. A diabolical howling, like fiendish laughter, deafened the horrified watchers.

Amid the chaos Ellie was aware of Henry stirring. He moaned and started to sit up. Finding himself facing another and far more appalling manifestation, he yelped and fainted again.

Deafened and sick, Ellie reached out. Her hands found Donald's, groping for hers. They stood with hands locked over Henry's prostrate body, unable to move forward, unwilling to retreat.

The lights had gone out except for the fiery glow that illumined the far end of the room. The black shape of the "monk" was silhouetted against it; he had turned and was standing quite still, but the very outlines of his body expressed unspeakable terror. There were faces in the whirling cloud that glowed with infernal fire—faces several of the watchers knew. A woman's face, beautiful and terrible, her hair lifted like a living flame; the face of a white-bearded man whose teeth were bared in a devilish smile; and, foremost among the other shadowy shapes, that of a dark, sallow man whose wavering features betrayed a terrible resemblance to another face Ellie knew. The howling laughter seemed to shape itself into words—not spoken sounds, but concepts that moved directly from mind into mind.

"My son!" the great, empty voice boomed. "Welcome! The old blood runs true!"

The "monk" recoiled as if he had been stung. He

tried to retreat and tripped over his skirts. Two black shapes, like arms, but longer and horribly flexible, shot out of the fiery cloud toward him. He screamed hideously, and fell, writhing on the floor as the snaky tentacles squirmed toward him.

Something small and light darted forward and pounced. Ellie's eyes weren't working too well; at first she thought it was one of the cats, its size distorted by the strange light. Then it rose, shaking disheveled hair back from its face, and Ellie recognized her aunt. Kate was holding the parchment. She turned to the nearest table and began rummaging among the litter.

Under any other circumstances the search would have had its comic aspects. Papers, withered apples, cat toys, potted plants flew in all directions as Kate burrowed frantically. It took far less time than it should have for her to find what she was after. Ellie couldn't see what it was. A small flame sprang up, hardly discernible in the greater crimson light. Then with a sudden flare it fed and grew. Kate had set fire to the parchment.

It was old and dry, but it burned faster than it should have, almost as if it had been soaked in oil. Kate dropped it, nursing scorched fingers; before it could drift to the floor it was gone.

With it went the crimson light and the faces. The voices rose in an ear-splitting shriek and died. The bulbs in the chandelier overhead sprang to life.

Kate was the first to speak.

"Well, that takes care of that. Goodness, what a mess. It will take me a week to clean up this room. I only hope Roger hasn't had a heart attack. Two in one week, in my house, would really set tongues wagging."

"Roger?" Ellie repeated.

Donald tried to free his hands. Ellie hung on to them; it was the doctor who reached the recumbent body and turned it over. The place where the face should have been was still a featureless expanse of blackness, but now they could see it for what it was. Dr. Gold lifted the black veil and exposed McGrath's face. It was as white as his bedraggled moustache, but after a moment the doctor announced,

"He's fainted, that's all. We'd better call the Rescue Squad, though."

"I'll call." Kate stepped unconcernedly over Henry's body and picked up the telephone, which was one of the objects she had flung aside in her search for matches. It was buzzing angrily. As she dialed, she started giving orders.

"Get that costume off him, Frank, before anyone sees it. And hide the gun. And—hello, Jimmie? This is Kate. Would you please come on out right away? No, I'm fine, thanks. How's your back? Oh, good. . . . Ten minutes? Thanks, Jimmie." She hung up the phone. "And do something with Henry. I will not have the place strewn with bodies, like the last scene of an Elizabethan tragedy. It creates the wrong impression."

"What do you want me to do with him?" Donald asked.

"Wake him up and get him out of here. Or get him out of here and then wake him up. The important word is 'out.' Here, Frank, I'll help you—"

But the doctor pocketed the gun before Kate could reach it.

"I just want to look at it," she protested.

"What good would that do? Roger probably borrowed it, the same way he did the horse. Any jackass can get hold of a gun these days, that's one of the things that's wrong with this country. Nothing personal, Kate—"

"Oh, yeah?" Kate replied.

"How did you know it was Roger?" Ellie asked. She knelt down by Henry's recumbent form and prodded him. They would have to wake him up; she didn't want Donald to hurt himself trying to drag Henry's dead weight.

"Oh, I suspected it all along," Kate said airily— and, Ellie suspected, untruthfully. "I knew for sure when that—uh—that character in the black whiskers called him 'son.' He was the spitting image of Roger under all that hair. I recognized the nose."

"Most amazing case of mass hypnotism I've ever seen," Dr. Gold muttered.

"Damn it, Frank, you can't squirm out of it that easily!" Kate glared at him. "Call yourself a man of science, and you won't even admit the evidence of your own eyes—"

The arrival of the ambulance ended a heated discussion on scientific methodology.

III

"I think Roger will have sense enough to keep his mouth shut," the doctor said. "He knows how a story like that would affect his—"

"He'll keep *his* mouth shut!" Kate was indignant. "Maybe he will, but I won't. I'm going to sue him for about a million dollars. Did you see the scorch mark on the floor? Six or eight square feet of tile all burned to a crisp. Not to mention invading my property and dragging all his dissolute damned relatives in uninvited—"

They were sitting in the kitchen, having agreed that restoratives for shocked nerves were in order. Henry was clearly intent on drinking himself into a coma as quickly as possible. He had reached the stage of maudlin good fellowship and kept patting Kate on the head. She endured this stoically; Henry had had a greater shock than he deserved and he was behaving comparatively well—perhaps because he had managed to wipe from his memory the most unacceptable parts of the evening's adventures.

"Really shouldn't leave that footstool where it is," he told Kate, for perhaps the fifth time. "Hurt yourself one of these days. If I hadn't tripped on it when I was rushing at that fellow—"

"I know, Henry," Kate said meekly. "I'm sorry. Here, have another drink."

"No, but seriously," Dr. Gold said. "We must decide how much of this has to be made public. And we'd better agree on a story right now, before one of us gets carried away."

He looked meaningfully at Kate.

"Right on," Ellie agreed. "Kate, you know we can't tell the whole story. You may not care if the town thinks you're a psycho—most everybody does now—but other people have reputations to consider."

"Such as rising young physicians with wives to support," Donald said, stiff as an Egyptian pharaoh in his chair. "Will you marry me one of these days, Ellie, when we get around to it?"

"Uh-huh," said Ellie. "Now, look, Kate—"

"Somebody getting married?" Henry asked, blinking. "Thass nice. Congrashulations."

"Thanks, old chap," Donald said.

"Kate—"

As Ellie knew, appeals to Kate's better nature succeeded where threats and warnings failed.

"Oh, all right," she muttered. "I won't sue Roger. Actually"—she brightened—"I've got enough on him to keep him out of politics for the rest of his life. I'll threaten to publish the parchment—"

"But it's burned," Ellie protested.

"Roger doesn't know that," Kate said.

"We'll never know what was on it," Donald said. "I know, Kate, you had to burn it—I've got to hand it to you, I wouldn't have thought of doing it—but I wish I could have seen those names. If they were names . . ."

"They were," Kate said. "Just before the thing went up in flames, the names sprang out, fresh as the day they were written. Maybe heat was the catalyst. Or maybe . . . Six names. Guess what they were."

Donald said nothing. Ellie knew now why it had been so important to him to learn the names of the signatories to that infernal contract.

"All of them?" the doctor asked steadily. "Even—"

"No. Not Morrison. The sixth name was Beaseley."

"So Miss Mary was right about the Beaseleys," Ellie said. Donald slumped down in his chair with a sigh, and immediately sat up again, looking pained.

"Beaseley was only one of the names," Kate reminded her. "Miss Mary's ancestor was no better— worse, actually; he ought to have known better. It wasn't a regular coven. That requires a membership of thirteen—twelve privates and a general, who represents the devil. This was just a little private club of bad guys—and girls—who got bored with respectability and played nasty games. I hate to think what went on in Mr. Lockwood's charitable institutions—the old peoples' home, the orphanage—"

"Don't," Ellie begged. Donald took her hand.

"They got what was coming to them," he said, with grim satisfaction. "I'm glad to learn that modern, wishy-washy theology is mistaken. There ought to be a hell for people like that."

"Mass hallucination," the doctor began.

"We'll ask the workmen who'll repair my floor if they see any marks of burning," Kate said. "Won't that be interesting? Secondary mass hallucination . . . Frank, I'm not proposing or supporting the concept of a literal Hades, complete with fire and brimstone. But suppose—just suppose people who actively and deliberately espouse evil pass on, after death, into a spiritual state that corresponds to our conception of purgatory. We could see it only in the images we know; the reality would be unimaginable to us. Any mental contact with souls like those would be automatically translated, by our limited brains, into sensory impressions we can understand. I don't know whether I believe in survival after death, but I do believe in evil. And I sure don't want to end up spending eternity with people like Roger McGrath, much less his grandfather. I hope they go someplace else. But," she added in a soothing voice, "if you want to think of it as mass hallucination, go right ahead. The terms are unimportant. The point is that some of the manifestations were not produced by a physical agent. That's what confused the issue so long. We were trying to attribute everything to a single villain."

"That's right," Donald said interestedly. "Leaving aside the agent who was responsible for the first apparition—and may I say that he, or she, displayed admirable taste, selecting the best-looking *and* the best-behaved of all the old families. . . ."

Kate stared at the ceiling and whistled through her teeth.

"Leaving that individual aside," Donald continued, grinning, "there were three separate agencies involved. Ted played Lockwood, and the 'couple' on the lawn—that was a clever stunt, to suggest two people. The man who followed them . . ."

"A hallucination," Kate said sarcastically, glancing at the doctor.

"An impression," Donald said. "A lingering sensory echo of strong emotion, visible under certain emotional conditions. . . . You know, Kate, in a sense Ted could be regarded as the one who triggered the whole bag of worms, hallucinations included. By reenacting the old tragedies he stirred up things that had been quiescent for a hundred years."

The doctor shifted uncomfortably.

"It is certainly possible that Ted unwittingly brought Roger's mild persecution mania to a dangerous pitch. Roger would have interpreted the tricks as taunts, hints that someone knew the unsavory history of his family, and was about to betray it."

"But how did Roger know about the book?" Ellie asked. "And the parchment?"

It was, of course, Kate who supplied the answer.

"Perhaps he only knew that there was a dangerous, defamatory document hidden in a copy of that particular book. I can see the tradition being handed down, from father to son, after the book was lost or stolen, a warning to watch out for it if it ever turned up. We may find that Ted knew something of the tradition; he has an uncanny nose for scandal. That makes Ellie the real instigator of the whole business," she continued cheerfully. "If she hadn't found the book . . . if Ted hadn't seen it and remembered the old rumor—and decided to tease Roger and the others . . . if Roger hadn't learned about the book and let his paranoia run riot . . ."

"You can't make me feel guilty," Ellie said. "You're just trying to find scapegoats to cover up your own part in this. Throwing Donald at me in the guise of a yardboy was dumb enough, but that stunt with the romantic ghost—"

"I don't understand," the doctor said innocently. "What's all this about?"

"Never mind," Kate said. "Uh—let's get back to the ghosts. The only other genuine—mass hallucination—was the white lady on the stairs. Until this evening, I mean. John Wilkes Booth was Roger's first appearance. Ted would have done it much better. The monk was his tour de force. He must have planned that effect, Roger could never have thought of anything that ingenious.''

"I don't mind admitting it scared the socks off me for a second or two," Donald said.

Kate laughed suddenly.

"I was thinking about poor old Roger running around the house carrying that screen," she explained. "It was a copy of the original—balsa wood and paper—but it must have been awkward to handle. He didn't know where to put it, because he didn't know where we were going to be. That's why he turned on the intercom—hoping he would overhear us discussing our plans. He had been in the house for hours, before we locked up. We were stupid not to think of that.

"Ted must have planned to play the monk scene in the library. He would simply substitute his screen for the real one. In semidarkness it would pass for the original. You saw how it worked, didn't you? One of the panel designs was painted on thin strips of transparent plastic. The costume was black; in a dark corner that screen would have looked solid. When the light came on, the figure stood out as if it had materialized with the panel of the screen showing through it. It was the other way around, of course; the screen, not the figure, was transparent. McGrath simply stepped through the thin plastic. The sound of the hair dryer covered any slight crackle or crunch."

"The hair dryer bugs me," Donald grumbled. "I should have spotted that."

"I don't imagine you use them," Kate replied. "They're small and portable these days, small enough to be hidden in a full, flowing sleeve, and battery operated. So was the torch that gave the spooky light. I liked that, it was one of Ted's better ideas. Did you notice how the light slowly built up, instead of just turning on full?"

"I certainly did," Ellie said emphatically. "How did he do it?"

"Nipples," Kate said dreamily.

"What?" The doctor started.

"The kind that are on babies' bottles," Kate explained. "I used to baby-sit when I was young and poor, and one time I forgot to turn off the fire under a pan in which the lady of the house was boiling the next day's supply. To sterilize them, you know. I was reading a particularly interesting book and ... well, those plastic nipples simply dissolved into thin air. There was nothing left of them. Ted used something similar to mask his flashlight—a thin, translucent film of some kind of plastic that would slowly melt with heat. Beneath was another non-melting lens of a nauseating color. Oh, it was very well arranged. Roger wore built-up shoes, of course. He had to, the robe Ted made was too long for him."

"One question," the doctor said. "How did you happen to think of burning the parchment?"

"But that's the traditional method," Kate said. "Fire purifies. I know all about demonology and witchcraft."

"Hmmm." The doctor pondered. "Yes, I see. Unconsciously we all knew that. Racial instinct—the mind a vast storehouse of forgotten facts—so when we saw the parchment go up in flames, our collective minds—"

"Collective balderdash," Kate snarled. "And you had the nerve to mention marriage to me? Lucky for you I—"

"Marriage," said a deep, solemn voice. They all jumped, including Kate. Henry had been sitting so long in a paralyzed, happy stupor that they had forgotten he could talk. "Congrash—congrash—good luck, old man." Leaning sideways to pat Donald on the back, he slid slowly onto the floor, where he curled up and went to sleep.

"I'll put a blanket over him," Kate said, rising. "Come on. It's late, but tomorrow is Sunday, and nobody has to get up. Would you rather see the Giants' game first, or—"

"Oh, no, Kate," Ellie groaned. "Not now!"

"It's excellent therapy," Kate said firmly. Her eyes glowed with a fanatical fire as she turned to Ellie. "You like bombs—I'll show you some real bombs!"